Bertie and the Tinman

Books by Peter Lovesey

Sergeant Cribb series
WOBBLE TO DEATH
THE DETECTIVE WORE SILK DRAWERS
ABRACADAVER
MAD HATTER'S HOLIDAY
THE TICK OF DEATH
A CASE OF SPIRITS
SWING, SWING TOGETHER
WAXWORK

Peter Diamond series
THE LAST DETECTIVE
DIAMOND SOLITAIRE
THE SUMMONS
BLOODHOUNDS
UPON A DARK NIGHT
THE VAULT
DIAMOND DUST
THE HOUSE SITTER
THE SECRET HANGMAN
SKELETON HILL
STAGESTRUCK
COP TO CORPSE
THE TOOTH TATTOO
THE STONE WIFE
DOWN AMONG THE DEAD MEN
ANOTHER ONE GOES TONIGHT
BEAU DEATH
KILLING WITH CONFETTI

Hen Mallin series
THE CIRCLE
THE HEADHUNTERS

The Prince of Wales mysteries
BERTIE AND THE TINMAN
BERITE AND THE SEVEN BODIES
BERTIE AND THE CRIME OF PASSION

Other Fiction
THE FALSE INSPECTOR DEW
KEYSTONE
ROUGH CIDER
ON THE EDGE
THE REAPER

Bertie and the Tinman

Peter Lovesey

SOHO CRIME

All the characters and events portrayed in this work are
fictitious or are used fictitiously.

Bertie and the Tinman
Copyright © 1987 by Peter Lovesey

This edition first published in 2020 by
Soho Press, Inc.
227 W 17th Street
New York, NY 10011

Library of Congress Cataloging-in-Publication Data
Lovesey, Peter, author.
Bertie and the tinman / Peter Lovesey.
Series: The Prince of Wales mysteries; book 1

ISBN 978-1-64129-162-0
eISBN 978-1-64129-050-0

1. Edward VII, King of Great Britain, 1841–1910—Fiction.
2. Great Britain—History—Victoria, 1837–1901—Fiction.
I. Title
PR6062.O86 B48 2020 823'.914—dc23 2019041335

Printed in the United States of America

10 9 8 7 6 5 4 3 2 1

Bertie and the Tinman

CHAPTER 1

The Tinman asked, "Are they coming?" and reached for his revolver.

His sister Emily made no response. She stood at a bedroom window of Falmouth House, near Newmarket, staring down at the curve of the gravel drive between the lawns. It was Monday afternoon, 8 November, 1886, about twenty past two. She made no response because she didn't understand the question.

She was bone weary, but profoundly relieved that her brother had rallied after a frightening weekend. On Thursday evening he had come back from the races at Lewes complaining of a feverish chill. Next day his temperature had soared dangerously. Two doctors had seen him, and a nurse from Cambridge had been engaged. Not until Sunday evening had his temperature started to drop. Last night, thank heaven, he had slept. This morning he had sat up in bed when his regular doctor called. His temperature was right down. Some of his friends had called to see him and he had chatted happily. A few minutes ago he had told Emily to send the nurse for lunch.

"Are they coming?" What did he mean by that?

Emily heard a sound behind her. She turned.

The Tinman was out of bed and striding toward the open door in his nightshirt. He had the gun in his left hand.

Emily's throat contracted. She put her hand to her neck and cried out, "What are you doing?" She darted across the room toward him.

He backed against the door and it slammed shut.

She froze.

He had lifted the gun and pointed it toward his own face.

Until such a crisis occurs, nobody can know how they will react. Emily fought her paralyzing fear, flung out her arm and tried to stop him. She succeeded in pushing the gun aside. He grabbed her with his right arm, gripped her around the neck and thrust her against the door. They wrestled for what seemed like a minute.

She shrieked repeatedly for help.

He tightened the grip. Emily's arms flailed uselessly. Considering how ill her brother had been, his strength was extraordinary, superhuman. He held her on his right side while he turned his face to the left and moved the muzzle to his mouth.

She was powerless to stop him. She could only scream.

He spoke no other words. He pulled the trigger and the shot hurled him backward. He hit the floor.

Sobbing hysterically, Emily staggered across the room and tugged at the bell rope.

Were they coming? It no longer mattered to the Tinman.

CHAPTER 2

I must say, it's a queer thing to be sitting in my study on the last day of 1886, addressing someone not yet born, but that is what I take you to be. That is what you had *better* be. As for me, I am a dead man, or will be when you read this. And grossly libeled in the history books, I shouldn't wonder.

Not to prolong the mystification, my name is Albert Edward, and among other things notable and notorious, I am the Prince of Wales, the eldest son of Her Gracious Majesty Queen Victoria. To please Mother and Country, I wear a straitjacket. This uncongenial garment is known as protocol. It obliges me to consign this intimate account of certain adventures of mine to a secure metal box in the Public Record Office for a hundred years. So I can confidently inform you that I am dead. As are all the other poor, benighted spirits I shall presently raise.

Good day to you, then. Not a bad day to commence putting pen to paper. Christmas festivities over; too much fog about for shooting; flat racing finished for the year; and a certain lady who has been known to make agreeable incursions upon my time and energy is occupied for a season on the New York stage.

In case it surprises you that the Heir Apparent's waking

hours are not filled with official engagements, allow me to state that I do my share of laying foundation stones, inspecting lines of guardsmen and handing prizes to clever dicks in universities. I do my share and the Queen's as well, for it's no secret that the Empress of India practices her own variety of *purdah*. The year of 1887 will be the fiftieth of her reign, her Golden Jubilee, and who do you think is acting as host? The royal families of four continents will be in attendance, and my most daunting task is to persuade the principal subject of all the rejoicing to emerge from her drawing room at Windsor for an afternoon.

What a job! Like putting up a tiger without elephants or beaters.

Steady, Bertie. This is a memoir, not a letter of complaint.

It was seven weeks ago that I was given the shocking news that prompted me to turn detective. Yes, *detective.* Does that surprise you? It surprised me. I wouldn't have dreamed of such an eventuality until it grabbed me by the beard and fairly hauled me out of my armchair. Yet now that I reflect upon it, I see that my unique position fitted me admirably for the challenge.

On the afternoon of 8 November, 1886, the first report reached London by wire from Newmarket that Fred Archer had killed himself. You cannot imagine the sensation this caused. Archer, the greatest jockey ever to grace the Turf— and I am confident that you, a century on, will know his name, even though you have never seen his like—had blown his brains out with a revolver bullet. He was twenty-nine years old. This year he had won his fifth Derby, his twenty-first Classic.

How shall I convey the shock that devastated the nation?

Archer was a legend. Crowds gathered to catch a glimpse of him wherever he appeared. Women he had never met pressed passionate letters into his hand. Every owner in the kingdom wanted to retain him. He rubbed shoulders with the highest in the land. Well, the second highest, at any rate—Mama not being a frequenter of racecourses. Here, I must own to a personal interest. In April, 1886, Archer rode a doughty little filly by the name of Counterpane to victory in a Maiden Plate at Sandown Park: my first-ever winner on the flat. We were given a rousing ovation from the public. Sadly, two weeks later, Counterpane broke a blood vessel and dropped dead. I bore it with philosophy, yet looking back, I wonder if my filly's untimely fate presaged the tragedy that befell her rider.

I am told that when the dreadful news of Archer reached London, Fleet Street was impassable for the crowds massed outside the principal newspaper offices. Special editions of the evening papers carrying the bare statement that the great jockey was dead sold out in minutes. Extra-special editions were printed and the sheets were snatched unfolded from the bundles faster than the boys could hand them out.

It chanced that the day following, 9 November, was the forty-fifth anniversary of my birth. As usual, flags were hoisted across the land, gun salutes were fired and church bells rang out peals at intervals from an early hour, but the gun crews and the bell ringers might as well have stayed in bed for all the attention my birthday received. One topic, and one alone, engrossed the nation. In the city, members of the Stock Exchange fought with umbrellas for the first edition of *The Times*.

Those who obtained a copy read in the leading article, "A great soldier, a great statesman, a great poet, even a Royal Prince, might die suddenly without giving half so general a shock as has been given by the news of the tragical death of Fred Archer, the jockey."

How true! I was as shaken as any man, although I cannot forbear from pointing out that the remark about a Royal Prince was in deplorable taste, particularly on my birthday.

One never knows what unpleasant shocks lurk unsuspected in the newspapers. I still bristle at the memory of learning in 1876 from *The Times of India* of the proposal to confer the title of Empress on my mother. Neither she nor Disraeli (who accepted his own earldom the same year) had thought fit to tell me about the Royal Titles Act, and I protested vigorously to both, I promise you. In no other country in the world would the next heir to the throne have been treated with such disregard.

Notwithstanding my misgivings about the press, I wanted to know about Archer. I turned out before breakfast and pedaled my tricycle furiously up the drive at Sandringham to meet the delivery boy. Gave him a shock, I fancy. I didn't read the remarks in *The Times* at that juncture. It was all graphically reported in that more congenial organ, *The Sporting Life*.

"Many happy returns of the day, Bertie, my dear," piped my first lady as I repaired to the breakfast room. Dear Alix had made an exceptional effort to be on parade. I can reveal to posterity that the Princess of Wales is not noted for punctuality.

The table was heaped with presents in brightly colored boxes tied with ribbon. A jug of Duminy, *extra sec*, was by my place and a servant hovered for my order. Alix was cooing like a basket of pigeons.

"My birthday is blighted," I informed her.

I must explain that Alix was not aware at this juncture of the tragic tidings from Newmarket. The previous evening, she had retired early. I was entertaining certain of my birthday guests until late. I heard the news of Archer from Knollys, my secretary, about 1:30 A.M.

Alix turned pale. She is inclined to anemia, anyway, and now she was more starched than the tablecloth. "Not another scandal, Bertie?"

"Absolutely not. The very notion," I protested in an outraged tone.

"Then what can have happened?" She put her hand to her collar as another thought occurred. "It isn't—tell me it isn't—bad news from Windsor." Inopportunely, a hint of color returned to her cheeks.

"So far as I'm aware, Mama is in the pink of health," I answered coolly, and then repeated, "The pink of health." (Alix is rather deaf.) "'Long to reign over us,' as the Anthem perpetually reminds one."

She sighed slightly and leaned back. "What, then?"

I tossed her *The Sporting Life.*

"Took his own life?" she read aloud in that Danish chant of hers that makes everything she says sound like Little Jack Horner. "What an unexpected thing to do."

"Due to an aberration of the brain, if the report is to be believed," I explained. "The poor fellow was apparently suffering the effects of typhoid."

"Apparently. You sound skeptical."

"I am," I admitted, adding in a measured voice, "I am not unacquainted with the symptoms."

"Of course, my dearest," Alix affirmed with eyes lowered, doubtless recalling how my father, Prince Albert, rest his soul, died of the dread disease and I myself had practically succumbed to it when I was thirty.

I made a rapid summation that saved her the trouble of reading further. "It seems that yesterday morning Archer was pronounced better and was speaking normally to his friends and family. Sometime early in the afternoon, at Archer's own suggestion, the nurse left the room to get some lunch. Mrs. Coleman, his sister, remained in the bedroom. She crossed the room to look out of the window, and Archer got up from the bed with a revolver in his hand. She ran to him and struggled with him, but he put it to his mouth and shot himself."

"Dreadful," said Alix.

"Rum is the description I would use," said I. "I shall cogitate on this."

I sent word to the chef to prepare a full breakfast, as for a day's shooting. That is to say, bacon and eggs, and plenty of them, followed by Finnan haddock, followed by chicken, followed by toast and butter, helped down with plenty of coffee. With me, breakfast has to be like the evil thereof in the Bible: sufficient unto the day. I had a strong premonition that this day would make heavy demands on my constitution.

Breakfast was not long in coming, or going. I eat swiftly, and with relish.

To please Alix, I unwrapped a box of Corona y Coronas and a pair of carpet slippers that she unsportingly informed me were exclusively for use in my bedroom at Sandringham, and then I was left to ponder further the strange suicide of Frederick James Archer.

Typhoid?

I can vouch for its dramatic effect upon body and brain. When it poleaxed me, toward the end of 1871, I was delirious for days. I am told that I shouted at my attendants, hurled pillows across the room and broke into songs of the sort that you won't find in the English hymnal. Poor Alix had to be restrained from staying in the room with me on account of certain names I uttered in my ravings. Once she tried to enter secretly on hands and knees, and I felled her with a pillow. I was quite oblivious of my conduct, you understand. Even my devoted Mama the Queen was obliged to shelter behind a screen. I hovered between life and death for weeks on end. As the poet dramatically expressed it:

Across the wires, the electric message came:
"He is no better; he is much the same."

WHEN I *DID* RECOVER, THE whole Empire breathed a sigh of relief. There was a service of public thanksgiving in St. Paul's.

In Archer's case, if the account were true, there were no symptoms of delirium on the day of the tragedy. He so impressed his friends that they left him in the charge of the nurse and Mrs. Coleman. He calmly dispatched the nurse to lunch and then dispatched himself with a bullet. A queer case of typhoid, if you want my opinion.

I summoned Sir Francis Knollys. Where would I be without Knollys? A more loyal secretary never picked up a pen. A bit of a stuffed shirt now that he's past fifty, but a regular pal in a scrape, and we've weathered a few in our time. I could a tale unfold of Francis and his collection of garters, but he's saved me from a few warm moments, so no matter.

"I propose to attend the inquest," I informed him.

"The inquest?" he repeated obtusely.

"Into Archer's death. There will have to be one. Kindly make the arrangement, Francis."

"Of course, sir." He hesitated. "I presume you would wish your attendance to be unofficial?"

"If you mean a seat at the back, see that it's well padded."

I opened another present while he went to make inquiries. Mama had sent me the usual cuff links and a copy of *The Golden Treasury*, with the marker pointedly inserted against a poem entitled "A Renunciation." Hope springs eternal in my mother's breast.

Knollys was back before I had time to open another wrapping.

"It's today, sir. The inquest is this afternoon."

"That's uncommonly quick. I wonder what the hurry is."

"Unfortunately, you have a full day of engagements."

"When haven't I?"

"The Mayor of Cambridge is coming this morning to discuss the Imperial Institute Fund."

"Put him off, Francis. I'd much rather attend the inquest."

"The laborers on the Royal Estate are due to assemble in the mews for the customary dinner in honor of your birthday."

"The laborers? For God's sake, they don't require me in attendance to give them an appetite."

"Then there are your birthday guests: Lord and Lady Randolph Churchill, the Comte and Comtesse de Paris, Prince and Princess Christian—"

"Where precisely is this inquest taking place?"

Knollys made no attempt to muffle the sigh he gave. "Newmarket, sir. At Archer's private residence."

"At what time?"

"Two o'clock."

"Then I can be back by six at the latest. The Princess will entertain my guests, and I'll see them at my dinner party. Order the carriage."

Although I could think of jollier reasons for visiting Newmarket, I wasn't going to miss this morbid matinee for anything. Fred Archer had been in a few fast finishes in his time, but an inquest within twenty-four hours of his death was remarkable going, even by his standards.

As for my birthday visitors, I reflected as my carriage bowled along the road to Newmarket, I had no conscience about abandoning them for the afternoon. Randolph was fortunate to be received at all (and knew it) after his contemptible behavior in years past over some innocent letters I once penned to Lady Aylesford. (While I was abroad, in India, he came to my wife Alix with threats that he would publish them unless I brought my influence to bear on a divorce case in which his brother was the guilty party. I was so incensed that I challenged him to a duel, which of course he was not man enough to accept. For eight years after, I refused to dine at any house where he was invited.) Of my other guests, the Comte de Paris had come only to shoot pheasant. And the appalling, one-eyed Christian came on sufferance, because he was married to my sister Lenchen (Helena). Setting aside our family difference over Schleswig-Holstein, the man was bereft of the most basic tenets of social behavior. His favorite party piece was to produce his several spare glass eyes at dinner and range them on the table. If that didn't sufficiently disgust the company, he would pass around the bloodshot one he wore when he was suffering from a cold.

The Archer residence, Falmouth House, turned out to be an impressive mansion for a jockey, a multi-gabled redbrick structure in its own grounds on the Bury Road. He had built it three years before when he married the daughter of the trainer, John Dawson. But it proved to be an ill-fated home for the couple. Their infant son died there a few hours after birth in January, 1884, and the following November, his wife also died after giving birth to a second child. And now Falmouth House had seen a third fatality within three years of being built.

My carriage was met by a fellow in a Norfolk jacket whom I took to be one of Archer's family until he announced himself as Captain Buckfast.

Buckfast. Mark his name. I knew it from the racing calendar. He owned and raced horses, and was a close friend of Archer's. I assumed he was sent by the family to meet the royal visitor on account of his army rank. That's the usual form: find an ex-officer and push him forward. Buckfast was adequate to the task, if somewhat diffident. I would have said he was past forty, but my estimates of age have given me several unwelcome surprises of late. I find that I'm classing men of my own age as some years senior to me. I shall have to revise my estimation of what forty-five actually means in terms of thinning hair and thickening elsewhere. If you want to picture Captain Buckfast, he was possessed of a military man's mustache with waxed ends, behind which lurked a less dramatic countenance, brown eyes set widely apart and pale lips that didn't propose to smile without excessive encouragement. His most interesting feature was a crippled left arm that I learned later had been practically hacked off with a spear in the Zulu War.

Not wishing to advertise my presence, I sent the carriage

away and asked Buckfast about the arrangements. Once I had established the plan of the house, I had him show me to the bathroom. I'm pretty adept at hide-and-seek in country houses. After a quiet cigar, while the coroner went through the preliminaries downstairs, I planned to make my way to the dining room adjacent to the drawing room. From there, I could follow the proceedings through an open door without being observed by the press.

It didn't go quite as planned.

The cacophony of voices downstairs increased as more people arrived. Apart from the coroner and his officials, there were witnesses, the family, the jury and the press. When I judged from a sudden abatement of the noise that the inquest had begun, I leaned over the landing rail and heard the jury sworn in. The words weren't audible, but I could tell the different tones of voices. I soon picked up the measured accents of the coroner.

I decided to make my move down the stairs. Unfortunately, I had only reached the third or fourth when I heard the scraping of chairs.

I stopped as if petrified.

A door opened, and people came out into the hall below. They started up the stairs.

Mercifully, I was obscured from their view by the bend in the stairway. I turned and reclimbed those four stairs and pushed open the nearest door.

I was in a bedroom, which didn't surprise me. The room was occupied, which did. The occupant was lying in an open coffin. I was alone with the mortal remains of Fred Archer.

But not for long. The jury was coming upstairs to view the body.

CHAPTER 3

My first instinct was to look for cover. I had the choice of a large mahogany wardrobe or the space under the bed. Neither struck me as suitable. If a lady's honor were in jeopardy, I wouldn't think twice about climbing into a wardrobe or taking my chance beside a chamber pot, but this wasn't that sort of emergency.

I glanced toward the curtains and dismissed that possibility as well. I wasn't a performer in a French farce. My status in the nation obliged me to conduct myself in as dignified a fashion as circumstances permitted. There was nothing I could do except abandon all ideas of remaining anonymous.

I took up a regal stance (left thumb tucked behind overcoat lapel, right hand holding stick, hat and gloves at waist level) beside the coffin as the coroner led the jury into the room. He was giving them encouragement in a well-practiced manner. ". . . a dismal, but necessary, formality. However, gentlemen, the appearance of the deceased is not so disturbing as you might anticipate, the bullet having passed through the mouth and exited at the back of the head. So, if you please . . ."

They lined up on either side. To my astonishment, no one looked twice at me. They simply joined me beside the coffin. I could only assume that their melancholy duty had blinded them to everything else, even an encounter with the Heir Apparent.

The coroner made a small lifting gesture with his fingers that I supposed for a moment had some ritualistic significance. Then he repeated, "If you please . . ." and it dawned on me that he was gesturing to me.

Here I must intrude a sartorial note. In keeping with the somber occasion, I had dressed in a dark overcoat with black velvet revers and black necktie, and I was carrying a silk hat and black kid gloves. Either the coroner had taken me for an undertaker, or he was giving me the opportunity to pass myself off as such.

I didn't need any more bidding. Obligingly, I bent forward and lifted the piece of linen that covered poor Fred's face.

He was a pitiful sight. The last time I had seen him was a fortnight before, directly after he had lost the Cambridgeshire in a desperate finish, and he had looked extremely dejected then, far too troubled for a man who had won the Derby earlier in the year. It sounds trite to say that he looked decidedly worse now, and I had better explain myself better. It was unmistakably the Archer profile: the broad forehead, well-shaped nose, prominent cheekbones and neat, determined jaw. Still, essentially, a young man's face. I daresay rigor mortis produces strange effects, and no doubt what I noticed was nothing remarkable, but I swear that there was an expression on the features. An expression of terror.

"The jury may wish to examine the back of the head," the coroner said to me, jolting me out of my thoughts. There was no doubt of it; he took me for an undertaker.

I was starting to wonder if I was equal to the job when one of the jurymen, bless him, spoke up. "I suggest we defer to the medical evidence on this. None of us are used to looking at bullet wounds."

There were general murmurs of support.

"Very well," said the coroner. He turned to me. "In that case, that will be sufficient."

I replaced the sheet immediately, and took a step back.

"While we are here," the coroner told the jury, "kindly observe the window where one of the witnesses, Mrs. Coleman, will tell you she was standing before the fatality occurred. Also the night commode beside the bed where the revolver was apparently kept. And the hearth rug upon which the deceased fell. And now, with your cooperation, I propose to resume the inquest downstairs."

They shuffled out without another word between them, leaving me with the corpse. I must confess to feeling slightly piqued that they hadn't recognized me, but on balance it had turned out well. And the story of Bertie the undertaker would go down famously at my birthday party.

Looking back on my career as an amateur detective, I see that it really began when I was left alone in Archer's bedroom. Purely by accident, I'd been afforded a splendid opportunity of searching for clues to the mystery of his sudden death. I'm not given to rummaging through other people's possessions, you understand, but as the man in question was in no mind to object, I made an exception here. So before following the others downstairs, I opened the wardrobe.

The late Mr. Archer had a fine collection of suits, which I methodically searched. Unhappily for me, he also had an efficient valet who had emptied the pockets. I didn't find so much as a spare button. I turned to the tallboy beside the washstand. Nothing of interest to an investigator had been left there. I searched the small chest of drawers and the night commode without result. There wasn't a letter or a visiting card to be found. Not even a betting slip. I couldn't believe that any man led such a colorless life, least of all the most famous jockey in history. Someone had diligently removed every personal item, even photographs. Every bedroom I've ever slept in—and I speak from not inconsiderable experience—has had its display of family photographs on the tallboy: Mama and Grandmama and the Great Aunts and Our Wedding (which I generally turn to the wall). In this room of death there wasn't a picture of the late Mrs. Archer, or even the child so tragically orphaned. I left without a clue, but with my curiosity vastly increased.

Captain Buckfast was giving evidence as I descended the stairs. I moved unobtrusively across the hall and into the empty dining room, where a chair had been thoughtfully provided close to the open door. I was afforded a view of the coroner and the witness without exposing myself to the eyes of the press.

"About four years," Buckfast was saying.

"You were very intimate with him?"

"Yes, sir."

"You visited him frequently?"

"Yes."

"And accompanied him to America on a visit?"

"That is so."

"That was toward the end of 1884, after his wife died?"

"Yes."

"And you have formally identified the body upstairs as that of Frederick James Archer?"

"Yes."

"Now, would you tell us when you last saw him alive, and how he appeared?"

The invitation to provide some information of his own appeared to throw the worthy captain slightly off-balance. He was happier with one-word responses. "I was with him until about noon yesterday. He appeared to be much improved, so I went out. When I returned shortly after two, I heard that he had shot himself."

"Did you ever hear him speak of suicide?"

"Never."

"Did you think he was a man likely to do such an act?"

"No, sir."

"You had conversation with him in the morning?"

"Yes."

"Did he say anything that might have indicated such an intention?"

"No, sir."

The coroner paused. Buckfast stood rigidly waiting for the next question. If someone had shouted, "About face," I am sure he would have obeyed.

"You noticed nothing unusual in his conversation?"

"Only the wandering."

The coroner leaned forward to catch the word. "The what?"

"The wandering. He would converse to a certain extent and then seemed to wander."

"I see. How would you describe his state of mind when you left him at noon?"

"Happy and contented."

"Really?" The coroner picked up a pen from the silver inkstand in front of him, dipped it in the ink and made a note. He resumed, "The deceased had recently been depriving himself of food. Is that correct?"

"Yes, sir."

"Why, exactly?"

"He was wasting for the Cambridgeshire. He rode St. Mirin at eight stone, seven pound."

"This was an exceptionally low weight for the deceased to achieve?"

"Yes."

"He was a tall man for a jockey?"

"Five feet, eight inches."

"By 'wasting,' you mean shedding weight by starving himself?"

"And other methods," volunteered the captain.

"Could you be more specific?"

"He used Turkish baths. And his mixture."

"His mixture?"

"A potion he took."

"Of what, precisely, did this potion consist?"

"I couldn't say. He was very secretive about it."

"It was purgative in effect?"

"I think you'd find it so."

The coroner gave a thin smile. "I am most unlikely to try. Thank you, Captain. I have no more questions for you, unless the jury wishes to ask you anything."

A chair was found for the next witness, Mrs. Emily Coleman, the jockey's sister. She was deeply affected by the tragedy, and even the simple formality of identifying herself caused her difficulty. In appearance and manner she reminded me slightly of my youngest sister Beatrice, with her forlorn, yet winsome, look.

After an interval while we all shifted uneasily in our chairs, Mrs. Coleman found her voice, and then it was difficult to stop her.

"I live here, in my brother's house, and I was with him when he died. I have been with him constantly since he was brought home from Lewes races on Thursday."

"That would have been the fourth of November," the coroner put in to assist his clerk, but the lady hadn't paused.

"I didn't think he was very ill that evening, and he went to bed about half past eleven. The next day, he was unable to get up, so I sent for Dr. Wright, and he took his temperature and it was so high, he said he wanted a second opinion, but Fred refused. Dr. Wright spoke to me and insisted that Dr. Latham was sent for from Cambridge on the Saturday—"

"Sixth of November," interposed the coroner.

". . . and by this time poor Fred was wandering in his mind. He seemed to forget things he had said a few minutes previous. He wouldn't take his medicine. He just kept asking for his mixture. The doctors said he was suffering from a severe chill. They arranged for two nurses to come and help me. The funny thing was that by Monday he appeared to be much better. I had several long conversations with him."

At the rate she was pouring out words, I could well believe it. How much the patient had been allowed to contribute was another question.

"Although he was better, he still wandered in his mind at times, and he was very anxious whether he was going to get over it. Then about two o'clock he said he wanted to speak to me alone. He told me to send the nurse away, which I did."

"So we are coming to the fatal incident," said the coroner in a fortissimo observation that finally induced Mrs. Coleman to pause in her narrative. He was enabled to add, with less bellows, "Tell me, did you notice anything peculiar in his manner?"

"No, he was quite normal. It was nothing unusual for him to ask me to send one of the nurses away, and I thought nothing of it. After she'd gone, I walked toward the window and looked out. Fred suddenly said, 'Are they coming?' Then I heard a noise, and when I turned, he was out of bed and walking across the room, near the door. To my horror, I saw that he had a gun in his hand. I ran toward him and tried to push the gun to one side. He put one arm around my neck and thrust me against the door. I don't know where he got the strength from. He had the revolver in his left hand. Then he put it to his mouth and . . ." Mrs. Coleman bowed her head and sobbed.

At a nod from the coroner, another woman stepped forward to comfort the witness. I think we all felt profoundly sympathetic. No one who had heard the account could have failed to picture the horror of what Mrs. Coleman had endured. I could imagine what the more lurid newspapers would make of it.

When the lady had recovered sufficiently, the coroner said, "There are just a few more details the court requires from you. During this scene that you have just described, did the deceased utter any other words?"

"I've told you the only words he spoke."

"'Are they coming?'"

"Yes, sir."

"Did you speak to him?"

"I had no chance. I was screaming for help. Nobody heard me, because the door had closed in the struggle. I got help eventually by ringing the bell."

"How long did the whole transaction take, would you estimate?"

"Not above two minutes, sir."

"And how would you account for it?"

"He seemed to be seized with a sudden impulse. I can't put it better than that."

That concluded Mrs. Coleman's evidence. She was helped away from the chair.

What would you, dear reader, have been thinking at this stage? From the evidence given by Captain Buckfast and Mrs. Coleman, did Archer's behavior sound like a fit of delirium or an aberration of the brain, as the press had suggested?

The crime of suicide presents us with a dilemma. On the one hand, it is an abominable act, punishable by law if the miscreant is unsuccessful in his attempt. On the other, we feel the profoundest sympathy for the close relatives of an individual who has taken his life. This lures us into hypocrisy. If a man is stopped before he pulls the trigger, we send him to prison. If we are too late, we look for signs that he was temporarily insane. From the evidence thus far, it appeared likely that Archer knew what he was doing. I looked forward with interest to the medical witnesses.

First, however, we had Archer's valet, Harry Sarjent. It was he who had first answered the bell and come to the aid of Mrs. Coleman. He explained how he had seen his master lying on the hearth rug, and how he had picked up the revolver that had fallen from Archer's hand. His evidence was all about the gun. About a month previously, Archer had become nervous about a recent burglary in Newmarket and sent his revolver for repair. It had been given to him as a present by a grateful owner. He had loaded it himself and given the valet instructions to put it in the night commode beside his bed when he was at home. At other times, the valet was directed to sleep in the house, with the gun beside him. When Archer had returned from Brighton on the Thursday, the valet, in accordance with instructions, had deposited the revolver in the drawer of the commode.

The nurse, Charlotte Hornidge, came next, and she couldn't have been above nineteen, with a high color to her cheek and black curls thrusting from her cap, far too pretty a creature to empty a bedpan, in my estimation.

The coroner agreed with me, from the way he took off his glasses and cleaned them two or three times.

"I was sent to dinner at seventeen minutes past two," stated Nurse Hornidge, which impressed us all. Here, we thought, is a meticulous witness, as well as a decorative one. "Mr. Archer suggested it to Mrs. Coleman."

Perhaps poor Fred was out of his mind, after all, I thought. Any sane man would have sent his sister to dinner and asked the nurse to remain.

"I had hardly been downstairs one minute when the bell rang violently," she continued confidently. "I also heard cries of help, and a sound as if a pistol had gone off. I dashed upstairs and saw the patient lying on the hearth rug, quite dead. Mrs. Coleman was screaming. The valet was also present. He was just ahead of me."

"You say that your patient was dead, my dear. Did you examine him?"

"I saw that he was bleeding in his mouth. I looked in his eyes and felt his pulse, but I didn't examine him further. I waited for the doctor."

"Eminently sensible," commented the coroner with an ingratiating smile. "Now perhaps you would say something about his state of mind, as you perceived it that morning. Was he rational, so far as you could tell?"

"Oh, yes. When I spoke, he always answered rationally, but he was very low-spirited when I was nursing him. I remember a conversation when he told me he thought he was going to die. I told him to cheer up, because there was no reason to think he would die. He replied, 'I wish I was of your way of thinking.'"

"But you still found him rational? He didn't appear to you to wander in his mind?"

"No, sir."

"Not in any way at all?"

"Not in the least."

"You're quite certain?"

"Utterly."

I may be mistaken, but I thought the coroner sounded slightly less enchanted by Nurse Hornidge when he thanked her for her testimony and told her to return to her seat.

The final witness stepped forward. Dr. J. R. Wright of Newmarket was a silver-haired, crisply spoken man, who must have appeared many times before the coroner. His manner of giving evidence carried authority.

"I was Mr. Archer's medical man for fourteen years. He had pretty good health. I have never attended him for a serious illness until this case of typhoid. I was called to see him last Friday morning, the fifth of November, and I found him in a high state of fever, extremely restless. I prescribed for him and saw him again at two. By then the fever symptoms had increased. Indeed, his temperature was so very high that I suggested having a second opinion. The patient declined, but I took it on myself to send for Dr. Latham from Cambridge."

"He is an authority on fevers?" inquired the coroner.

"He is a colleague whose opinion I value," stated the doctor in a tone that made the question seem superfluous.

"Kindly proceed."

"Dr. Latham sent his carriage for me the next morning at seven-thirty. We examined the patient together. He was no better. His temperature was the same, and he was not prepared to be cooperative."

"In what way, Doctor?"

"He told us he didn't require another medicine. He wanted his wasting mixture."

"Why was that?"

"He had a delusion that a dinner he'd eaten three days ago was still in his stomach."

"Ah," said the coroner, removing his glasses and placing them on the table. "His mind was wandering."

"It is not unusual in cases of fever."

"I'm sure. Pray go on, Doctor."

"Dr. Latham attended again in the afternoon and told the patient he had typhoid fever, and he then became more quiet."

"You agreed on the diagnosis?"

Dr. Wright answered, "There is no question of it. Admittedly, the patient appeared to rally during the course of the weekend and his temperature fell on Sunday afternoon, but this is not uncommon. In fact, on Monday morning, he was better."

"When you say 'better,' do you mean that his temperature was normal on the morning he died?"

"Fluctuations in temperature are to be expected," answered Dr. Wright.

"I must have a more precise answer to my question, Doctor."

"The patient's temperature was normal yesterday morning."

"How was his behavior?"

"He was very low-spirited. He told me continually that he would die. I had a reassuring talk with him and left about nine-thirty. I was called back in the afternoon, about two-thirty. When I saw the deceased, he was on his back on the floor, covered with a sheet, quite dead. There was a wound at the back of his mouth. On examining the back of his head, I found an opening between the two upper cervical vertebrae. I was shown the revolver, and I have seen the bullet found on the dressing table, and I have no doubt that it was the bullet that passed through the spinal column, causing death."

"I am sure the jury has been greatly assisted by your evidence, Doctor. I have just one or two questions more concerning the state of mind of the deceased."

The doctor didn't need to have them. He knew what was wanted. "I would say that he was not delirious in his fever, so much as disconnected in his thoughts. It seemed from the commencement of the illness to take the form of depression. One must also take account of the weakened state he was in from reducing his weight by unnatural amounts. This, followed by the fever, so disordered his brain that he was not accountable for his actions. In other words, he was temporarily insane when he committed the act."

Approving murmurs were heard. It was as if the doctor had spoken for the whole of Newmarket, and there was no question what the jury's verdict would be.

Fred Archer was found to have committed suicide while in a state of temporary insanity induced by typhoid fever.

CHAPTER 4

Hold on to your hat and keep your wits about you, for we're about to make a backward leap. After that depressing inquest, I propose to treat you to a breath of fresh air and some sport. Of the four-legged variety, naturally. We'll project ourselves back a fortnight, and bring poor Archer briefly back to life, put him on St. Mirin and look at his last ride of consequence, the 1886 Cambridgeshire. My weakness for the Turf is well known, so in case this smacks of self-indulgence, let me assure you that the race is fundamental to the crime I shall unfold.

To Headquarters, then, on Tuesday, 26 October (Headquarters being the name by which Newmarket is affectionately known to all patrons of the Turf). A day for topcoats and mufflers: chill, slate gray and with a stiff breeze blowing off the fens. Not that October weather would deter the race-going public. They came in their thousands, trainloads from Liverpool Street and St. Pancras, the Midlands and the North. Personally, I avoid traveling on the day of a big race if I can possibly help it. I arrive on the first or second day of the meeting and stay overnight in my rooms in the Jockey Club. If affairs of state compel me to travel on race day, I make an outrageously early start. It's either that, or trail the last five miles in slow procession between the four-in-hand full of jovial "men" from Cambridge, and a trap containing a farmer and his giggling daughters. No thank you.

I wouldn't mention this to the good people who live there, but between ourselves, the town of Newmarket is a fearful disappointment when you first see it. It's little more than a stretch of the London to Norwich Road lined with dull buildings, most of them modern. The only edifice of interest is the Jockey Club, and that chooses to sit with its back to the High Street.

Mercifully, there's more to Newmarket than its buildings. From first light onward, the High Street echoes to the clatter of hooves as the trainers lead their strings to the gallops. See the breath on the morning air and the shimmer of well-groomed flanks and you'll know what animates this place. It has been linked with the horse ever since Queen Boadicea in her chariot led the Iceni against the Romans, but the credit for making it the headquarters of racing should be awarded to the Stuarts. That shameless old reprobate, King James I, built a palace and royal stables here and was rebuked for spending too much time at the races, as were his son and grandson, Charles I and II. They have my sympathy. Do you know, my mama the Queen has never patronized a Newmarket meeting? Before I was old enough to declare an interest, she had the old palace of Newmarket auctioned. It was demolished by the purchaser, and now a Congregational chapel stands on the site.

On this Cambridgeshire day, the High Street was practically impassable by noon. There is always a throng outside the Subscription Rooms, where the principal bets are laid. I had made sure of getting reasonable odds the previous night, so for the purposes of this narrative we can proceed at once to the Heath.

The Cambridgeshire is the last great race of the season, with a character all its own. It gives the final chance for a horse to impress before it goes to winter quarters, an uphill one-mile, two hundred and forty yards for three-year-olds and over, where sprinters and stayers can try conclusions. Fortunes are staked on the outcome. For a betting man, the good old Cambridgeshire has more to commend it than the classics. Form and the handicapper aren't infallible, thank the Lord, and there's a rich history of sensations. Catch 'em Alive was the winner in 1863, but in the weighing room afterward, calamity! His jockey couldn't draw the weight. They were about to disqualify him and award the stakes to the second, when someone thought of examining the scales. Would you believe it, some blackguard had tampered with them by fastening sheet lead to the bottom of the weight-scale. Another drama that outraged many was Isonomy's two-length win at 40-1 in 1878, after that foxy old trainer John Porter kept his form from the touts for a twelvemonth. Fred Gretton, the owner, is said to have netted £40,000. Is it any wonder that I sent my horses to Porter? And I'll give you one more Cambridgeshire controversy: Bendigo's win by a head in 1883, believed by no one except his backers, and precious few of them, if truth be told.

Back to 1886. The day couldn't have started in finer style. My filly, Lady Peggy, easily carried home my colors at 10—1 in the Maiden Plate for two-year-olds, putting the crowd in bonny humor and one hundred guineas in my pocket. Amid a chorus of loyal acclaim, I took myself and several of my party down to the unsaddling.

Archer was the jockey. For me, nothing can equal the pleasure of leading one of my own into the winner's enclosure, and I don't mind admitting that my heart swelled when the champion jockey dismounted and stood beside me and my steaming filly. As I write these words, I have a tinted photograph on my desk that brings it vividly to mind, Archer in my colors, the purple with gold braid and scarlet sleeves, and the gold-fringed black velvet cap.

I'm racking my memory to see if I can possibly recall any sign that he was under strain. It's difficult. The pinched look is common to all jockeys except boys, and Archer, as you know, had wasted more than usual to make the weight for his Cambridgeshire ride. He was an inch and a half taller than I and weighed all of six stones less (though I've never aspired to be a jockey).

The only sign of anything untoward was that he was talkative. I must tell you that the greatest jockey in history wasn't noted for his conversation. He generally saved his breath to cool his porridge, as the saying goes. Yet here in the unsaddling enclosure, surrounded by the usual gogglers and fawners, I was treated to a regular torrent of words.

"She's a plucky one, your Royal Highness," says he. "I wouldn't call her a classic prospect, but she'll earn some tin if you pick her races carefully. Tidy work over the last furlong, wasn't it? When I started to ride her with my hands, she half stopped and pricked up her ears as if she wondered what it meant. Then she did all I asked. Wasn't it a tonic to watch?"

"Emphatically," I answered. "But let's give the jockey some credit as well."

"Thank you, sir."

"You must be feeling confident," I commented, fishing for information.

"Cock-a-hoop, sir."

"So should I chance a tenner on St. Mirin?"

"Every tenner you can spare, sir. I haven't won a Cambridgeshire yet, but I've never had a prospect like today."

Lord Edward Somerset, the owner of the favorite, Carlton, happened to be one of my party, and close enough to hear this. "Get away, Fred!" says he. "You won't beat my colt and you know it. Yours hasn't learned how to gallop. Alec Taylor tried them together and Carlton took it by a street."

"I heard, my Lord," commented Fred impassively, as he

loosened Lady Peggy's girth, "but did you take the riders into account? The lad on St. Mirin was a novice."

"Where did you discover that?" asked Somerset, flushing to the tips of his ears.

"From the horse's mouth," responded Fred in all seriousness. He paused before he added, "The poor beast was never off the bit." With that, he lifted off the saddle, touched his cap and left me laughing, and Edward Somerset purple faced.

"Pig obstinate," Edward commented when the jockey was out of earshot. "He was offered the ride on Carlton and he refused."

"Do I detect a dwindling of confidence?" I asked.

"Not on your life."

Nonetheless, I dispatched one of my party to Tattersall's ring to put fifty on St. Mirin at 10-1. In the Subscription Rooms the previous evening, I'd already backed an elderly outsider, The Sailor Prince, at 25-1 for sentimental reasons (he was the son of a horse called Albert Victor, and *my* A. V. went through Dartmouth, and my other boy George is in the Navy still).

Edward Somerset's story of the trial between Carlton and St. Mirin was true, and pretty common knowledge. Both colts were trained at Manton by Alec Taylor and regarded as useful three-year-olds. One morning on the Marlborough Downs, observed by touts from all the sporting press, he raced them over a measured mile, and Carlton came out an easy victor.

Why, then, was Archer so confident of St. Mirin taking the Cambridgeshire? And why so talkative? Uniquely in his career, he had made sure every newspaper blazoned his confidence: "The crack jockey fancies his mount immensely."

Certainly St. Mirin was well sired, by that plucky Derby winner, Hermit, out of Lady Paramount. It had promised well, but hadn't won anything as a two-year-old. If I'm any judge of horseflesh, it was too light about the loin and flank to possess much stamina. I like an animal with something behind besides ribs.

My thoughts returned to St. Mirin's hindquarters when the Cambridgeshire entrants were paraded in the saddling enclosure known to all Turfites as the Birdcage. Prominent there was the animal's owner, the Dowager Duchess of Montrose, as formidable a female as ever graced the Turf. She is known unkindly, but not inaptly, as Six-Mile Bottom, and if St. Mirin had been half so generously endowed as she in that portion of the anatomy, the race would have been as good as over.

Did that strike you as an ungallant observation? The fact is that Carrie Montrose had long since put herself beyond the pale. Before I was born, she scandalized society by insulting my mother the Queen. This was over the so-called Bedchamber Plot in 1839, when Mama, encouraged by Lord Melbourne, stoutly refused to dismiss certain of her Whig ladies-in-waiting, and so frustrated Peel in his attempt to form a Tory administration. Mama doted on Lord Melbourne, you know, and thanks to her firmness, he was returned as Prime Minister. At the Ascot races she invited Melbourne to sit beside her in her carriage for the drive up the racecourse. This was all too much for the young Duchess of Montrose and another Tory woman. They stepped brazenly forward and hissed the Queen. Mama was incensed. She said such creatures deserved to be horsewhipped. If you ask me, there was intemperance on both sides. Mama wouldn't like it said, but she and Carrie Montrose have much in common. The difference is that Carrie's tantrums take place in public.

On this Cambridgeshire afternoon, the Duchess had wrapped herself in a sable coat that must have decimated the wildlife of Canada. She was haranguing Archer as he waited to mount St. Mirin, and half the racecourse could hear it: "I want no sleeping in the saddle, Fred. He's a horse in a million and I adore him, but don't spare the whip if he slackens."

Stony faced, the greatest jockey of the age kept his eyes on the horse in a million. No one knew exactly how much the Duchess had paid him as a retainer, but it was close to five figures for a claim of any sort, so he was well compensated for any embarrassment.

On the far side of the Birdcage, Edward Somerset issued final instructions to the elder of the Woodburn brothers, who was riding Carlton, with only six stone, thirteen pounds, compared with St. Mirin's eight stone seven. In Tattersall's ring, Carlton remained the clear favorite, although his price had lengthened slightly. St. Mirin, for all the confidence bestowed in him by Archer and his owner, was some way down the betting. Melton, the 1885 Derby and St. Leger winner, was being heavily backed at 100-6, in spite of his in-and-out form and the nine stone, seven he was handicapped. Tyrone, of whom I knew little, had come in at 8-1. St. Mirin's on-course price had lengthened to 100-8.

The signal was given to mount, and we patrons of the Turf made the best speed we could to our points of vantage. I called for my hack and cantered up the hill to the finishing post. The Cambridgeshire, I must explain, takes a different course from the rest of the day's program. It starts near the new stand at the Rowley Mile and proceeds up a stiff rise, "on the collar" all the way, to the part of the Heath known as the top of the town. A forty-minute interval is given after the finish of the previous race to allow the public to foot it up the hill, but few who make the effort are likely to be satisfied with what they see. A really good view of the Cambridgeshire is difficult to come by. You need to be on the roof of a brougham at the very least to look down the steep gradient to the start. The carriages reach all the way past the rails. I'm afraid the groundlings catch only a glimpse of the jockeys' jackets, unless they miss the finish altogether and station themselves opposite the Red Post, about two furlongs from home.

My carriage was by the winning post. Good-humored shouts and applause hailed me as I clambered up to the box seat and focused my race glasses on the advance flag at the start. The starter's assistants were still trying to get some semblance of order into the field, so I put down my glasses and took a warming sip of brandy. I defy anyone not to feel dry-mouthed with anticipation at the sight of that emerald band of freshly mown turf stretching away across the Heath.

Carlton or St. Mirin?

Lord Edward Somerset or the Duchess of Montrose?

Sixteen had cantered to the start, one of the smallest fields in memory. I mounted the roof of my carriage and got another cheer. I secured my top hat more firmly, for there was the devil of a wind blowing up the course, likely to trouble all but the strongest. Several others of my party who had joined me on the roof did likewise.

I held my glasses steady and picked out the start again.

They were moving toward the tapes. There was some hesitation as one reared up and tried to turn. The jockey was quick to assert his control.

The flag fell. The familiar, irresistible shout went up.

I trained my glasses on the multicolored line as it stirred and rippled like the tail of a kite. Without a doubt they were charging up the course, yet they scarcely appeared to progress at all. For an agonizing interval it was impossible to tell who had taken up the running, then the name Carlton was on everyone's lips. I shifted my glasses to the left. The colors of Mr. Somers, as Edward is known—blue, with white diamonds—definitely showed in front on the lower ground. It was already obvious that Carlton was setting a scorching pace. They had all settled down to their work, and I couldn't make out who was second for a long time.

Then I glimpsed St. Mirin, tucked in usefully behind the

leader; you'll understand that I have a sharp eye for a scarlet sleeve, and the Montrose colors are all of that hue. Tom Cannon, on Melton, was close up. The three favored horses had chosen to make their running together on the lower ground, pursued by several others, while another group, including Tyrone and The Sailor Prince, had elected to strike out on the right.

As they approached the Red House, the favorite still led, and those wily horsemen, Archer and Cannon, were preparing to challenge. I gripped my glasses and shouted with the crowd. I could see young Woodburn desperately trying to liven Carlton with some rib roasters, but Somerset's colt appeared to be straining to master the hill.

The three fixed in my focus were raising a veritable cloud of steam. The wind and the gradient were taking a toll of them all, and there were still two furlongs to run. Carlton's stride was visibly shortening. Was St. Mirin's? I feared so.

To another roar from the crowd, Melton moved out to challenge the leader. Cannon's *eau-de-Nil* jacket appeared to show in front. He was sitting well. Melton had a glorious action and Tom didn't need to be told he was on a good thing.

Then, by Jupiter, the scarlet of St. Mirin showed! He drew level with Carlton. He challenged Melton. He dashed into the lead. Too soon? I wondered. Better than being boxed up, I tried to tell myself. I ground my teeth in apprehension at Archer's temerity. I'm a dreadful faint heart when watching something my money is on.

Tom Cannon is no slouch. He has collected every classic in his time. In 1882, he took the 2000 Guineas, the Derby and the Oaks, and he's been runner-up to Archer as champion jockey more times than I cared to remember at this stage of the race. He was making a fight of it now.

The whips were out. They were so close that I could hear the drumming of hooves and see the mud kicked up. Carlton appeared to have shot his bolt, which subdued some of the crowd, yet there was still a tremendous din around me.

I suffered agonies as Melton edged closer to St. Mirin. Cannon has a reputation for gentle handling, yet I tell you, in that final furlong he flogged his mount as soundly as ever Archer punished a horse. Nor, it goes without saying, was St. Mirin spared the whip. Whatever the result, Carrie Montrose would have no cause to complain, for Archer obeyed her instructions impeccably.

And I should have trusted him to find enough. Who else but Archer would one depend upon to get up in a neck-and-neck finish? He was the master. When the horse was off the bit and dashing full pelt for the post, Fred knew precisely when to use the whip and how to stand on the stirrups and get so far forward that it was practically his cap that first crossed the line.

Fifty yards from home, Melton faltered. In his Derby year, he might have held on, but as a four-year-old carrying top weight he couldn't sustain the effort. He threw up his head, and I knew he was beaten.

What a fright he had given me!

I lowered my glasses and cheered St. Mirin and his rider.

How often has it been borne home to me that nothing in this sport is certain? From nowhere, it seemed, a blur of black and Indian red appeared on the far side. Something was challenging St. Mirin on the top ground. It had come out of the ruck and was finishing faster than Carlton and Melton. Damn my eyes, it was faster than St. Mirin!

Archer must have seen the danger at the edge of his vision. His head didn't turn, but he used the whip again. St. Mirin and its challenger passed the post together. I was opposite the line and I couldn't separate them.

"What was it?" I demanded of one of my party.

"The Sailor Prince, sir."

The Sailor Prince! My outsider at 25-1!

Do you see what I meant about the Cambridgeshire? This animal's form was laughable. It was the oldest horse in the field, a six-year-old that had run the race twice before and never finished better than ninth!

The crowd had lapsed into the buzz of anguish and frustration that follows an unexpected result. Few had backed either St. Mirin or The Sailor Prince, but I was doubly satisfied. Whatever the outcome, I'd picked the winner. Now, which would it be?

These things always take longer than you expect, and I hate suspense, so I got down from my carriage to seek an opinion from the jockeys.

By the time I arrived in the weighing room, Archer was stepping off the scales, pale, flecked with mud, eyes downcast.

"Well, Fred, what's your opinion?" I asked straight out. "Come on, man, don't play the oyster."

Hearing my voice, he looked across, twitched his features into something that was intended for a smile, and said without much exultation, "I believe I held him off, sir."

I noticed Tiny White, the lad who had ridden The Sailor Prince, give a slight shake of the head, but nothing else was said until we all stood outside waiting for the numbers to be hoisted in the frame. Then Sir George Chetwynd came up to Archer and asked his opinion, and the champion contradicted his earlier verdict and said, "I was beaten. I allowed Tom Cannon to kid me."

He was right. A moment later The Sailor Prince was declared the winner by a head. It was the oldest horse ever to win a Cambridgeshire.

I told Archer to have no regrets on my account, as I'd backed the winner, and then I asked him the meaning of his remark about Cannon.

"I shouldn't have taken him on so early," said he. "Mine had nothing more to give when the outsider made its run."

"You didn't disgrace yourself, Fred," I tried to assure him.

He gave me a bleak look and spoke the last words I ever heard him utter: "I wish I agreed with you, sir."

I took it as a typical Archer remark after losing a race he believed he should have won. Poor beggar, I thought, you've got another rough ride in prospect when Carrie Montrose catches up with you. I wouldn't care to receive one of her tongue-lashings. Almost as daunting as a summons to Windsor after a night out with the Marlborough House set.

I don't know what Carrie had to say to Archer, but that same evening she sold St. Mirin, the colt she "adored," to the Duke of Westminster for 4,500 guineas.

And the real story of the race had yet to come out.

CHAPTER 5

After the inquest, I remained for some time in the dining room of Falmouth House, not wishing to reveal myself to the gentlemen of the press. Looking at my surroundings, it seemed eminently reasonable that Archer should have decided to equip himself with a revolver, for the sideboard practically groaned with silver trophies and the walls were crowded with paintings. Four of his Derby winners were represented there in oils, with the prime position over the mantelpiece awarded to Arnull's portrait of Bend Or, and no wonder, considering the phenomenal manner in which the big chestnut colt overcame Robert the Devil in 1880. Did you ever hear the story of what happened to Archer before that celebrated race? If you're a serious reader (i.e. without a sense of humor), you have my permission to skip the next paragraph or two, because it has no bearing on the mystery, but if, like me, you are partial to a spot of amusing gossip, read on.

To some, Fred Archer was a paragon among jockeys, but the plain truth is that he was uncommonly hard on his mounts. He didn't hesitate to use whip and spurs to vitalize a horse unwilling in its work, and one, aptly named Muley Idris, took its revenge one morning after a training gallop.

It seized his right arm in its jaws, swung him off his feet and would have trampled him if someone hadn't come to his rescue. The limb was a fearful mess and the Derby was only three weeks off. Archer's doctor referred him to Harley Street, and the specialist he saw happened to be Sir James Paget, a man so ignorant of sport that if you mentioned Epsom, he thought of a laxative remedy. Sir James dressed the wound and put the arm in a splint and told Archer it should be better in three weeks.

"But shall I be right for the Derby?" Fred inquired.

"I think you can go."

"Yes, but can I ride?"

"Better drive, my boy, better drive."

With admirable self-control, Fred said, "I fear, sir, you have not realized who I am."

Sir James peered at his pad and said, "I see I have the honor of receiving a Mr. Archer . . ."

"Yes, Sir James," said Fred, "and I think I should tell you that what you are in your profession, I am in mine. If I ride Bend Or, I could earn in the region of two thousand pounds."

"Two thousand?" said the consultant, after a thoughtful pause. "And you say we are coequals. I've never charged that for a horse bite, but for you, Mr. Archer, I'm willing to make an exception."

To complete the story, Archer started that Derby with a near useless right arm supported by an iron splint. Around Tattenham Corner, he was in fifth place, six lengths adrift of Robert the Devil. In the last furlong, he reached for his whip, but the pain in his arm obliged him to drop it at once. Miraculously, by dint of voice power and extraordinary horsemanship, he persuaded Bend Or to shorten the advantage yard by yard and finally get its nose in front. He remarked to me later, "Bend Or wasn't the best I ever rode, sir, but he was the gamest. We pulled that one out of the fire."

Dedicated detective story readers, resume here. Quite properly, the room also contained a bronze statuette, on a table against the window, of that beautiful animal, St. Simon, which missed its chance to run the Derby, but retired unbeaten and never seriously challenged. The sculptor, I noticed, was Boehm, of whom more anon. I was still facing the window when I said aloud, "Rather a pantomime, wasn't it?"

Captain Buckfast (I'd spotted his reflection as he entered) answered, "I beg your pardon, sir."

"The inquest," I enlightened him. "A performance of make-believe—with the ending everyone wanted." Since he didn't respond to this neat analogy, I turned and said, "You don't really believe the verdict, do you?"

I was being unfair, I admit—his future monarch inviting him to question a British jury's decision. The poor fellow was struck dumb. His mouth gaped, and his brown eyes registered something between mystification and panic. To restore confidence, I issued an order (which never fails with the military): "Show me over the house, Captain, and I'll explain. Has everyone departed except family and servants?"

They had, and I started my tour of inspection in the cellars. My respect for the late owner increased even more when I saw his champagne—I would estimate over two hundred dozen of vintage stock, tidily racked. "He took it in moderation," Buckfast assured me in the reverential voice one uses of the recently departed.

"At what hour of the day?"

"Lunch, sir."

"And of what did his lunch consist?"

"A glass of this and one sardine."

"One sardine?"

"Yes, sir."

"And after that? A dose of castor oil?" I quipped.

"No, sir. That was for breakfast."

He was completely serious. I decided not to pursue the intimate workings of Archer's digestion. "If I recollect, you said in your evidence that you have known him four years."

"Yes, sir."

"As a friend?"

"I like to think so."

"A friend in whom he confided?"

"On occasions."

I was doing no better than the coroner at drawing him out. I must have pulled a face, because he added defensively, "I'm known for my discretion, sir."

"Of that I have no doubt. Would you go so far as to say that, since the death of his wife last year, you were closer to Archer than anyone else?"

"I would, sir."

I waited.

Eventually he cleared his throat and volunteered, "I looked after his business affairs, his racing engagements and so forth."

My silence was more productive than my questions.

He added, "When I say 'looked after,' I must make it clear, sir, that Fred made his own decisions. He simply left the paperwork to me."

"So he wasn't much of a hand with pen and ink?"

"He was illiterate. He could barely scratch his own signature."

We moved upstairs to the drawing room where the inquest had taken place. This, too, was hung with oils and engravings, including portraits of two of Archer's patrons, Lord Falmouth and the Duke of Westminster. Then my attention was diverted by a familiar item on a card table, a silver cigarette case mounted on a crude chunk of metal that an inscription informed us was a portion of a shell that had burst on the deck of the gunboat *Condor* when my old pal Charlie B. (Lord Charles Beresford) found fame at the bombardment of Alexandria. I have an identical one. Lord knows how many Charlie distributed.

I made some witty remark about it to Captain Buckfast and he began to relax a little. He escorted me around the room, pointing out the Classic winners, and we exchanged memories of some of Archer's notable triumphs. Buckfast took a rather touching pride in each success. His reserve, I decided, wasn't born of stubbornness, so much as loyalty to a great man of the Turf who happened to have been his friend, and I liked him better for it.

"Fred's record will take some beating," I remarked, fresh from reading the obituary columns. "Thirteen years in succession as Champion Jockey and over 2,700 winners."

"Twenty-one of them Classics," Buckfast chipped in.

"Pity about the suicide," I added casually. "I can understand the decision to arrange the inquest so soon—or I think I can. Was that your doing, Captain?"

"The family's," said he. "Mr. Archer, Sr., and Fred's brother, Charles. Once this appalling thing occurred, they wanted to, em—"

"Bury him as soon as possible?"

Buckfast cleared his throat and murmured confidentially, "He was used to the intrusions of the press, but the family are not."

"Quite. They don't want the newshounds in full cry."

"Exactly, sir."

I nodded and remarked, "I think everyone cooperated admirably."

He either missed my irony or decided to let it pass. He smiled a little awkwardly and said, "Would you care to see the Turkish bath, sir?"

The Turkish bath, where by all accounts poor Archer spent the greatest part of his time at home, was an outhouse beyond the kitchen containing two tiled rooms. We presently stood in the hot-air chamber among the plumbing and wooden slats, and in that more secluded place talked of the real significance of the inquest.

"I should like to expand upon my earlier remarks," I offered. "I've no reason to believe that anyone at the inquest was dishonest. I merely observe that some of the evidence was inconsistent. Let's take the nature of the illness that had afflicted poor Archer."

"Typhoid fever."

I arched an eyebrow. "So the doctor conveniently informed us. Conveniently, because it is well known that typhoid induces hallucinations of the brain. I suffered it myself."

"The whole nation suffered with you, sir."

"How kind of you to mention it."

After a suitable interval, Buckfast asked, "Are you skeptical of the diagnosis, sir?"

"Perhaps you recall the doctor saying in evidence that he and his colleague diagnosed typhoid on the Saturday afternoon."

"Yes, indeed."

"How strange, then, that Mrs. Coleman wasn't informed. She believed her brother was suffering from a severe chill. Isn't that what she said?"

"There seems a discrepancy, certainly . . ."

"When were *you* informed that he was suffering from typhoid?"

"Yesterday, sir."

"After he shot himself?"

"Well, yes."

"Not on Saturday, when the doctor claimed the diagnosis was made?"

"No, sir."

"Doesn't that strike you as queer?"

Buckfast hesitated. "I'm in no doubt that he was very ill at the week's end, sir. Feverish. A very high temperature."

"Undoubtedly," I concurred, "for a couple of days. He was poorly on Saturday and Sunday, but yesterday he was sitting up having conversations."

Buckfast nodded. "Perfectly true, sir."

I said in a reasonable tone, "It sounds most unlike the typhoid I experienced. I was at death's door for three weeks. A severe chill I can believe, but typhoid . . ."

Buckfast stood erectly, saying nothing.

"Of course," I went on, rather enjoying this (you can see me blossoming as a detective, can't you?), "if one were to stand logic on its head and reverse cause and effect, a possible explanation emerges. Suicide equals brain fever equals typhoid. A well-intentioned family doctor may see it as his duty to confirm such a diagnosis."

Buckfast thought it proper to defend the medical profession. "There was the matter of the wandering."

"Ah, the wandering," said I. "Everyone was at pains to mention the wandering. It is, after all, a well-known symptom of typhoid. Everyone, that is to say, except the nurse."

"I thought she spoke of it," said Buckfast with a frown.

"The coroner did, when the nurse was giving evidence. He particularly asked her whether the patient wandered in his mind. She denied it. She said she was utterly certain that he didn't."

"Perhaps she was absent from the room when it occurred," the Captain responded.

"Possibly," said I, and then suggested, not without irony, "Shall we move on? The ventilation in this place leaves something to be desired."

We removed ourselves to the conservatory, passing Mrs. Coleman on the way. I don't think she could have overheard us in the Turkish bath. She effected a passable curtsy, and I returned a nod, as one couldn't smile in the circumstances. In feature and build she was very like her brother had been, though better nourished. She was still red-eyed from weeping, reminding me that the family wouldn't be overly pleased at having the inquest verdict questioned. However, if Archer, as I suspected, had been terrorized into taking his own life, someone was responsible and should be made to answer for it.

Among the ferns and palms I rapidly located the only bentwood chair furnished with cushions, and dispatched Buckfast for a bottle of Archer's vintage bubbly. As I reasonably pointed out, the owner had no more use for it. Knowing Archer's reputation for tightness—not for nothing was he known as the Tinman—I privately doubt whether he would have offered us so much as a glass of beer while he was alive, but I don't believe in speaking ill of the dead, so I gave him the benefit of the doubt and uncorked his champagne when it was brought. I also offered Buckfast a cigar. Not often do I hand out my specials to virtual strangers. However, a notion was forming in my brain that the Captain could be of service to me. When he had poured me a glass, I invited him to take the stool opposite. Without fuss he wedged a matchbox between his knees and struck a light with his good hand and offered it to me. The hand shook a little as it approached my cigar, but whose wouldn't? All in all, he exemplified what is best in the British army officer: resource, good manners and loyalty to the Crown.

"Tell me about yourself," I invited him warmly. "Are you a family man like me?" (That *like me* is my way of putting a man at his ease.)

"No, sir." (It doesn't always succeed.)

"What is your status, then?"

"I'm a bachelor with rooms in London. Jermyn Street."

"A good address," I told him. "Not far from mine. I have a place in Pall Mall."

"I know, sir."

"And you had some time in the army? The Guards?"

"Cavalry, sir. The 17th Lancers. I was wounded in the Zulu War, at Kambula."

"Rotten luck."

"I got in the way of an assagai."

I shook my head in sympathy. "A savage beast."

"It was a spear, sir."

"I was referring to the native who threw it, Captain. So you returned to England—on a generous pension, I hope?"

"It suffices, sir. I have a modest private income."

"And you know enough about racing to earn a penny or two?"

He gave the suspicion of a smile. "One never knows enough, unfortunately."

"How true!"

He added, "I owned a colt that won the Guineas and came second in the Derby."

"Oh? Which was that?"

"Paradox."

I was more than a little impressed. He was speaking of one of the outstanding thoroughbreds of recent years. "You owned Paradox? I thought Brodrick-Cloete owned Paradox."

"I sold it as a two-year-old."

"Pity. What did you get for it?"

"Six thousand. I bought it as a yearling for seven hundred."

"Not bad! I can see why Archer cultivated you. Let's drink to Paradox." We touched glasses and I looked searchingly into his eyes. "I want to confide in you, Captain," I informed him without ceremony. "From all I heard this afternoon, I don't believe Archer was deranged by typhoid. I think he shot himself deliberately. Does that shock you?"

He was silent for a moment. "Why should he do such a thing, sir?"

I lowered my glass and leaned forward. "That's the crux of it, Buckfast, that's the crux of it. I'm hoping you can enlighten me. We heard he was low-spirited. Is that true?

When you left him at midday yesterday, he was happy and contented. Weren't those your very words?"

"Well, yes. That was my clear impression, sir."

"Yet the doctor and the nurse reported that he was low in spirits. He told them he was going to die."

Buckfast lowered his eyes for a moment and rested his chin on his fist in an attitude of thought. "They must have been speaking of much earlier. The doctor left by half past nine. By noon, when I went out, Fred was much improved. You could ask Mrs. Coleman."

"I don't think we should trouble her now."

"I wouldn't have dreamed of going out if I'd thought he was depressed, sir. I cared about Fred. I've seen him through some dreadful times—slanderous attacks by people who should have known better, the deaths of his first child and his wife. I took him to America to recover from the grief. When you've seen a man in the depth of despair, you know the signs. He was at peace when I last saw him. I swear it."

From a normally reticent man, this was a singularly moving speech. Buckfast had gone quite pink as he uttered it. He took out a handkerchief and wiped the corner of his eye.

I refilled his glass. "Now that he's gone, what do you propose to do?"

"I've hardly had time to consider, sir. I've been showing the coroner over the house and preparing for the funeral. After that, no doubt I'll be asked to assist the executors in going through his papers."

"After these duties have been dispensed, would you consider rendering a service to me?"

He didn't move a muscle, but his eyes shone like the Koh-i-Noor. I believe he thought I was about to offer him a position as my racing manger. "Whatever you deem that I'm capable of performing, sir."

I said, "I, too, had a strong regard for Archer, and I'm not satisfied that what we heard today was the whole truth. I shall be making some inquiries of my own—in the strictest confidence—and you are best placed to assist me in this enterprise."

He looked a shade crestfallen, I thought, but to his credit he said at once, "It will be my honor and my pleasure, sir."

"Not much pleasure, I suspect," said I.

"What can I do to help?"

I put aside my glass and sat forward. "Of all the words that were spoken at the inquest, three intrigue me mightily. Why? Because they were the last that Archer ever spoke."

"'Are they coming?'"

I nodded. "A simple question, but what a dread significance it has in the circumstances. 'Are they coming?' What could he have meant by it? The coroner seems to have missed the point completely. Presumably he dismisses the words as the rambling of a demented man. Demented? Or tormented? That is what we have to discover, Captain."

His eyes had widened. "So you believe he was expecting someone to come to the house, sir? Someone real?"

I answered, "I doubt if he was referring to the Four Horsemen of the Apocalypse. Mrs. Coleman was at the window looking out, and Archer thought she'd seen some visitors who so alarmed him that he reached for the gun. Captain, have you any notion who they might have been?"

He shook his head. "Every jockey is vulnerable to criminal elements, sir. There are plenty of low types on the fringe of racing."

I nodded. We both knew the temptations open to jockeys, and Archer had more than once been asked to explain a curious result, but he had satisfied the Turf authorities each time. In sixteen years of racing he had only once been suspended, and that was when he was a lad of fourteen.

I asked, "Did he have any enemies among the jockeys?"

"Not that I ever heard. Rivals, yes. Fordham, Cannon, Wood. He gave no quarter on the racecourse, and they knew it. But they respected him."

I took out my watch. I'd already lingered longer than I intended. My birthday guests would assemble in the ante-room at Sandringham in under three hours. "Very well. We obviously have some serious detective work ahead of us. Are you game? You're at liberty to say no if you wish."

"I'll do anything I can to be of assistance, sir."

"Good. What's your Christian name?"

The question discomposed him a trifle. "Charles, sir."

"Is that what your friends call you?"

"They call me Charlie, sir."

"That's good enough for me. Well, Charlie, I'm Albert Edward. Bertie to my intimates, but you'd better continue to call me sir."

"As you wish, sir."

"These are your instructions. Search your memory minutely for any incident concerning Archer that might suggest he was under threat. You say his executors will want your help in sorting through his papers in the next few days. Study those papers before you hand them over, even if it means staying up all night. Look for anything of possible significance in the accounts, the correspondence, his betting book. I shall want a report when I see you next, and, I hope, some promising avenues of inquiry."

"Will that be at the funeral, sir?"

"I think not, Charlie. I'll be sending an equerry."

"Then how shall I report to you? By letter?"

"Lord, no. We'll meet privately. This is a highly secret investigation." I got up and reached for my hat. "What was the name of that valet—the fellow who placed the revolver in the night commode?"

"Sarjent, sir."

"I'd like to see him if he's still about. And would you have my carriage called? It's waiting in the lane beyond the church."

I have a reputation for being fastidious in regard to dress, and I suppose it's justified. I don't have a large wardrobe by the standards of European royalty, but what I have is the best, and I make a point of keeping it so. When Sarjent arrived, I said, "Do you know who I am?"

I needn't have asked. He was out in goose pimples at the sight of me, a tall, willowy young man of about twenty-five. "I believe so, your Royal—"

"How long did you work for Mr. Archer?"

"Four years, sir, first as a groom."

"He must have thought well of you. It was your job to guard the house when he was away?"

"Yes, sir."

"Did you ever notice anything suspicious? Intruders, that sort of thing?"

"Never, sir."

"What exactly did Mr. Archer say when he asked you to guard the house?"

"He said he didn't want it burgled while he was away, sir."

"A reasonable sentiment. And are you as good a valet as you are a guard?"

"Yes, sir."

"Then take this hat and coat and brush them soundly. I want them back in ten minutes, in the front hall."

He was back in less, which was unfortunate, as I was just emerging from the cloakroom to a fanfare of rushing water. When he had helped me into the coat, he dropped the florin I tipped him with and retired blushing.

My co-investigator, Charlie Buckfast, made a more timely entrance.

To round off our business, I told him in confidence, "I'll arrange to see you in London in a week or so. Occasionally I have engagements in the metropolis, of a private nature."

He said impassively, "My rooms in Jermyn Street are at your disposal anytime you wish, sir."

I winked and said, "I have hopes of you, Charlie."

CHAPTER 6

And now we shall trip the light fantastic together. Consider yourself invited to the County Ball at Sandringham on Friday 12 November, 1886. Let's rattle the chandeliers with my favorite dance, the Triumph. It's meant to be danced with vigor, you know, and Signore Curti and his instrumentalists will give no mercy until I signal them to stop. In case you were thinking of sitting out, I must warn you that I'm a tyrant in my own ballroom. No one is permitted to shirk.

I take Lady Randolph Churchill's hand and lead her on to the floor. If I'm any judge, Jennie's spirits need a lift. She's been unusually subdued since she arrived, and the whisper is that she and Randolph were barely speaking before they got here. The age-old problem. I wouldn't be Randolph for all the tea in China when she shames him with those exquisite violet-tinted eyes. But through the white lace gloves, Jennie's hand is warm to my touch, and I feel not the slightest tensing of the fingers when Randolph turns to Lady de Grey and invites her to make up a set. Cunning old Randolph, a politician in all things. Gladys de Grey is a black-haired beauty straight off a Goya canvas, all passion and fire, but she was married for the second time last year,

and is so besotted with her noble earl that she's the safest
woman in the room for Randolph to be seen with.

Before Curti raises his baton, I spot a few malingerers
behind the columns where they're apt to take cover when
the Triumph is announced. "The footmen have instructions
to take the names of all deserters!" I shout, and repeat the
phrase in French for the benefit of the Duc de la Trémouille.
It terrifies him into snatching the plump forearm of the wife
of the Lord-Lieutenant and hauling her into a set led by my
dear wife Alix and the Comte de Paris.

I smile at Jennie. "Ready, my dear?"

"Whenever you say, sir."

Is that meant to be suggestive? I can't be certain, but I
give her the look that never fails to redden a pretty cheek.
Then I nod to Curti, and the opening chord is sounded.
Every gentleman bows, every lady curtsies, and that is the first
and last stately movement in the dance. We hurtle into the
briskest gallop you can imagine, skirts and coattails flying.
Jennie and I lead the set, down the middle and up again,
past a blur of red and black jackets and taffeta gowns of
every color. She is obliged to cling to me in order to stay
upright, and I won't deny that this is one of the attractions
of the dance. In this account of my adventures I mean to
be frank about liaisons, and I shall be, so you must take my
word for it that I've never bedded Jennie—our intimacies
are exclusively platonic. That is, up to the time of writing.

We stand back to watch the less boisterous dancing of the
next pair, the Comte and Comtesse de Paris, who are my
principal guests. Poor dears, they have been living at Sheen
House since their expulsion from France. Who would be
a pretender to the French throne? Mind, even a staunch
anti-Republican must have reservations about the Comtesse,
who smokes a pipe (not during the dance) and helps herself
to my cigars on every imaginable pretext.

My sympathies toward the royalists from across the

Channel are well known, and in certain circles notorious. When I offered Chiswick House to the Empress Eugenie after the fall of the Second Empire, I was called to Windsor to explain myself. I was informed that my action was diplomatically inept, which gave me an opportunity to respond that as I was never taken into the confidence of the diplomats, I could scarcely be blamed for upsetting them.

As we progress, I glance at Jennie, but her eyes are on Randolph or the lady he is dancing with, so I turn my gaze toward the far end of the ballroom, where I meet a penetrating look from a face ravaged by sixteen years of heroic service to me: Sir Francis Knollys. Who would believe that Knollys was capable of diverting me from the fascinating Lady Churchill?

This, you see, was the day of Fred Archer's funeral at Newmarket. Impossible for me to attend, so I sent a gigantic wreath and Knollys. And now I'm extremely impatient for his report.

I decide to exercise the prerogative of mercy and limit the reprises of the dance to two, and my guests limp to the nearest chairs. Unfortunately, supper is not due for twenty minutes. When I have returned Jennie to her spouse, I tell Signore Curti to give us a slow quadrille, which at least will supply an opportunity of communication. Then I beckon to Knollys.

We make up a square consisting of myself and Alix, Prince Christian and my sister Lenchen, the Comte and Comtesse de Paris, and their young daughter Hélène, the Princesse d'Orléans, partnered by Knollys. The tempo is undemanding, so each time I step sufficiently close to Knollys I can discreetly slip him a question.

"A fitting send-off for the Tinman?"

"Indeed, sir. Upward of thirty carriages."

"Plenty of wreaths, I daresay?"

"More than I could count. They blocked the hall and stairway of the house."

At this, Knollys steps aside and I find my uncouth brother-in-law fixing me with his one good eye. Christian has aspirations to be a Turfite, and he must have overheard, because he says in a voice audible to the entire set (save possibly Alix), "You must be speaking of the dead jockey. Where was the poor fellow buried?"

Lenchen flaps her hand at her clodhopping husband and says, "This is hardly a topic for the ballroom, my dear."

Knollys, embarrassed, mumbles something about the local cemetery, and young Hélène says brightly, "Cemetery? *Que veut dire ceci?*"

Alix, who picks up the child's piercing remark, and is always grateful of an opportunity to join in the pleasantries, provides our French guests with a definition of the word, and then supplements their vocabulary with some others, such as *mausoleum, sepulcher* and *crypt.* Meanwhile, I'm close enough to Knollys to ask, "Did you make a list of the wreaths?"

"So far as possible, sir."

"Apart from mine . . . ?"

"Lord Falmouth, his first patron."

"Naturally, and . . . ?"

"The Duke of Westminster."

"Oh, where?" says Alix, looking around the room. "I haven't seen him."

"The Marchioness of Ormonde," continues Knollys, who is as accustomed as I to Alix going off on tangents. "Count Kinsky."

"So 'andsome!" murmurs the Comtesse, equally at sea.

"Sir George Chetwynd."

It amounts to a catalog of the racing aristocracy. After I've heard it out, I say with confidence, "My wreath was the largest, I presume?"

The sequence of the dance constrains me to wait for an answer, and when it comes, it's Knollys at his most diplomatic: "Yours had pride of place, sir."

I blink in surprise. "Not the largest?"

He shakes his head.

I say in his ear as we pass, "Tell me, who so far forgot himself as to send a wreath larger than mine?"

"The Dowager Duchess of Montrose."

"Carrie Montrose!" I say in outrage.

"Who is this Montrose?" asks the Comtesse.

"Mes sentiments, exactement," I tell her.

Supper is taken in the dining room. The band of the Norfolk Regiment play Bizet, while I play host to my French guests—not to mention the three hundred others who swoop on the *Mousse de Saumon aux Concombres* and the *Ortolans à L'Aspic* as if they haven't seen food in a fortnight. I suppose the dancing gives them an appetite. The Duc de la Trémouille attacks the *Noisette d'Agneau à l'Anglaise* as if he were taking revenge for Waterloo.

After the strawberries, the plates are cleared, coffee and cigars are handed around and I become an object of surpassing interest, for no one may rise to respond to a call of nature until I get up from my chair.

I stand and make an expansive gesture that signals relief for all who need it. This is also the cue for frisky debutantes to slip away from their chaperons and make assignations in the corridors.

I cross to the table where Francis Knollys is seated with some kindred spirits, among them Christopher Sykes and Lord Arthur Somerset, who is known to us all in the Marlborough House set as Podge.

Before the dancing resumes, I mean to obtain a more coherent account of the funeral. The cortege, Knollys informs us, consisted of six funeral carriages of family mourners, the hearse itself, a large brake loaded with wreaths and floral tributes and up to twenty private carriages. Although the principal racehorse owners had not considered it appropriate to attend, the Turf was honorably represented by Mr. Tattersall, of the famous firm; John Porter and Tom Jennings, two of the most distinguished trainers of recent years; Tom Cannon, Fred's old rival in the saddle; and my co-investigator, Charlie Buckfast. Wholly unfit to be included in such company (I'm compelled to mention the monster because he will figure in our story) was Abington Baird, the notorious amateur rider known as the Squire.

The cortege left Falmouth House at 2 P.M. and drove the mile or so into town along the road beside the Heath, past a continuous line of stable lads, who showed touching respect for the great Fred by posting themselves like guards of honor at a state funeral. In the long main street of Newmarket, where every shop was closed, with blinds drawn at all the windows, the townsfolk stood three and four deep, oblivious of the rain. The tide of people at the cemetery gates delayed the cortege for some minutes, for the police had stopped the public from entering. Only the immediate family entered the small chapel for the funeral service. Then Archer was laid to rest in a plot lined with laurel leaves and white chrysanthemums, beside the graves of his wife and infant son. I heard that his father was too distressed to attend.

"Was anything said about the suicide?" I ask Knollys.

"By the vicar, sir?"

"By anyone at all."

"It was generally spoken of as a dreadful tragedy."

"Not as a mystery?"

"Not that I heard, sir."

"Podge" Somerset has been listening keenly, yet draws back now and takes an unwarranted interest in his cigar, as if it just flew into his hand. I'm not standing for that kind of evasion.

"What do you know about it?" I ask.

"Nothing worth saying at all," he hedges.

"Out with it, Podge. You may be well padded, but you're very transparent."

He flushes scarlet. "I would only care to comment, sir, that I'm not surprised Archer shot himself. He was in very bad odor after the Cambridgeshire."

"Oh? Who with?"

"My brother Edward for one."

"What does Edward have to complain about? His horse was well beaten."

"It was stopped."

I stare at him in amazement. He's telling me that Carlton, the 4-1 favorite, was not allowed to win. You often hear ill-founded accusations after a favorite fails to please, but this comes from the owner. If true, it warrants a Jockey Club inquiry, at the least.

I'm trying to follow the logic of what he's just suggested, but he's lost me. Even if Carlton *were* stopped, why should Archer be blamed? Woodburn was the rider, not Archer.

He explains, "Woodburn was bribed by Archer to throw the race."

I'm speechless.

He adds, "Since his wife died, Archer had nothing to live for except his racing. Winning the Cambridgeshire became his obsession. He would use any means. He decided Carlton was the main threat, so he paid Woodburn to lose, but he reckoned without the outsider. He was devastated. That's why he killed himself, Bertie."

After a moment to contain myself, I say, "Podge, do you know what you're suggesting—that the greatest jockey in the kingdom was corrupt?"

"I say it, sir."

Christopher Sykes, that beanpole of a fellow with sad eyes and the longest face you ever saw, who was manifestly sent into the world to be a victim of practical jokes, and unend-ingly tries to convince me otherwise, asks Podge, "Have you spoken to Woodburn? Have you accused him to his face of taking a bribe?"

"My brother has."

"And . . . ?"

"The man denies it. Naturally he would. His livelihood is at stake."

"Then you have some other proof?"

Podge begins to flounder. "Not exactly proof, but I'm darned sure we could obtain it if we tried. Now that Archer's dead, it seems churlish to pursue it."

At this, I see red. "That's decent of you, I must say! You and your brother slander a man who is scarcely in his grave and then admit you haven't a shred of proof to support you. But you're such fair-minded fellows that you're not even proposing to supply the proof. Fair-minded, my arse! You're a muckraker of the worst sort, Somerset, and I've heard as much as I can stand."

With that, I march back to the ballroom, and as I go, I'm sorry to say, I strike panic into numbers of my guests, who step backward and press themselves against the wall—always a sign that I'm glaring at people. You may think I was unduly harsh on Podge considering that I'd practically commanded him to expound his theory. Perhaps I was. I had a strong respect for Archer. In my opinion he was neither bad, nor mad, and I shall prove it.

While the first waltz after supper is in progress, I compose myself by sitting with the Earl and Lady de Grey, or Fred and Gladys as I know them. Fred is the best shot in England, and that's saying a lot, but it *is* the lot, so far as anyone is aware, except possibly Gladys. She dotes on him, so perhaps there's more to the little man than we give him credit for, though between ourselves, he caught her on the rebound, lucky fellow. She was married first to the fourth Earl of Lonsdale, who treated her disgracefully. His sudden death was a blessed release for Gladys. She's still only twenty-seven, and, I don't mind repeating, a fascinating creature. I ask her to dance.

I'm still brooding over Podge's monstrous allegation. Even supposing the unthinkable were true, and Archer actually did pay a bribe to another jockey, the thwarting of his plan was hardly grounds for suicide. All right, the Cambridgeshire was about the only race of note that he never won, and the wasting he was willing to endure to make good the omission was extraordinary, even obsessive, to use Podge's phrase. Yet at twenty-nine he could have looked forward to other Cambridgeshires. Plenty of jockeys go past forty. Why stake his reputation, indeed his life, on the outcome of this one race?

Gladys de Grey interrupts my brown study by remarking, "Perhaps in this case feminine intuition may be of assistance."

I frown. "What makes you say that?"

She smiles. She looks bewitching in a diamond tiara, with a rope of antique pearls wound in triple around her neck and suspended in a long loop from her bare shoulders across her bosom to the level of her waist. She tells me, "Like every other woman in the room, I've been watching you, sir. It's evident that you have something on your mind. Would I be right in divining that it is not unconnected with a sad event at Newmarket?"

"Good Lord, Gladys, how the deuce . . . ?"

"I have my sources."

I affect a stern look. "Don't be evasive with me, young lady, or . . ."

Another smile dawns. "Or what, Your Royal Highness? How do you deal with evasive females—shut them up in the Tower, or is that a thing of the past?"

The dance is coming to an end. I signal to Signore Curti to prolong it, and I confide to Gladys, "The punishment I propose for you is far more severe than a spell in the Tower. I shall force you to dance with me until you promise to cooperate."

She says solemnly, "How could I *not* cooperate with a man who dances as divinely as this? I am utterly at your mercy, sir. I shall tell all. I saw you in earnest conversation with a certain gentleman who arrived late for the ball, so I asked Charlotte Knollys where her brother had been today."

"Ah."

She sighs. "Now you're no longer impressed."

"Untrue. Let's put this intuition of yours to the test. Where would *you* look for an explanation of Fred Archer's suicide?"

She raises her eyebrows as if the answer is obvious. "*Cherchez la femme,* I should think."

I stop dancing and cause a shunt down the length of the ballroom. "A *woman*. Archer had no time for women."

"He married one," says Gladys flatly.

"Yes, but she died."

". . . leaving him alone in the world with a beautiful house and oodles of money. Of course there was a woman ready to fill the gap."

"Name her, then."

Gladys smiles wickedly and recites a verse that was current a year or two ago:

"Isn't Craw a lucky boy
With Carrie Red and Corrie Roy?
Corrie Roy and Carrie Red—
One for the stable and one for the bed."

I'd better translate. "Craw" was the late Stirling Crawfurd, a distinguished figure of the Turf, and Corrie Roy won the Cesare-witch for him. "Carrie Red" was his buxom and energetic wife.

I say with a gasp of disbelief, "Carrie Montrose?"

Gladys nods.

I've given up any pretension of dancing. I lead her to the side of the ballroom. "Gladys, that's grotesque! Carrie Montrose must be almost seventy!"

"Sixty-eight. Why is it grotesque if an old woman desires a young man, when the reverse is so acceptable?"

I sidestep that one. "Are you serious—about Carrie Montrose?"

Her brown eyes lock with mine, and she almost dares me to challenge her. "Believe me, she was actively pursuing him. She offered to marry him."

"How can you know this?"

"I listen, Bertie. What else is there for a respectable married lady to do but take an interest in what the not-so-respectable ones are doing?"

She follows that with a penetrating look. The fact has not escaped me that she has addressed me for the first time as Bertie. I escort her back to the best shot in England, thinking, after all, that they are well matched.

CHAPTER 7

The ball ended officially at 2 A.M. on Saturday morning. After the last carriages had left, my houseguests amused themselves for a while with my barrel organ, until, toward 3 A.M., I bade good night to the ladies and led the gentlemen to the smoking room. I have noticed many times that there's nothing like a smoking-room party in the small hours to bring out the true character of one's associates. Randolph got up a noisy game with the French in the bowling alley next door; Christian sank into my favorite armchair and snored; Knollys went straight to the brandy; Podge Somerset, wishing he were a million miles away after his dressing-down, wandered about the walls studying my Leech pictures as if he had never set eyes on them in his life; and the Great Xtopher (Sykes) tried to prove himself indispensable by poking the fire.

Sykes it was who brought up the subject of Archer again. I suppose he was interceding on Somerset's behalf, trying to suggest that there might after all be something in the story of bribery, although you can never be certain with Christopher. He's learned to distract me when the brandy is being served. One evening after dinner at the Marlborough Club, when tedium was setting in, I acted on a whim and tipped my glass of brandy over his head. Nothing remarkable in that, except that the fellow bore it like a philosopher, letting the liquid trickle down the length of his face and beard onto his dress shirt and dinner jacket, before turning a damp face to me and saying in his solemn voice, "As your Royal Highness pleases," and causing every one of us to howl with laughter. I'm still helpless if I picture it. Naturally, it became a party turn. Now no evening is complete until Sykes has been dowsed with brandy, a full decanter if possible, or had my cigar stubbed out on the back of his hand. His response is always that impeccably obliging, "As your Royal Highness pleases," and hilarious to hear.

Before a glass was put in my hand, he said, "There was something I meant to mention earlier, sir, about the Cambridgeshire, but the opportunity passed."

I eyed him without much show of interest.

He moved as close as he dared. "Touching on the possibility—the remote possibility—that the race was not to the fastest, so to speak, I heard from a certain source that a personage not unknown in Turf circles made a tidy sum by backing the outsider that won."

"So what?" I commented. "I backed it myself at 25-1."

"Sir, this individual netted fifty thousand on the race."

"Fifty thou?"

"He spread his investment over several bookmakers. He dined at Romano's the same evening and was boasting to all and sundry about his coup."

"Well, don't be so blessed mysterious, Christopher. Who was this lucky blighter?"

"Baird, sir."

After a moment's hesitation I said warily, "Do you mean Abington Baird? The Squire?"

Sykes gave a nod and followed it with a grave stare—and no one in my circle can stare more gravely than he.

I'm not sure how I received this information. I may have

whistled, or vibrated my lips like a horse, or uttered a profanity. At any rate, I took the point about Baird. If that monster of iniquity had backed the winner, questions indubitably had to be asked.

It won't have escaped you, I'm certain, that Baird's name has already been raised. He was mentioned to me by Knollys as one of the mourners at Archer's funeral. And now, in case you suspect me of prejudice, I shall enlighten you about Mr. Baird's reputation.

He is a young man still in his twenties, of immense wealth, some three million pounds, which he inherited on his twenty-first birthday. His father and uncles, the seven sons of an impoverished Scottish farmer, built their fortunes out of coal, iron and the railways. The family firm of William Baird & Company now owns and mines vast areas of Western Scotland, and those brothers who founded it represent all that is estimable in the Scots character: energy, enterprise and foresight, governed by thrift and piety.

Unhappily, none of this except the money was passed on to the next generation—by which I mean George Alexander Baird, known in racing circles as Mr. Abington or the Squire. He was sent to Eton and Cambridge to be educated as a gentleman and drove his tutors to the point of despair. If rumor is true, he didn't attend a single lecture while up at Magdalen. He went elsewhere for his schooling, to gambling dens and low public houses and penny gaffs. He consorted with women of doubtful repute. He surrounded himself with an odious gang of roughs and pugilists and took a fiendish delight in giving offense to decent people. One of his favorite tricks upon entering a restaurant or public house was to knock off a stranger's hat or snatch his cigar. Were the victim so rash as to protest, he was liable to have his nose bloodied by one of the Squire's pugilistic following. The latter, I may say, included Mitchell and Smith, champions of England.

It occurs to me on reading over the previous paragraph

that certain newspapers obsessed by stories of indiscretions in high places might be tempted to make invidious comparisons. They had better be advised that there is an absolute distinction between private high spirits and public rowdyism.

One would not claim to be a saint, of course, any more than asserting that Baird has utterly gone to the devil. The Squire's saving grace is that he is a capital horseman, probably the finest gentleman rider (I use the word *gentleman* only to distinguish him from professional jockeys) in the kingdom. While at Cambridge, he maintained a string of hunters, took part in the University Drag, and inevitably rubbed shoulders with Newmarket trainers. The Turf excited him as nothing else. His chief ambition was to emulate Fred Archer. To this end, he first became an owner and spent vast funds on acquiring good horses to ride. He followed Archer from meeting to meeting, studying his style and tactics. Ultimately, he persuaded the champion to tutor him, blithely paying, it is said, the most extravagant fees ever asked for riding lessons, for the Tinman was never cheaply bought. The Squire got good value, however; he learned how to steal that precious yard in a close finish, and equally how to catch the judge's eye by getting up on the horse's neck. Last year, he rode almost thirty winners.

Yet the outlay on his racing must vastly exceed the returns. He keeps horses all over the country—many registered under other names—on the principle that when there is a meeting in the vicinity, he will always have a ride available. He has not the foggiest idea how many he owns. Each time a selling race takes place at a meeting he attends, he buys the winner. When Lord Falmouth's horses were put up for sale a couple of years ago, the Squire went through the catalog with Archer and outraged the Turf aristocracy by buying the pick of the collection. So it was fitting, if not in character, that the Squire should have attended Archer's funeral.

There is no question that he admired Archer—reason

enough, one would think, to pay final respects, even if he wasn't well-known for respecting anyone. Yet this story of a thumping win on the Cambridgeshire, coming after Podge's bizarre accusation, troubled me deeply. Was it possible that Archer had known something and tipped The Sailor Prince? The Squire must have felt confident, to go to the trouble of spreading his bet over several bookies. A win of fifty thousand was fairly small beer to a millionaire, but it impressed the world at large. His main reward was the prestige of picking the outsider, and he'd made sure it was public knowledge. The Squire craved esteem as a Turfite, so no wonder he had broadcast his success in Romano's. The question was whether he regretted making it public now, in the light of Archer's violent death. Had his boasting in some way precipitated what happened? Was it out of guilt that the Squire had made his appearance at the funeral?

I inquired of Sykes, "How did you hear about this?"

He nervously fingered his beard and glanced about the room. "From my sister-in-law Jessica, sir. She got it from one of her acquaintances."

I chuckled. "That can't be right."

"Why not, sir?"

"Jessica doesn't have *acquaintances*, does she?"

Christopher reddened. His elder brother, Sir Tatton Sykes, had married the lively Jessica Cavendish-Bentinck when she was eighteen, he forty-eight. Ten years on, Tatton was mentally in his dotage. He subsisted on milk puddings and early nights. Jessica, still in her prime and believing there must be more to life than a bowl of tapioca and sweet dreams, leased a large house in Grosvenor Street and gives some of the gayest dinner parties in London. To the gossip-mongers, Lady Tatton Sykes is known as Lady Satin Tights, and I don't think she minds a bit.

Poor Christopher! It all but choked him to mention his scarlet sister-in-law. He said, "Her informant was a, em, gentleman friend who happened to be in Romano's the evening Baird was there."

"Am I not to be told his name?"

"In all humility, sir, it might be more profitable to know the name of the young lady who was at Baird's table."

"Conceivably. Who was that?"

"She calls herself Miss Bliss, I believe. They appeared to be on intimate terms."

"Miss Bliss? Sounds ominously like one of the sisterhood."

"I understand she has not descended to that, sir. She is a music hall artiste."

I was so grateful for this information that I refrained that evening from pouring brandy over Sykes. If inquiries had to be made, Miss Bliss, the music hall artiste, sounded a more approachable subject than the Squire. My heart had sunk at the mention of that reprobate's name. Can you imagine my situation trying to conduct a discreet conversation with such a loudmouthed barbarian?

In bed that night I decided on my course of action. I was due to visit London the following weekend. On the pretext that Satan finds some mischief still for idle hands to do, my dear mama and her advisers are indefatigable in devising ever more obscure ways of occupying my hours. The latest is the Wellington Statue Committee. I ask you! Some years ago Wyatt's hideous equestrian statue of the old Duke was removed from the arch at Hyde Park Corner and carted off to Aldershot, and ever since there has been a debate as to what should be put in its place. The committee was formed to devise a competition to find a less objectionable replacement, and I was considered the ideal chairman. If I learned anything from this experience, it was that sculptors and soldiers should be kept apart.

Did you detect a note of bitterness there? This has been a momentous year in the destiny of the nation, with two changes of government and the great debate over Gladstone's

Home Rule Bill. As the future King, I wish earnestly to keep abreast of the affairs of state, yet I am compelled to wheedle tidbits of information from ministers like Lord Rosebery and Sir Henry James, who happen also to be my friends. They and I are obliged to be so damnably furtive about the business as to feel a sense of guilt.

Anyway, the great decision over the Wellington Statue took me to the Smoke. On these occasions, I stay at Marlborough House, where congenial companions are always within call and the servants are handpicked for their loyalty. This time, I sent word to Captain Charlie Buckfast that I would call privately at his rooms in Jermyn Street on Friday night.

Then I made preparations. I surprised one of my gardeners by asking to borrow a set of his oldest clothes. Having kitted myself in boots, kersey trousers, doeskin waistcoat, serge jacket, greatcoat, muffler and billycock hat, I left Marlborough House on Friday evening by the tradesmen's entrance and walked to Jermyn Street. It is a little-known fact that I am not unused to walking the streets of London in the clothes of a workingman. A year or two ago, in my capacity as member of the Royal Commission on the Housing of the Working Classes (another of HM's ideas for filling my time), I ventured incognito into some of the worst slums of St. Pancras. I can tell you I felt safer on that occasion than I did this evening walking through St. James's. I got some decidedly antagonistic looks.

Captain Buckfast lived above Boyd's, the fruiterers. I was obliged to step over two boxes of oranges to reach his door—a change from a red carpet. I was starting to congratulate myself on the success of my disguise when the door was opened by a butler who promptly bowed so low as to show me his back collar stud. I muttered, "Not here, you buffoon," and it so shocked him that he broke wind. This is one of the hazards of bowing, as anyone who has attended an investiture will know.

When I got upstairs, Buckfast at least had the grace to look bewildered at my appearance. The first thing I asked was whether this was his regular butler, and he admitted that he'd hired him for the occasion. I was highly displeased, and I let him see it.

I tersely instructed him to give the man his marching orders, not for what had occurred downstairs, which can happen to the best of us, but because, damn it, I had specified a private visit. While he dealt with that, I took stock of the place: very much the ex-soldier's, neatly arranged, with colored engravings of cavalry officers at symmetrical intervals around the walls; zebra hides on either side of the fireplace; some native spears, a Zulu drum; and, reflecting his Turf connection, a painting of Paradox, with Archer up. I picked a spill from a Chinese vase on the mantelpiece, lighted it and started a cigar.

"Can I rely on you at all?" I asked when Buckfast returned, full of apologies. "Did you find out anything at the funeral?"

"I have to admit I didn't, sir. The weather was most inclement."

How that had obstructed him, I didn't ask. "Have you sorted through Archer's papers, as I asked?"

"Yes, sir."

"And . . . ?"

"I found nothing irregular."

"But you can tell me how much he was worth?"

"Somewhere near sixty thousand pounds, I would estimate."

"Are you sure? I read a couple of years ago that he had a quarter of a million."

Buckfast shook his head. "An exaggeration, I'm certain, sir. He was never worth as much as that. Of course, he sank enormous amounts into building Falmouth House."

I waited to see if anything else was forthcoming, but it wasn't. If you got three sentences together out of Charlie

Buckfast, you were doing well. I admonished him gently. "Charlie, you disappoint me. How are we going to form an investigating team if all the discoveries are down to me?" Not without relish, I told him first about the Somerset family's suspicions over the Cambridgeshire result, then the Squire's boastings in Romano's. "Do you know the Squire, Charlie?"

"He's no friend of mine, sir."

"I'm glad to hear it. But he was a friend of Archer's, so you surely met him on occasions?"

Buckfast shook his head. "I'm not sure that Fred ever thought of Baird as a friend. Most times, he was an infernal nuisance. Never missed a chance to claim acquaintance."

"What about this story, then? Is it possible that Archer told him to back The Sailor Prince?"

He put his face through a series of pained expressions as he tried to come to terms with this odious suggestion. "I suppose it's not impossible."

I had the advantage of him. I'd already thought the unthinkable. "The opportunity was there at the Newmarket meeting. They were both on the racecourse all the week."

Charlie Buckfast's blood pressure was rising visibly. He blurted out, "I can't believe that Fred stopped his horse, sir. I simply can't believe it. His whole career would be at risk. He'd rather be dead than . . ." He let the words trail away as he realized what he'd said.

I told him, "I think a visit to the music hall is indicated."

CHAPTER 8

Let's give Buckfast his due: his mustache twitched at the prospect of the Heir Apparent visiting a common music hall, but otherwise he took it as an ex-officer should. "I presume, sir, that this must be in the course of duty."

"You have it, Charlie."

I told him about the connection (if that doesn't sound indelicate) between the Squire and Miss Bliss. He confessed he had never heard of Miss Bliss.

"Nor I."

"How shall we find her, then?"

I smiled in a cryptic fashion. "Last Sunday morning, Charlie, I attended Divine Service at Sandringham in the company of Lord Randolph Churchill, Prince Christian and a handful of red-eyed survivors of the County Ball. The Sub-Dean of the Chapel Royal was sent from Windsor to give the sermon. For a text, he used the parable of the ten virgins—not the most fitting choice. I could have taken it irreverently, Charlie, but I did not. I listened to the word of the Lord, and in future I shall apply it in my daily life."

"To be a wise virgin?" said Buckfast.

I gave him a sharp look. "To be prepared."

"Ah."

"A sound principle for detective work, wouldn't you agree?"

"Absolutely, sir."

"So today I have come prepared. I sent for a copy of that useful periodical, the *Era*. I studied the music hall notices, and I find that a Miss Myrtle Bliss is appearing twice nightly at Mr. George Belmont's hall, the Sebright, in Hackney Road."

"Hackney Road?" Buckfast mouthed the words in a whisper, as if they ought not to be spoken aloud. He was so dismayed that he quite omitted to compliment me. For the benefit of my readers in the provinces, the road in question runs from Shoreditch out to Cambridge Heath, not the worst of East London, by any means, but still a locality where people of Buckfast's class—not to mention mine—venture at their peril.

The reason for my workingman's attire was now apparent, and we presently attended to his. We opened a trunk and found a Chesterfield overcoat that he hadn't worn since the seventies and a pair of army boots that we dipped in water to remove the shine. The hat was more of a challenge. We were obliged to use the only black bowler he possessed. After crushing it out of shape and liberally applying goose fat and ash, we finally had a titfer sufficiently shabby.

I looked at his cavalry mustache and said, "That's got to come off."

He was aghast. "It took years to cultivate, sir."

He was so reluctant to submit to the scissors that I was persuaded to see what difference it would make to dismantle the spiked ends. We softened the wax over a bowl of steaming water and I prised the hairs apart with a silver toothpick. He bore it with fortitude. I assured him when it was done that the bedraggled effect was pure working-class.

We left Jermyn Street about eight o'clock. I first proposed that we take a cab to Shoreditch High Street and hoof it from there but quite failed to realize that no cabman would stop for the likes of us in clubland, so we were compelled to walk to Oxford Circus to look for a bus. All this was novel to me, and I enjoyed it immensely.

"This strikes me as more dangerous than Hackney Road," I remarked as we strode up Regent Street in our hobnailed boots, getting distinctly unfriendly looks from the well-heeled West Enders.

"It might be safer if you stepped aside and gave them precedence, sir," Buckfast suggested.

He was right, of course. The habit of a lifetime is hard to break.

While we waited in Oxford Street for the Clapton bus, I admitted, "This may be a wild-goose chase, Charlie."

He responded with impeccable good manners. "Speaking for myself, sir, it's a privilege, whatever the outcome."

The fat woman in front turned and took a hard look at both of us. I fear we were not wholly convincing as members of the great unwashed. I won't go into the embarrassment created on the bus when I proffered a sovereign for our two threepenny fares. Thank heavens Buckfast had a spare shilling.

As it was not a particularly cold evening, we sat on the upper deck, where we could talk more freely. And talk more freely Buckfast did, after I offered him a cigarette, quite abandoning his usual reticence. He was interesting on the subject of Fred Archer's relations with the fair sex. He told me that eager females went to extraordinary lengths to contrive meetings with Archer up to the time of his marriage and beyond. I don't know what it is about the ladies who patronize racing, but many a jockey had been offered an extra ride after the last race, if you'll pardon a smoking-room expression. Fred, of course, was better looking than most with his dark hair, glittering brown eyes and superior height. According to Buckfast, he often had invitations of the most brazen character pushed under his door. As a matter of routine when booking into hotels, he would ask the staff not to reveal his room number to inquirers of either sex. Even so, he was often obliged to change hotels to avoid his fair pursuers.

"Charlie, my dear fellow, you make these women sound like the hounds in full cry," I commented.

"Sometimes they were."

I pondered a moment. "Now there's a thought."

"What's that, sir?"

"'Are they coming?'"

I meant the remark in jest, but I didn't see Buckfast smile under his drooping mustache. I suppose as a military man, he lacked imagination. Personally, I was highly amused by the vision of a pack of lustful ladies advancing on Archer's house.

I asked, "Did he never allow himself to be caught?"

"Setting aside his marriage?"

"Naturally."

"No, sir. To my knowledge, he resisted them all. He was unfailingly charming, but implacable."

"I wonder why."

"There were more important things, sir."

"Winning races, you mean?"

"And holding on to his money. Women don't come cheaply."

The bus took us along Holborn and through the city, past Liverpool St. Station and out to Shoreditch. As it started along Hackney Road, we looked out for the lighted front of the music hall. Progress was slow along the narrow thoroughfare, for most of Shoreditch seemed to have left its shopping until late, crowding the barrows at the curbside and crossing the road without the least regard to traffic. Tantalizing aromas of hot soup, pies and roast chestnuts wafted up to our level, and I was so distracted (not having taken Buckfast up on his offer of a meal) that I missed the Sebright when it finally came in view. My hawk-eyed companion pointed it out, a narrow entrance framed by crowds of plaster cherubs festooned with colored lights.

We left the bus and were immediately accosted by two painted females reeking of cheap scent, one of whom linked her arm in mine and said, "Gerna tike me in, Tubby? Yer won't be sorry, m'darling."

I said firmly, "That's open to question, madam, and I don't propose to risk it."

To which she retorted, "Listen to 'im. '*Don't propose to risk it.*' Oojer think y'are, then? Lord Muck?"

I didn't enlighten her. We shouldered a passage through the throng of orange sellers, piemen and whores, paid our shilling for a seat in the front and passed inside.

I'm glad to report that the Sebright is a music hall in the old style, with tables for the patrons, where you sip a pot of beer and sup on pease pudding or pigs' trotters if you wish, while the performers entertain from the platform. I say "the old style" to distinguish it from such aberrations as the revamped London Pavilion, which are increasingly appearing in the West End. What a confounded liberty to masquerade as music halls when they force you into a row of tip-up seats with just a ledge to hold your beer glass and, as likely as not, with your view obstructed by the hat in front of you. It appears to me that the managers are interested only in cramming as many people as possible into their dreary "palaces of variety." From which you'll have gathered that I'm a stout supporter of the traditional halls. Years ago, I made a private visit to Evans's in Covent Garden and watched the show from a screened box, and I was ravished by the experience. I've been many times since, to all the more accessible halls. And I regularly invite my favorite artistes to perform at Sandringham and Marlborough House, though I'm bound to say that private entertainments lack something in atmosphere. One's dinner guests can be so infernally stuffy.

Buckfast and I found a convenient table out of the glare of the lights, yet not too close to the promenade. This, I may say, was my first experience of music hall as an anonymous member of the public, and I relished every moment. We took a chance on sausages, fried onions and mash, and helped ourselves to mustard from an enormous, gruesomely encrusted jar. What a toothsome treat it made! And what a splendid novelty to eat a meal with one's hat on!

No one in a regular music hall pays undue attention to what is happening on the stage until the top billings appear. There's a steady din of conversation punctuated by laughter; the waiters and potboys move among the tables; and the patrons are at liberty to get up from their seats and promenade. In fact, Belmont, the proprietor, was touring the auditorium during the acts, cigar in hand, saying to the patrons, "What do you think of that for thirty bob a week? Not bad, eh?"

I was mainly occupied in clearing my plate and ordering a second helping, but of course I kept an ear open for the chairman's announcements. He was on a raised chair at a table just in front of the orchestra, at the foot of the stage. Thus far, he'd introduced Sam Redman, a comic with blackened face who spoke on a monotone and hardly paused for breath; Marie Lloyd, the singer of "The Boy in the Gallery," said to be no older than sixteen; and a pair of lady gyrists or "voltas," who swung from ropes suspended over our heads and did nothing remarkable except show their legs in pink tights. Most of the turns, it has to be said, would have been hooted off the stage in a better class of hall. But then music hall isn't only what happens up there on the stage; everyone is noisily involved, from the chairman in his white tie to the brawny stevedore out for the evening with his doxy.

I won't tax your patience by taking you right through the bill. Sometime toward ten o'clock came the rap of the hammer followed by, "And now, ladies and gentlemen, beauty and obedience—the adorable Miss Myrtle Bliss and Cocky."

"And Cocky?" I piped in surprise. I hadn't expected a double act.

I spoke more audibly than I intended.

"And Cocky, old cock," retorted the chairman, to hoots of amusement from the audience.

I was about to shout something back when Buckfast silenced me by pushing a cigarette between my lips. He was right, of course. I'm occupationally accustomed to being the center of attention. It was no way for a plainclothes detective to behave, and once I was over the affront, I appreciated what he'd done. Charlie Buckfast was going to be a valuable companion, for all his want of humor.

As he struck a match for me, I said for his ears only, "I was expecting her to be a singer."

"And I, sir," he agreed.

How mistaken we were! Miss Bliss was a bird trainer, would you believe, and Cocky was a white cockatoo that performed like a human with bits of apparatus, including a miniature tricycle and a tiny drum. To be truthful, it wasn't a very arresting turn until, through no fault of mine, I became part of the performance.

This was how it happened. The spotlight unexpectedly shifted from the stage to the audience, dancing about our heads, and then, for some reason unfathomable to me at the time, settled on our table. Thereupon Cocky gave a piercing screech and flew straight toward me, nipped the cigarette from out of my mouth, soared into the gods and presented it to someone in the gallery. That got the biggest cheer of the evening. Apparently it was one of his regular tricks.

I must have made quite a spectacle of myself, for it's no joke to find yourself with the limelight shining down on you and a large cockatoo flying toward your face.

Miss Bliss made a show of scolding the bird and told it to say sorry to the gentleman, but I flapped my hand to show I wanted nothing more to do with Cocky. The evil creature turned its back and said something I didn't catch that got belly laughs all round.

I haven't told you yet that Miss Bliss was an uncommonly pretty black-haired creature in a fetching lemon-colored gown with a silver girdle. She had white, elbow-length gloves and a large white hat with a pale yellow ostrich feather. When the act finished, she gave me a most disarming smile.

I called a waiter and asked him for pencil and paper. At the feel of a florin pressed into his palm, he was eager to oblige.

"My dear Miss Bliss," I wrote, "I write as one who was not only captivated by your charming performance this evening, but was privileged to take a small part. I was the smoker of the cigarette that your parrot cleverly snatched away. I consider myself honored to have contributed in a small way to your success tonight. And I would be doubly honored if you would agree to join me and my companion for supper."

I folded it and handed it to the waiter.

"Who is it for, mate?" he asked.

I was about to tell him curtly that he was no mate of mine, when Buckfast chipped in with, "Miss Bliss, the young lady who just performed."

"Myrtle? You're too late." He grinned and added, "The bird has flown—and Myrtle with it."

"What?"

"She must have left the building by now. She appears at the Royal Eagle in half an hour."

"Damnation!" I *knew* that music hall performers appeared on several bills the same night. If I'd studied the *Era* systematically, instead of chucking it aside the moment I found her name on the bill for the Sebright, I'd have known she was likely to be rushing off to another hall. So much for my resolve to be a wise virgin.

"Where the devil is the Royal Eagle?" I demanded.

"City Road—as if you didn't know."

Buckfast said sharply, "If we knew, there would be no point in asking."

"Strike a light, mate—don't you know the song? 'Up and down the City Road, in and out the Eagle; that's the way the money goes—'"

I said, "Is it far?"

"No. Hoxton. You can walk it in twenty minutes, easy."

Easy was not the word I would have used as we shouldered our way through the crowds along Hackney Road, stepping over drunks and beggars and being importuned repeatedly by pimps and opium dealers. Stopping to ask for directions was positively dangerous in such a neighborhood, and thank heavens we were fortunate in the persons we consulted. Resolutely, we persevered as far as Old Street and so through to City Road, which was no more salubrious, I may tell you.

The Royal Eagle was another honey pot for streetwalkers and hawkers of every description. Before we went inside, I glanced at the bill and saw that Myrtle Bliss was indeed performing, with "feathered friends." Her name was at the bottom of the bill here, which meant second billing. Top, I noted wryly, was "Marvelous Disappearance of a Lady."

We moved around the side of the building to the pass door. It cost me a sovereign to gain admission that way, and even then the harridan on guard tested the coin with her teeth before she would let us through. Miss Bliss, we were advised, had her own dressing room at the top of the stairs. Luxury, indeed! The reason was shortly explained.

When I knocked, there was a screech from Cocky, or so I assumed, but it was followed by a pandemonium of squawks and shrieks. I opened the door and stepped into a veritable parrot house. It was a riot of color and earsplitting noise. There must have been six large parrots the size of Cocky; and uncountable smaller ones perched on every conceivable place where claws would grip. They screamed and swayed and flapped their wings. One of them called out, "Shut the door!" and I obeyed.

Miss Bliss spoke from behind a Japanese screen. She had to shout to get any hearing at all, and it was apparent that she mistook us for some other person. "Didn't I tell you not to come in sudden like that? You know it starts them off. Oh, stow it, Binky. You'll give me another headache." And when Binky persisted, "All right, you noisy perisher, I'm going to strangle you now!"

Suddenly she was no longer a disembodied voice. In fact, there was rather more body than either Buckfast or I were prepared for, because she was wearing only a bodice, drawers and stays when she darted out in pursuit of the noisiest parrot, an evil-looking red-and-yellow macaw perched on a chair back. She threw a towel over it and thrust it into a cage, where it abruptly stopped its hullabaloo. That bird was no less startled, I can assure you, than Captain Buckfast and I.

The shock was not unwelcome. Myrtle Bliss, in stays, was by far the prettiest sight we'd had all evening. Her figure revised the laws of science as I understood them. It was buoyancy without immersion, mass that defied gravity. And to run your eyes along the length of her legs was to understand infinity.

Unabashed, she glared at Buckfast and me and said, "Who the blazes are you?"

I said, "The Prince of Wales." I hadn't intended to give myself away, but I'm a creature of impulse. I adore surprising pretty young women, and at that moment I wanted nothing else but to make Myrtle Bliss shriek like her birds and take cover behind the screen.

It didn't happen. She said, "And I'm Florence Nightingale. Who's this—the Archbishop of Canterbury?"

Buckfast said, "Madam, take care how you speak to His Royal Highness."

She hesitated, and then said, "You're a couple of loonies. Stay where you are. These birds have got sharp beaks, you know."

I said, "I know from experience, my dear. One of them had my cigarette in the Sebright."

She clapped her hands and said with manifest relief, "*That's* who you are, you artful beggar! I thought I'd seen your face before. For a moment I thought you *was* the Prince of Wales."

I gave Buckfast a restraining look. Now that it was established that we weren't lunatics, but artful beggars, Miss Bliss seemed ready to be friends, and I had no objection. I could understand why the Squire had treated her to supper in Romano's. She was about twenty-four, I would guess, with glittering brown eyes, black hair in ringlets and a most engaging smile. I said, "We'd like to take you out to supper."

She giggled, fingered her drawer strings and said, "Dressed like this?"

To show decorum, I said, "Good Lord, no. We'll wait downstairs."

Buckfast, still thinking along more practical lines than I, asked her, "What will you do with your parrots?"

She said, "I'll put them to bed first."

Cautiously, I asked, "Where precisely?"

"Here. They sleep here while I'm engaged. All except Cocky. He comes home with me." She gave me a saucy look. "He's very privileged."

Buckfast said in a shocked voice. "Do you propose to bring the cockatoo to supper?"

She said, "We'll go to Mr. Hollis up the road. He's used to Cocky."

So it was settled, and I was thankful; none of the places I knew for supper would have welcomed us dressed as we were, with or without the bird. In Hollis's oyster house in the City Road, Cocky perched on a coatrack and observed a discreet silence.

Myrtle (we were soon on familiar terms) had put on a large black plush hat with a dash of crimson in the trimming, a black dress cut distractingly low at the front, and ruby-colored beads and earrings. She was liberally scented with frangipani. She sat facing Buckfast and me at a table screened on three sides by dark-stained wooden boards.

We ordered, talked for ten minutes about Cocky, who it emerged was a greater sulfur-crested cockatoo, and then I brought the conversation around to animals in general and racehorses in particular. Myrtle admitted to liking a "flutter on the gee-gees" when she could afford it. So I told the story of my old friend Sir Ernest Cassel, when he started as an owner and asked Lord Marcus Beresford's advice as to what should be inscribed on the side of his horse boxes. Ernest is justly proud of his knighthood and wanted to know whether it would be appropriate to add the letters K.C.M.G. after his name. "Oh, it's quite clear," said Marcus. "You put K.C.M. on the outside, and the gee goes in the box."

Myrtle gave a screech of laughter that startled even Cocky, and I followed up my story by asking whether she'd won anything on the horses lately.

"As a matter of fact, I have," she told us. "I backed the winner of the Cambridgeshire."

"The Sailor Prince?" said I, trying to sound surprised. "How very clever!"

"Bertie, I knew it couldn't lose," she admitted. "A gent of my acquaintance told me to put on every penny I had. I didn't do that, but I stumped up a week's wages and got a very good price."

"This gentleman—was he by any chance Mr. Baird, the Squire?"

She was saucer-eyed. "How did you know?"

"Oh, it's common knowledge that he fleeced the bookies,

and good luck to him." I winked across the table. "Do you happen to know his secret, Myrtle?"

"What?"

"I mean, where he got his information."

She said with awe in her voice, "For God's sake, keep your voice down, Bertie. He'd kill us both for gabbing about it in a place like this."

I said, "Later, perhaps—in another place?"

She said flatly, "You're an optimist, and no mistake."

She refused to be pumped any more on the subject of Baird, so we did full credit to Hollis's oysters, and very scrumptious they were, fresh from Colchester that morning. Without thinking anything of it, I ordered champagne. What else can one drink with oysters? Hollis first offered us quinine water, which I informed him wasn't fit for the parrot to drink. I insisted on champagne and suggested he send out for it. He wanted some assurance that we could pay for it, so I took out a handful of sovereigns and gave him one.

This transaction was productive in more ways than one, because I happened to notice Myrtle's eyes on the money, and her pupils had dilated like a hunting cat's. So, I thought I understand what excites you, young lady, and what drew you to the Squire.

Hollis was gone for a long time and finally returned with a bottle of non-vintage with a very inferior label that cost me five shillings. Once or twice in the next hour, as Myrtle and I conversed merrily about the music hall and our favorite comic turns, with Buckfast out of his depth, I felt the touch of Myrtle's shoe against mine, and believe me, it wasn't accidental. When the time came for us to leave, and Buckfast obligingly went to collect our coats, Myrtle leaned toward me and said, "Can't you get rid of that old poopstick?"

I murmured, "With the greatest of ease."

While Myrtle was retrieving Cocky, I told Buckfast in the

kindest terms that his duties were over for the night, and I would pursue the inquiry independently.

"Is that altogether wise, sir?" he asked.

"Charlie," I responded, "this is an avenue that only one of us is at liberty to venture along."

So we parted outside, Buckfast to try his luck at the cab stand and I to try mine with Myrtle. She had lodgings in Mile End Road, not the best of addresses, but convenient for her music hall engagements, and, she volunteered with a playful pull at my beard, blessed with a very understanding landlady.

Myrtle made no bones about inviting me in. We groped our way up a creaking staircase to the top floor, and she asked me to hold Cocky while she found her latchkey.

She let us in and reached for matches and a lamp, which presently showed me an attic room of modest proportions containing a bed, wardrobe, table, washstand and T-shaped perch, where I thankfully transferred Cocky. In the absence of any chair, I stood awkwardly holding my hat while Myrtle found some seeds for the bird.

That done, she turned to me and said, "Well, Bertie, it's too perishing cold to stand about. I'm getting straight into bed." She then started unbuttoning her dress.

You may think that good taste demands I should end my chapter here, but there is more of significance to tell, even at the cost of some embarrassment to myself. As you peruse these lines, kindly remember, as I endeavored to, my serious purpose in being there.

I decided that now might be the last opportunity for questions, so as Myrtle continued to disrobe, I said, "You hinted in the oyster house that you knew why The Sailor Prince was a certainty for the Cambridgeshire."

She lifted her skirts over her head and said, "Lord bless you, Bertie, you're not going to talk about horses now!"

I said, "I understood that *you* were going to."

She was down to her stays again. She draped the dress over the bed rail and said, "You'll have to ask the Squire."

I said, "That's no answer, Myrtle."

She came over to me and casually started unbuttoning my coat and jacket. "You're used to wearing better togs than these."

"Don't be evasive, miss."

She said with gentle mockery, "Masterful!" and started on the waistcoat. "Bertie, all I know is that it was a very close secret. The Sailor Prince was a much better horse than the bookies knew. The Squire spread his bets so as not to spoil the odds." My overcoat, jacket and waistcoat joined her garments on the bed rail.

"Was it a fixed race?"

"Would you loosen my stays?"

I obliged, manfully endeavoring to keep the investigation foremost in my thoughts.

As Myrtle eased the corset over her hips and stepped out of it, she offered, "I could try and find out, if you want."

"When will you see the Squire again?"

"Tomorrow."

At this juncture in the proceedings, my concentration wavered. It's no secret that I've battled gamely all my life with mixed success against my amorous nature. The sight of Myrtle in chemise and drawers would have made a saint think twice about paradise, but I had more to endure than the visual provocation, for she had hitched her thumbs under my braces and slipped them off my shoulders. The borrowed trousers dropped like a flag at sunset.

She commented, "Nice underwear. Why don't you take it off?"

"I don't trust your cockatoo."

She shook with laughter. "Oh, Bertie, he only takes cigarettes!" She wrenched off her remaining clothes and stood gloriously, glowingly naked. "Come to bed as you are, then."

Such cheek. Such cheeks.

The cultured element among my readers will be relieved to learn that I didn't do quite as the lady suggested. I first removed my boots.

How long it was before we were interrupted, I cannot say, except that it was not long enough, either for Myrtle or for me. There had been steps on the stairs several times already, so we paid no attention to a particularly heavy-footed approach until the door was thrust open without even the courtesy of a knock and someone staggered in, collided with Cocky's perch and knocked it over and crashed on me like the Tay Bridge.

Myrtle, heaven knows how, managed to squirm from under me and ignite the lamp. The cockatoo, quite berserk, was on the pillow pecking tufts of my beard. The intruder was lying across my back in a posture I shall not attempt to describe.

When the light came on and Myrtle bravely removed the bird, I managed to extricate myself. Our uninvited guest was fortunately not a heavy man.

In fact, he was a famous gentleman rider. We both knew him.

"The Squire!" whispered Myrtle.

He opened his eyes and said, "Where am I, Marlborough bloody House?"

Then he shut them again. He was as drunk as the moon in a puddle.

CHAPTER 9

Considering my situation at the end of the last chapter, it may surprise you to learn that I duly attended the Wellington Statue Committee meeting on Saturday morning. I have always been punctilious in attendance to my duties. *Ich Dien,* as you probably know, is the motto of the Prince of Wales. I serve, no matter what has occurred the night before, never ceasing to amaze my intimates when I rise early after a demanding night. But there's nothing remarkable in it. With me, it comes down to priorities—generally, pressure on the bladder.

This was the committee's first opportunity to examine the plaster models submitted by the sculptors. After a couple of hours, dusty debate over whether the likeness to Wellington mattered more than the anatomy of the horse, we chose Mr. Boehm's design and adjourned to brush the plaster off our suits. The momentous decision as to which direction the statue should face was postponed until the following Saturday, when we agreed to reconvene at Hyde Park Corner. Such are the great affairs of state which occupy me. Prime Ministers of each persuasion, Disraeli and Gladstone, have repeatedly urged the Queen to initiate me into the responsibilities to which I am heir. I am still not permitted to see the contents of a Foreign Office dispatch box. Every impediment possible is put in the way of my travels. "Any encouragement of his constant love of running about," Mama wrote to Disraeli, "and not keeping at home, or near the Queen, is earnestly and seriously to be deprecated." Yet what incentive am I given to keep at home?

When the meeting was over, I told my coachman that I had some shopping to do in Jermyn Street, and after he had conveyed me there I would not require him to wait. He's a trusted servant, totally discreet. How one relies upon such people! Many's the time he's driven me to addresses I wouldn't care to see printed in the Court Circular.

Charlie Buckfast opened his own front door this time, and I don't mind admitting that I chuckled at the sight of him, for I'd caught him repairing his mustache. One side was waxed, and the other hung limp.

I said, "Is it as late as that?"

He didn't understand.

I said, "Your face is at half past three."

Once inside, I settled into one of his leather armchairs and allowed him to continue with the repairs while I gave an account of the night's adventure. In all important respects, it was a truthful account. If you notice any small discrepancies in what follows, it is because I have always believed that good taste ought to govern one's conversation.

"Once I had escorted Miss Bliss back to her lodgings," I explained, "I commenced to examine her—in the legal sense of the word, you understand. That, after all, was my reason for being there."

Buckfast stood in front of his sideboard mirror combing the unkempt half of his mustache. "That goes without saying, sir."

"Naturally, Charlie."

His eyes met mine through the mirror. "And was she . . . forthcoming, sir?"

"My word, yes—it was give-and-take for the best part of an hour, Charlie."

"Did something emerge?"

I gave a sniff. "I rather think that your wax is becoming overheated."

He snatched up the fireplace tongs and rescued the tin from the edge of the grate.

I told him as he teased out the whiskers again and twisted them, "Myrtle and I were rudely interrupted in the middle of our exchange. Someone burst through the door, staggered across the room and fell onto the bed."

"Good Lord! That must have been uncomfortable, sir."

I said with emphasis, "I got up from the chair where I was seated and went to the bed to protest. The man was obviously drunk, as one would expect. But I did not expect to recognize him, Charlie. It was Abington Baird, the Squire."

Buckfast turned from the mirror, and the mustache sagged again. "But how on earth . . . ?"

"He'd made an arrangement to meet Myrtle on Saturday, and she assumed he meant Saturday night, after she finished her music hall engagements. She wasn't prepared for the small hours of Saturday *morning*, and nor was I. I mean, one simply doesn't blunder into a lady's room like that in the middle of the night. It's not as if it were a house party."

"Outrageous," Buckfast agreed. "Did he recognize you?"

"Oh, yes. He wasn't *that* inebriated."

"What did you do, sir?"

"What did I do? My first instinct was to leave at once. Heaven only knows what a scoundrel like Baird would make of one's predicament, however innocent the explanation. Then I had a second thought. Up to this moment, I'd been extremely reluctant to confront the fellow, whatever his involvement in the Archer mystery. Now, I had the advantage of him. For once, he was away from his gang of roughs and pugilists. Like most bullies, he's a different man deprived of his support. I told Myrtle to bring me the jug of water on the washstand. She was splendid. She knew what to do."

"Tipped it over the Squire?"

"The lot. Sobered him up in seconds."

"Stout work! Was he willing to answer questions?"

"*Willing* is not the word I would use. He was persuaded."

Buckfast gave one of his rare smiles. "A little arm-twisting, sir?"

"No, no. I abhor violence. I gave him a cigarette and stepped back like a bombardier." I grinned, but Buckfast was slow to comprehend, so I explained, "Cocky the cockatoo performed his music hall turn."

"Ah."

"The Squire cooperated splendidly after that."

"So you were enabled to question him about the Cambridgeshire?"

"I was. First, I confirmed that it was true that he won all that money on The Sailor Prince."

Buckfast remarked without much tact, "I thought everyone in London knew about that."

"Captain, any detective worth his salt checks everything at the source."

He colored perceptibly.

"I proceeded to ask what caused him to repose such confidence in a horse at 25-1. He gave an offensive laugh. I've never been so close to the man before. He has a profoundly disagreeable countenance, Charlie. Those thick lips like saveloys under that snub nose. Quite revolting."

"What was his answer, sir?"

"He said he'd heard that I backed The Sailor Prince myself. I told him *my* reasons were entirely sentimental, making clear by implication that his were not."

"How did he respond to that?"

"With an enormous belch."

"How disgusting!"

"Quite."

"Did you persist, sir?"

"Of course, Charlie. I'm a serious investigator. I asked Myrtle to bring Cocky's perch a little closer to the bed, and that worked wonders. The Squire told me that The Sailor Prince had been showing better staying power in training this season than it had ever possessed before. It was a revelation. William Stevens, the Compton trainer, couldn't explain it, but he had the sense to keep its form from the touts."

"Stevens? I can believe it," said Buckfast. "The Stevens brothers are up to every kind of trick."

"They entered it for the Liverpool Summer Cup and told the jockey to drop in on the rails behind the leader and not try anything spectacular. The Sailor Prince finished well up in third, behind the two dead heaters, but it could have won at a canter, given its head."

"So it didn't attract much attention."

"Exactly, Charlie. They didn't race it again before the Cambridgeshire."

There was a pause while Buckfast once more performed the twisting operation. He faced me, fingers pinching the spike into shape. "Is that approximately even, sir?"

I nodded, and he applied the wax.

Finally he turned from the mirror fully restored and remarked, "When you said 'they' didn't race the horse again before the Cambridgeshire, who exactly did you mean, sir?"

Charlie Buckfast was nobody's fool.

I told him, "That's the crux of it. When the Squire was speaking about the way the horse was prepared for the race, he didn't use *they*, he used *we*. The first time I remarked on this, he told me he kept some horses of his own with Stevens, and he regarded the Yews at Compton as a home away from home. He said he'd often watched The Sailor Prince at work."

"Who is the registered owner, sir?"

"William Gilbert, of Ilsley."

"Ah."

"Do you know him?"

"I know that he's a neighbor of the Stevens brothers."

"Well, you've obviously worked it out," I said. "The real owner of The Sailor Prince is the Squire, and it's registered in Gilbert's name."

Buckfast was impressed. "Did you get him to admit as much, sir?"

"With a little help from Cocky. He has scores of horses registered in other people's names, and pays handsomely for the privilege."

"That's a tremendous risk, isn't it? He could be disbarred from racing if the stewards got to hear of it."

"Yes, but remember what happened the last time he was warned off."

(Here, I'd better supply the story, for although it's well known in Turf circles, I doubt if it will pass down into history. The Squire, like his idol, Archer, is an aggressive, not to say ruthless, rider. His behavior on and off the racecourse has made him countless enemies among the racing fraternity, and no wonder, for when he isn't showing the way home to their horses, he's gallivanting with their wives, most of whom go quite giddy over him—or, more likely, his millions. Matters came to a head in a Hunters' Selling Flat Race at Birmingham in 1882, when the Squire won at a canter and was accused of foul riding by the rider who had finished last, and happened to be Lord Harrington. The Squire had apparently made abusive remarks about Harrington's riding and threatened to put him over the rails. When it was over and Harrington protested, the Squire said, "I thought you were a bloody farmer." As a consequence, he was reported to the Jockey Club and we decided to teach the blighter a lesson. We warned him off every course in the country for two years. How do you think he responded? He had the infernal cheek to let it be known that he proposed to buy the Limekilns—the gallops at Newmarket that are the finest anywhere, and practically hallowed ground. We in the Jockey Club were horrified at the prospect. Imagine this outlaw in a position to dictate which trainers used the gallops. He might have fenced the Limekilns off, or even plowed them up! We were compelled to enter clandestine negotiations with the Squire to secure the lease on terms that wouldn't beggar the club, and of course, he was reinstated before his ban was up.)

Buckfast said, "I daresay he secretly bought The Sailor Prince during the time he was warned off. It repaid him handsomely."

He poured me a glass of dry sherry and asked what else I'd learned from the Squire.

I responded judiciously, picking my way with care. I had a job for Buckfast that he might not welcome. I'm not renowned for my tact, but I felt some subtlety was wanted here. "He spoke up for Archer, wouldn't hear a blessed word against him. He said Fred had nothing to be ashamed of over the running of the Cambridgeshire. That rumor Lord Edward Somerset is putting about, to the effect that Fred paid a bribe to stop the favorite, Carlton, is a diabolical slander, in the Squire's opinion. Fred was offered the ride on Carlton, and he turned it down because he was convinced St. Mirin was the better horse."

"He's right about that," Buckfast conceded. "Fred thought he was on a certainty."

I continued in the same vein, "The Squire said he had a friendly exchange with Archer on the day of the race. Archer advised him strongly to back St. Mirin."

Buckfast put aside his sherry as if it were poisoned.

"Charlie, you look skeptical," I said. "As a matter of fact, Fred gave me the same tip."

He cleared his throat in a way that signaled disagreement.

"Out with it, man," I said.

"Well, sir, I have no doubt that Fred gave you a tip, but I question whether he was so generous to the Squire. They were not the bosom friends that the Squire would have you believe."

"The Squire was Fred's protégé," I pointed out. "Have you forgotten the riding lessons?"

"The most expensive riding lessons I ever heard of. Purely a business arrangement," said Buckfast dismissively. "The Squire paid well, and Fred was never averse to earning some extra."

"Fred in his capacity as the Tinman," said I.

"Exactly."

I remarked as if the thought had just occurred to me, "Wasn't there talk a year or two ago of Archer and the Squire going into partnership in Newmarket? A joint racing establishment?"

Buckfast winced as if I'd struck him. "The talk was all on one side, sir. Fred would never have sullied his reputation in such an ill-starred venture. He was furious with the Squire for putting the story about. People believed it, unfortunately. The Duke of Portland was one."

"Silly arse," I said. (Arthur Portland had acted prematurely when he heard the gossip and ordered Archer to send back his cap and jacket. Fred never rode in the Portland colors again.) "What you're saying is that the Squire was an embarrassment to Fred. Last night, he was claiming to be his one true friend."

"That's utter bilge—begging your pardon, sir."

I said teasingly, "Do I detect some personal animus here, Charlie?"

He answered, "I have never met the Squire, sir. I have always contrived to keep out of his way. I doubt if he's aware of my existence."

"Perfect," I said, and never meant it more sincerely, "because I want you to follow him."

His face was a study. I could have thrown a penny into his mouth. "Follow him?"

"Go to the places he frequents. They shouldn't be difficult to locate. The Greyhound at Newmarket is one. Romano's in the Strand is another. Where there's a barney going on, it's ten to one you'll find the Squire and his crew. Have another glass of sherry, Charlie. You look as if you need it."

He said, grappling with the unthinkable, "What would be my purpose in being there?"

"It stands out, doesn't it, Charlie? The Squire isn't being honest with us. You just told me he was talking utter bilge. We can't let him get away with it, can we?"

Buckfast rubbed the side of his chin and wetted his lips. "I suppose if you think he had some influence on Fred's suicide, sir . . ."

I said, "Never mind what I think. What do you think?"

After a moment's consideration, he answered, "He's a dangerous man."

"Undeniably."

"And it isn't just the Squire. There are all those others—Charlie Mitchell, Jem Smith—men whose profession is physical violence. They follow him everywhere. You must have seen them on the racecourse, sir."

"I saw them in the City Road last night," I told him.

"They were there?"

"Waiting under a lamppost for the Squire to complete his assignation with Myrtle. She spotted them from the window, at least a dozen of the ugliest specimens of humanity I have ever seen. It was quite impossible for me to return to Marlborough House, as I intended."

"What did you do?"

"I remained there all night."

"With Myrtle and the Squire?"

"Not with the Squire. After an hour, we encouraged him to leave. I helped him downstairs and bolted the door after him. It was the only possible course of action. His mob cheered him raucously when he appeared, and presently moved off, thank heavens."

"But you remained?"

"Solely to protect a lady at risk, Charlie. I don't underestimate these ruffians, and neither must you."

"No, sir."

"You're there to observe, not to provoke any unpleasantness. Be inconspicuous."

His hand went protectively to his mustache.

I said in a mild, reasonable voice, "It's got to come off, hasn't it, Charlie?"

"Off, sir?"

I nodded.

He was aghast. "Completely?"

"Every whisker."

He turned back to the mirror and regarded himself. "I suppose it is a prominent feature."

I said, "At two hundred yards or less. Heaven knows what the Squire and his gang would do with it if they suspected you of eavesdropping."

There was a moment's horrified silence.

I added, "Myrtle offered me her services as a spy, but I'd much rather rely on you, Charlie."

He went to a drawer and took out a pair of scissors. Such is the devotion to duty of the British cavalry officer.

As he snipped, I said, "I wouldn't want you to think that I shall be out of the front line, Charlie. I intend to mount an assault on a different flank. I shall arrange to visit the Dowager Duchess of Montrose."

He cut off a huge handful of whiskers and said, "The Duchess? Whatever for?"

Echoing Gladys de Grey's remark, I said, *"Cherchez la femme,* Charlie."

CHAPTER 10

Each Sunday afternoon, the affairs of State permitting, I make it my custom to tour the Sandringham estate. My weekend guests—there are always guests—are at liberty to join me if they wish, but old friends (the Earl of Carnarvon, Lord Herschel and Sir Henry James on the occasion of which I speak) generally feel at liberty to leave me to it. Upon a bleak November day, the twenty-first, I muffled myself like a cabman, for a brute of a wind was blowing off the Wash. In such conditions I generally head for the greenhouses, only there isn't so much as a rotten tomato to see at this end of the year. So we resorted to the sawyer's yard, where there is always a fire burning, and it was there that I discovered a lad scarcely above twelve years of age reading a copy of *Reynolds's Newspaper*.

I don't know if you will have heard of *Reynolds's*. I hope to heaven it will be defunct and forgotten by the time these lines are read, for it is a vile publication, a rag that promulgates wicked libel and defamation week by week in the name of socialism. Lest you think I exaggerate, let me quote from an article of last May referring to my son Eddy, destined one day to be King:

> *. . . A duller, a stupider lad never existed. He cannot even read with any degree of grace or dignity the written speech which is put into his hand and which is reported next day in the newspapers as his own.*

Now, while I am the first to admit that Eddy's powers of concentration leave something to be desired, it is a matter of record that after his naval training the boy was admitted to Trinity College, Cambridge, and is soon to be offered a commission in the Tenth Hussars. How can any responsible journalist pen such vitriolic stuff when we, Eddy's devoted parents, are doing all in our power to prepare him for the responsibilities of State? I can tell you, poor Alix would be inconsolable if she knew the scurrilous abuse that is read each Sabbath in millions of homes up and down the country.

That was not all. Judge for yourself the quality of the journalism as I quote the remainder of the same article:

> *The Prince of Wales and other "members of the royal family" who venture to favor the public with their views upon current topics have also their speeches prepared for them by the official speech writer. You have only to dress up a donkey or an ape, and call it "king" or "royal," and half the females in the land will start into a paroxysm of admiration, praising the lovely ears, and the finely molded hoofs and the delicate skin, and the refined ways, just the same as if it were the most Godlike of created beings. Many of these poor people are ready for a lunatic asylum; but of course, so long as they are merely in the stage of idiocy, and their friends consent to support them at home, the State need not burden itself with the charge.*

So you can understand my reaction when I chanced upon

the young sawman reading *Reynolds's Newspaper*. I snatched it from his grimy hands and soundly boxed his ears with it. Then I warned him that he could seek employment elsewhere if he was ever again found with it in his possession on my estate. He was quick to understand. He assured me that he only read it for the racing results. How I wish my Eddy were so quick-witted.

The head sawman, who is not slow, either, took the opportunity to divert any blame coming his way by offering to beat the boy and burn the offensive paper. I didn't allow it. As I explained, I had already administered a summary chastisement. As for the newspaper, it was the lad's property, albeit at a cost of one penny, and I proposed to teach our young socialist a lesson in practical politics. I respected property, so it was against my principles to permit his newspaper to be destroyed. I would confiscate it instead. I handed it to Jarvis, my estate manager, promising the boy that when he left my employ, which need not be for many years if he improved his ways, he could ask for his paper to be returned, and it would be handed to him.

At the end of the afternoon, Jarvis asked what he should do with the wretched newspaper, and I was somewhat at a loss until I thought of Knollys. "Hand it to Sir Francis," I said. "He will commit it to some place of safekeeping."

Next morning, after my guests had made their farewells and been conveyed to the station, Knollys buttonholed me in the front drive.

"That, em, copy of *Reynolds's Newspaper,* sir."

"Of what?" I said, hazily recalling the incident. The previous night, I had yarned with my guests in the smoking room until the fire turned to ash. "Ah, yes. You put it somewhere safe?"

Now it was Knollys who became vague. "The newspaper, sir?"

"What else? We're not talking about pink elephants, Francis."

There was an uncomfortable pause, then Knollys responded, "The newspaper in question was handed to me, sir. I was given to understand that you had suggested I took charge of it."

"So I did."

He said in that disapproving tone that bears an uncanny resemblance to my mother's, "It is not a pleasant organ—not the organ one would desire to see at Sandringham, sir."

"Emphatically not," I agreed.

"One would not wish Her Royal Highness or the young princesses to discover it by some mischance."

I didn't like the drift of this. I gave a grudging nod.

He continued, "After it was given to me, I examined it page by page. Some of it was extremely offensive. The remarks about Your Royal Highness—utterly uncalled-for."

I said, "I haven't seen them."

Knollys declared forcefully, "Nor will you, sir. I took the liberty of destroying them."

"You *what?*"

"I cut out the only possible item for your scrapbook—and burned the rest."

I was outraged. I shouted, "Damn you, Francis! You had no right. You're worse than incompetent. You're a destroyer, an anarchist," but really I blamed myself. After my homily in the saw yard on the sanctity of property, I should have made sure that the confounded newspaper was put away safely. If the boy grew up to start the revolution, mine would be the responsibility.

Knollys was white at the gills. I suppose I had been too heavy-handed. To soften the rebuke, I said, "You might as well show me the piece you decided to keep. Is it amusing?"

He said, "I wouldn't describe it as such. It is one of the leading articles."

"The subject?"

"The late Mr. Archer and his will."

I pricked up. "Then I should like to see it at once."

He fetched the scrapbook from his desk. The cutting was already pasted in. Under the title "A Jockey's Fortune," it announced that on reliable authority Fred Archer was stated to have left a fortune of over a hundred thousand pounds. Most of what followed was tedious and predictable socialist claptrap about the racing fraternity making piles of gold while the laboring classes starved, without a word about the thousands who are afforded employment by the sport. Archer, it suggested, was a poor stable boy who should have remained poor. He had betrayed his class by hobnobbing with "lords, dukes and even princes, while by certain of his countrymen he had for years been worshiped as a sort of demigod."

I looked up and remarked to Knollys, "The usual joyless propaganda."

He said, "If you read on, sir, I think you may find something to interest you."

I did. It was the very next sentence: "A certain frowsy old dowager duchess of sporting proclivities is said to have been nearly marrying him."

Carrie Montrose.

"My word," I said, spluttering with laughter, "I wonder if she's seen this."

Knollys commented dryly, "I wouldn't care to be the one who drew it to her attention, sir."

I was chuckling over Carrie's sporting proclivities for the rest of the morning, and it was quite some time before I began to grasp the importance of the statement. Lady de Grey had told me that Carrie Montrose, at the advanced age of sixty-eight, had been pursuing Archer with a view to matrimony and I had scarcely believed it, yet here it was in a newspaper read by millions. Strange things happen, but I doubted whether *Reynolds's Newspaper* employed Gladys de Grey to write its editorials.

In point of fact, *Reynolds's* went much further than Gladys had suggested. The Duchess was "said to have been nearly marrying" Archer. Amazing, if true. I should say amazing if Archer had seriously entertained the match. Granted, Carrie was extremely rich and had inherited from her second husband possibly the finest racing stable and breeding stud in the country. Granted, Archer had an eye to making money. Moreover, he was a lonely man since the death of his wife. And Carrie had flattered him by stumping up an enormous retainer for years. Granted, all that. I still couldn't picture them as bride and groom, sixty-eight married to twenty-nine. Six-Mile Bottom carried over the threshold by the Tinman.

However, I was glad to have the information, for whatever it was worth. It gave my forthcoming meeting with Carrie an extra piquancy. She didn't know it yet, but she would be entertaining me and Charlie Buckfast to dinner at her town house in Cheyne Walk the following Saturday. The arrangements had to be discreetly handled, so it was all being done through Sykes's sister-in-law, Jessica, who was known to Carrie. I hadn't mentioned it to Knollys. Fortunately, he still has sense enough not to interfere in my private dining engagements.

Nor does he open my letters. I mention this because on Tuesday when the post was brought to me, there was a pungent aroma of lavender emanating from the stack. Intrigued, I picked out the source, a scented envelope of a most vulgar shade of blue, with a London East postmark and the word *Pursonall* doubly underlined above a curiously misspelled attempt at my name and address. I was not long in deducing that it came from Myrtle Bliss.

She had first written *Your Royl*, then scored it through and substituted *Dear Burte*.

Wot a jolly time we had Fridy nite! Arnt you a sorsy begger and no mestake! Wooden it be a lark to meet agen? I bin

invited to Noomarkit Sundy with the Sqyre so if you want
to here all about it, be shore to cum and look me up next
week-Chewsdy about 11. Cocky sez bring yore smokes. Hes
got a new trick to shew you.

Love,

M

Much as I appreciated the sentiments in general, the style
and orthography shocked me—in fact, caused me to ask
myself how I could have been so impetuous as to encourage
such an attachment. At the risk of appearing snobbish, I
must say that on paper the lady lost most of her charm. All
things considered, I preferred to rely on Charlie Buckfast for
news of the Squire. I didn't respond. If I have learned one
lesson in life, it is that letter writing to the fair sex, whether
they are literate or not, is fraught with snares.

That apart, the main excitement of the week was the safe
delivery on Monday, 23 November, of a son to my youngest
sister Beatrice. I visited her at Windsor on Wednesday (not
to mention Mama, and I prefer not to, for it was the usual
sermon on self-restraint). I traveled back to Sandringham for
my youngest daughter Maud's seventeenth birthday party on
Friday. Birthdays are joyous occasions, and I would be the
last to complain, except that with seven in our family and
over thirty nephews and nieces we do little else but send
cards and eat cake. I left for London late that night for the
inevitable meeting on Saturday morning of the Wellington
Statue Committee.

I was eager to hear from Buckfast after his week as a
shadow to the Squire, and I'd arranged to call at his rooms
in Jermyn Street at six o'clock on Saturday evening, in good
time to have his report before we left for our dinner engagement with the Duchess. Inconveniently, he was not at his
address when I arrived, and I was obliged to stand for twenty
minutes exchanging pleasantries with the greengrocer about

the nourishment in potatoes. I'm a great advocate of the humble potato.

When a four-wheeler eventually pulled up and a fellow stepped out, I had difficulty at first in recognizing Charlie Buckfast. Without the mustache, and in an ill-fitting Norfolk jacket and cap, he could have passed for a loader at one of my Sandringham shoots, except that he ignored me totally and stared up and down the street before he put the key in the door. He didn't even have the elementary good manners to step back and let me enter first. He fairly bolted inside and left me to make my own way in and close the door after us.

I would certainly have taken objection if I hadn't seen his expression. I'm well used to looking at nervous faces. I come across them all the time, like red carpets and the smell of fresh paint. Charlie's wasn't merely nervous; it was *hunted.* And the first words he spoke when we got upstairs had a horrid familiarity.

"Are they coming?"

I was standing by the window. I stared at him for a moment. Then I turned and looked out.

He said, "Don't move the curtain, for God's sake!"

Below, in Jermyn Street, the growler had moved off. Someone in a dark green ulster and billycock was coming out of the tobacconist's opposite. A couple in evening capes were crossing the road. I could see nothing to provoke such alarm in my co-investigator, and I told him so.

He said, "They followed me up from Newmarket. They looked right into the compartment before the train left, and I saw them get on as it was pulling out. At Liverpool Street, I jumped off the train before it came to a halt and fairly sprinted to the barrier, with them in open pursuit."

"Good Lord! Who were they?"

"Two of the Squire's henchmen, his minders, as he calls them. One is a prizefighter, built like an ox. He's fond of displaying his scars, and the scars are confined to his fists, from battering his knuckles against other men's skulls. The other is taller and younger, with the coldest gray eyes you ever saw. Can you see them yet, sir?"

I glanced down at the street again. "Hide nor hair, Charlie."

He waited, expecting any second to hear me say otherwise. "Please God, I gave them the slip. I changed cabs near St. Paul's."

"Do they have any idea who you are?"

"I think not. But I'm a marked man. Last night, there was dogfighting in the back room of the Greyhound. He has this murderous Staffordshire bull terrier called Donald, which he unleashes on any of the local strays his men can round up. I wouldn't call it fighting—more like ratting. There's betting on how long they last."

"And you were there to see it?"

"No, sir. I took the opportunity to break into Bedford Lodge, the Squire's headquarters."

"You broke into the Lodge! By jove, Charlie, I salute you. Are we on to something?"

Buckfast had poured two whopping brandies. He handed me one, stealing a glance out of the window at the same time. "I'd stake my life on it, sir. I've been listening all week to the Squire's bragging. If half of it is true, Fred Archer must be stoking the fires of hell. The Squire says there isn't a jockey in England who can't be squared. He says Archer and Charlie Wood were in his pocket and now he wants Cannon."

This was devastating. I said in a voice thick with shock, "Archer accepted bribes from the Squire? Is that what you're telling me, Charlie?"

"That's what I heard more than once, sir. He and Wood were regularly pulling races, and the Squire was putting up the money."

I felt a wave of nausea at the very idea. Rumors of a conspiracy, a "jockeys' ring" involving Archer and Wood and certain "professional backers," had surfaced two years ago but were disbelieved by all except that vengeful old Turfite, Sir George Chetwynd, whose own runners had been afflicted that season with in-and-out form. Chetwynd had gone so far as to interrogate the two jockeys (they denied the charge) and publish a notice in the sheet calendar of the Jockey Club asking the stewards how they proposed to deal with the allegations. The stewards responded that they required clearer evidence of malpractice, and for a time Chetwynd was in uncommonly bad odor over the business. Now, apparently, his complaint was vindicated.

The last thing I wanted was to drag Archer's name through the mud.

And there was worse to come from Buckfast: "The Squire claims that he didn't need to put up large bribes once the jockeys had taken the first payment, because they were terrified of a Jockey Club inquiry. Their livelihoods were at risk. They had so much to lose."

"Unlike the Squire, whose reputation reeks to high heaven," I commented acidly.

"He bought his way out of suspension once. He could do it again," said Charlie.

"No doubt of that. With his millions, he has the Jockey Club by its ears. What I don't understand is why he bothers to cheat. What's in it for him?"

"The same thing puzzled me, sir," Charlie admitted. "My first thought was that he took a malicious delight in fleecing the bookmakers. Then I heard him say something else, a remark that made me see the logic in what he was doing. He said Fred was an idiot to blow his brains out just when he was offered the finest opportunity of his life."

"Opportunity? What kind of opportunity?"

"A partnership with the Squire."

I closed my eyes and said something sacrilegious.

Charlie gave a shrug. We both remembered the talk of a joint racing establishment. And you, my reader, ought to remember it, too, if you're paying attention, because I mentioned it in the last chapter.

Charlie said, "The bribes were just the bait. The Squire was planning from the start to trap Fred into signing an agreement. He idolized Fred. To be a partner with him was recognition, the supreme accolade. A contract was drawn up and Fred was being blackmailed into signing it. The Squire kept saying that he still had the document and he couldn't bring himself to destroy it. That's why I broke into Bedford Lodge."

"To steal it?"

Charlie looked slightly pained. "To annex it, sir. I managed to force a window in the boxing saloon and gain access to the main part of the house. The lights were burning in every room, but no one appeared to be about. I was looking for a study, or at least some room where a writing desk was situated. The entire house is in a disgusting state, with empty bottles and glasses and cigar butts and half-chewed bones strewn about, and the fireplaces heaped with ash and cinders."

"Didn't you find anything?"

"I gave up looking downstairs, sir."

"You tried the bedrooms?"

Charlie nodded. "I thought possibly the Squire would keep anything of value beside his bed. I located his room without difficulty. Unfortunately, it was occupied at the time."

"He was at home in bed?"

"Not the Squire, sir. Two of his men, naked as cuckoos."

"Fellows?" I pictured the scene all too shockingly. "Whatever next?"

"They were a pair of his pugilistic friends, believe it or not, sir—the two who are currently pursuing me."

"Charlie," I said sympathetically, "I understand everything now."

And everything, to put it at its most tame, was unsatisfactory. In spite of our strenuous efforts on Archer's behalf, his reputation looked blacker than when we had started. We still had nothing of substance to assist us, and Charlie Buckfast couldn't any longer be used to keep tabs on the Squire.

He asked me what I proposed to do, and after a moment's reflection, I fished the scented letter from my pocket and allowed him to read it. "I want this thing settled," I said. "If there *is* a document proving that the Squire was pressing Archer into a partnership—and poor Fred shot himself rather than sign—I shan't rest until I've seen it. I think we shall have to resort to Myrtle Bliss."

Charlie looked exceedingly dubious. "She's just a music hall performer, sir. She doesn't have my background or military training."

"She has one incalculable advantage over you, Charlie—the entrée to the Squire's bedroom."

He couldn't argue with that. I suggested it was time he dressed for dinner with the Duchess. At the prospect of venturing out again, he made a few demurring noises, but I was swift to remind him of his obligations as a gentleman, not to say an ex-officer. He withdrew to his bedroom.

It was toward half past seven when we left. I manfully offered to step into the street first, and when I'd made sure there was no one suspicious lurking, I hailed the first hansom that came along and negotiated a fare. Charlie crossed the pavement at speed and climbed in, and we set off at a canter in the direction of Chelsea.

Never having visited Carrie Montrose before, I was unable to give the cabman precise instructions as to the location of the house. The street is numbered, but who wants to own a house that is known by a mere number? The Duchess's is named Sefton House, after her late husband's Derby winner.

We had some difficulty in locating it, a common enough experience in a public carriage, when the wily cabdriver takes every advantage to relieve you of more than the fare you agreed. We were driven the length of the Walk—quite half a mile along the Thames embankment (for the houses overlook the river)—and most of the way back before he stopped the horse outside the Duchess's gate. I handed him the one and six we had agreed, and a threepenny tip, and he had the cheek to demand sixpence more for the extra distance. Buckfast and I had already got out, and I was damned if I would be tricked into paying any more. The driver's revolting language disgusted me, and I asked him for his number, which I was unable to see in the darkness. It was a disagreeable, but not uncommon, scene. Buckfast, evidently embarrassed by the business, opened the wrought-iron gate of Sefton House and went through.

Next, I was conscious of a strangled shout that I swear uncurled the hair on the back of my neck. The voice was Charlie Buckfast's, manifestly in trouble, and it came from inside the garden of Sefton House. I guessed at once what was happening, for I called upon the cabdriver to render assistance, whereupon the cowardly fellow whipped up his horse and deserted me. The sounds of heavy blows came from the other side of the high brick wall. I looked up and down the Embankment, but no help was within call. A groan of unspeakable character was conveyed to me as I considered how to act.

I flattened myself to the outside of the wall. Criticize me if you wish, but isn't it beyond dispute that most heroes are people with no imagination? As a sensitive man, I was graphically, painfully aware of what was happening to my unfortunate associate, and it was presently confirmed when two roughs came through the gate dragging the dead weight of poor Charlie, his heels scraping the ground. Both were muffled to the ears and wore long coats and billycock hats.

One had the build of a prizefighter, with a back like a leather armchair. The other was taller, better proportioned. I can't be more precise. That stretch of Cheyne Walk is almost unlit.

In fact, I entertained a slight hope that the lighting was so poor that I wouldn't be spotted, but it was not to be. The squat man looked my way and shouted, "Get him!"

Thinking back, my best chance was probably to have dashed through the gate and up the path to the front door of Sefton House. The Duchess or one of her staff might well have heard the commotion and opened the door in readiness. Instead, I rashly started along the Embankment toward the Albert Bridge. Running is not a pastime at which I excel. In the first two strides I lost my hat. I lost my breath in the next and was collared from behind by my pursuer. When I say "collared," I mean it literally. I was grabbed by the collar and practically garotted into the bargain as an arm like a rifle butt clamped against my throat.

The brute hauled me back toward his confederate, who, to my horror, was in the act of pushing Charlie Buckfast over the Embankment wall into the Thames.

I shouted. "You'll kill him!"

The only response was the tightening of the clamp on my throat.

I saw Charlie tipped over the wall. I heard the splash as his body struck the water. There was no cry. Whether he was conscious, I cannot say. He put up no fight, and that's not the way a cavalry officer would want to go.

It was two against one now.

The shape of the figure by the wall was outlined for a moment against the moonlight reflected along Battersea Reach. It was positively simian in aspect.

I tried to speak, but my vocal cords were unable to function under the pressure.

The ape shuffled toward me and grabbed one of my arms. I was propelled toward the Embankment wall and thrust

CHAPTER 11

Whoever wrote that line "Sweet Thames, run softly, till I end my Song," should have been dropped headfirst into the evil river. His song would have ended there and then.

I can tell you from personal experience that *sweet* is not an accurate description of the Thames. I would allow brackish, foul and emetic, but not sweet. We are told that Mr. Bazalgette's marvelous system of drainage has transformed the river from an open sewer to a natural waterway, and all of London is grateful to him for that, so I shall put the blame on Nature for the unendurable taste of the pints of noxious fluid I swallowed that November night.

I spluttered and floundered. My clothes and shoes weighted me, and I was in the gravest danger of drowning. I have absolved Mr. Bazalgette of responsibility for the state of the water, but the same gentleman is guilty of another charge, for he designed the Embankment, and there isn't a decent handhold for a drowning man to grasp along its entire length. I can remember when it was a wharf equipped with iron hooks and rings and even lengths of rope dangling helpfully. Since Bazalgette's improvements, the hapless struggler in the water is confronted with massive granite blocks forming a rampart, an unscalable wall where his hands claw unavailingly at weed and slime.

If you ask what kept me afloat, I am convinced it was willpower. I was damned if I would allow myself to perish in such squalid circumstances. I'm told that a drowning man sees his whole life pass across his brain like a magic lantern show. I can only speak for myself and tell you that I had a vision of the editor of *Reynolds's Newspaper* at work on a gloating obituary on the moral of my sinking into the sludge. That vision saved me. I struck out like Captain Webb, the channel swimmer, in sight of Calais.

For perhaps fifty yards, I kept up a resolute breaststroke, until, praise be, my hand came in contact with a solid obstruction, a wooden structure, a floating jetty used by the penny steamers. I grasped the post on the nearest corner. It was as sweet an embrace as any in my experience.

I succeeded in dragging myself out at the second attempt and lay blowing like a grampus for an interval of uncertain duration, utterly spent, nauseated from the intake of water. At length, I propped myself into a sitting position and listened for voices above. If my attackers were waiting up there and found me alive, they wouldn't hesitate to throw me back. Hearing nothing for some while, I crawled across the jetty and located the steps leading up to the Embankment wall. Water streamed from my clothes as I ascended. Near the top, I paused and listened.

Not a sound.

I raised my head to the level of the wall. There wasn't a living soul in sight. I clambered over and staggered across the road toward the houses of Cheyne Walk. At the gate of Sefton House, I listened again before entering. All was silent. I tottered up the path and rang the Duchess's door bell.

It was answered by a maid in uniform. She took one look at me in the porch light, said, "Jerusalem!" and slammed the door in my face.

Admittedly, I was an unprepossessing spectacle. My head and evening jacket were coated in mud, slime and waterweed. One sleeve had torn at the seam as I'd pulled myself onto the jetty. I had lost my bow tie, hat, both shoes and one of my gloves. A pool of water was forming at my feet.

I pressed the bell a second time. When there was no answer, I crouched and shouted through the letter slot, "This is the Prince of Wales. Let me in at once!"

I watched and listened for the response, and my announcement certainly elicited some excitement in the house. Presently the light in the hall grew dimmer as a bulky form stepped toward the door. A pair of eyes met mine on the other side of the opening, and the voice of the Dowager Duchess of Montrose said, "If you don't get off my doorstep this minute, I'll call the police to you!"

This had descended to farce.

As if I had not heard, I inquired, "Did you, or did you not, invite me to dinner?"

There was a pause.

The door eased open a mere two inches. Her face glared through the gap. She flung the door wide open and said, "You're a caution, Your Royal Highness! You and your practical jokes."

I lurched across the threshold, far too weak to argue.

She curtsied, caught a whiff of the river, and abandoned decorum. "God help us, the smell of him! Stay where you are, Your Highness. Don't move a step in those filthy clothes, and keep away from the wallpaper." She sent the maid for newspapers and a bath.

You won't wish to be put to the blush by a copious description of the next few minutes any more than I will. Suffice to say that such is the force of the Duchess's personality that I was persuaded to stand on a copy of the *Morning Post* and strip to my sodden undergarments. She contrived in the cause of decency to place her ample form between me and the team of domestics who carried a hip bath into the hall and filled it with jugs of steaming water from the kitchen, whereupon they all retired, leaving me to complete my undressing in privacy and step into the water. Despite the novel surroundings, never was a bath more welcome.

While soaping my hair, I had a most disquieting thought. Charlie Buckfast.

Suppose he had not drowned and was afloat in the Thames, expecting to be rescued! It seemed unlikely, for I'd heard no sound when I was in the river, but I couldn't in all conscience abandon the poor fellow if he had the slightest chance of survival. I sat forward in the bath and shouted for the Duchess.

It occurs to me that you may feel I was tardy in bringing my thoughts to bear on Charlie Buckfast. If so, I beg to remind you of what had just occurred. Not merely had I made a miraculous escape from the Grim Reaper. Down there in the Thames, the destiny of the nation had been in jeopardy. By triumphing over death, I had preserved the line of succession and ensured, God willing, that I will be spared to undertake the great responsibility for which I have been preparing all my life. I won't say I was fully conscious of these matters at the time, but afterward they tended to crowd out other thoughts.

Let's give credit to Carrie Montrose, for when I called her name, she appeared very rapidly from behind one of the half-opened doors leading off the hall. Unfortunately, she was not so rapid in apprehending what I was saying. My concern about Buckfast made no appreciable impression. She was not interested in Buckfast. Incredibly, she still appeared to believe that the episode was one of the practical jokes for which I am well known. Worse, silly woman, she had somehow convinced herself that I had devised it with the wicked intention of revealing myself to her in a state of nature. She was pink with excitement.

I told her, "Captain Buckfast may be drowning at this minute!"

She said with a most inappropriate outburst of laughter, "You should be on the stage. You're better than Henry Irving." She wagged a finger at me. "Let's stop pretending, shall we, Your Royal Highness—or may I call you Bertie? You came alone."

In desperation, I howled, "Duchess, will you kindly order your servants immediately to conduct a search along the riverbank?"

She hesitated, frowning, and I entertained a fleeting hope that she understood. Then she said, "Do you really want me to get rid of the servants, Bertie? So early in the evening?"

As I've mentioned more than once, Carrie Montrose is a lady of mature years. Moreover, she is built like a barge horse and colors her hair a revolting shade of orange. She wears it high, in tight curls bunched over her brow, topped, for this occasion, by a cluster of pink and green ostrich feather tips. Her dinner gown was of tomato-red velvet with lace epaulets and a profusion of roses, butterfly bows and gathered frills extending over what one prefers to assume was a bustle, to end in a long train. She wore white gloves and carried a Japanese fan. The effect was as bizarre as our conversation.

I said, "A man may be drowning out there. Hand me a towel, for pity's sake, and I'll give the order myself."

Still refusing to believe me, she said, "Don't you care about dinner? It will be ruined."

I'm afraid I said something unparliamentary about the dinner. But this was an emergency that demanded more than mere words. Since no towel was forthcoming—and to make clear how serious I was—I stood up in the bath. I've never been coy about my body. I've nothing to be ashamed of (quite the contrary) and I made no attempt to cover up. I folded my arms across my chest and faced her.

For once in her life, the redoubtable Duchess of Montrose

was bereft of speech. She opened her fan and covered the lower part of her face in awe. I took it to be awe, anyway.

I said, "Will you speak to the servants, or shall I?"

She shot out of the hall and gave the orders. I lowered myself thankfully below the water again, for it was drafty.

When my hostess returned, she was holding a bath towel which she told me had been warmed. She also provided me with bottle-green silk pajamas, a woolen dressing gown in a Tartan design, and slippers. I assured her that I was in a fit state to use the towel without assistance, and she withdrew to the sitting room, leaving me to ponder how it was that an elderly widowed lady living alone could produce a completely new set of gentlemen's night clothes, in my size and precisely the materials and colors I most favored.

But to more serious matters. Dreadful to relate, when the servants returned, they had no news of Charlie Buckfast. Five of them had searched with lanterns for upward of an hour. They said a strong tide was running now and it was likely that he had been carried far upstream. Recalling how I had insisted on his accompanying me, in spite of his apprehensions, I felt conscience stricken. I retained a slender hope that by some miracle the shock of immersion had brought him around, and like me, he had managed to swim to the landing. Optimism leads one at times to make the most improbable assumptions, for I had conveniently overlooked poor Charlie's crippled left arm.

The Duchess, cognizant at last of what had happened, said, "Shouldn't we send for the police?"

This wasn't a suggestion I welcomed. I am the first to applaud the work of the men in blue, but I expect them to perform it without reference to me, except over matters of ceremony. It would be unthinkable for the Heir Apparent to become involved in a police investigation. I was once called as a witness in a case of divorce, and although my part in the sad affair was entirely innocent and trivial, I can't begin to tell you the rumpus my appearance caused—and that was in the civil courts. Imagine the field day the press would have reporting that the Prince of Wales had been involved in a brawl on the Thames embankment. And—perhaps even more shocking—that he had been on a private visit to the Duchess of Montrose.

In hot water such as this I mix my metaphor and grasp at any straw. I deflected the Duchess by asking for a servant to be sent to Jermyn Street to see if by some miracle Captain Buckfast had escaped with his life and returned home. This was arranged. The same man was instructed to call at Marlborough House to collect a change of clothes for me.

Without much concern for the delicacy of my position, Carrie Montrose persisted. She pointed out that what I had witnessed was murder, or attempted murder at the least, and it would be next to impossible, not to say an offense, to keep it secret. The attackers ought to be apprehended as soon as possible. Captain Buckfast was a fine gentleman, a Turfite, and she had the highest regard for him. And as a loyal subject of the Crown, she could not allow the Prince of Wales to be thrown into the Thames outside her own doorstep. She had another suggestion. By a happy chance, one of her neighbors was the Metropolitan Police Commissioner, Sir Charles Warren, "a most approachable gentleman, and totally discreet." Wouldn't it be sensible to speak informally to Sir Charles about the attack? He, of all people, was capable of handling the matter in the strictest confidence.

When the servant returned with news that Captain Buckfast's apartment was in darkness, and there was no answer to the door bell, I consented to send for Warren.

This left me a desperately short time in which to change my clothes and decide how much I would tell. Should I reveal, for example, that Buckfast had spent the past week shadowing the Squire, and that our two assailants were almost certainly the men who had pursued him from Newmarket? It was bad enough having my name linked with Carrie's, but the Squire's as well? I shuddered.

In that divorce case I just mentioned, counsel advised me to answer the questions truthfully and volunteer nothing that was not asked. It is a sound principle.

Sir Charles Warren arrived dressed unnecessarily in full uniform, from cocked hat to high boots, and with all his decorations displayed, which at half an hour's notice was an impressive tribute to his military training. I'd met him thus arrayed on a couple of occasions, but you don't get much chance to assess a man when he bows and you wish him good day and move on to the next to be presented. He is a soldier, a Royal Engineer, who rose to the rank of general, and his appointment to the police was quite recent. He was brought in as Commissioner to deal more effectively with public demonstrations after his predecessor allowed the unemployed to run riot through Oxford Street, breaking windows and looting shops. Sir Charles had useful experience in Bechuanaland, dealing with unruly Boers. He is not a man to tolerate bad behavior.

We went into the dining room to eat. Sir Charles's appearance is intimidating, but so, I am told, is mine. He has a massive mustache in the Prussian style, curling below the edges of his mouth, a truly exceptional silver-brown growth that is distractingly different in color from the hair on his head, which is jet-black and pomaded into a severe, straight line across the forehead. As if that were not sufficiently arresting, he sports a monocle that causes him to frown. However, I am perfectly capable of frowning too.

I sometimes find it expedient in dealing with generals to gain a moral victory at the outset, so I advised him that the K.C.M.G. that he correctly wore suspended from his neck was partially obscured behind his sash, which was at least half an inch broader than necessary. Surprising how often my knowledge of decorations and ceremonial comes to my aid. It quite discomposed him.

While the meal was being served, I took the opportunity to point out that Warren was fortunate to be dining with us. If our worst expectations were confirmed, he was about to eat a dead man's dinner.

He was in the act of swallowing a piece of bread. He had to take water to help it down.

At his request, after the servants had left us, I related my story, describing the two attackers as well as I was able, but venturing no opinion as to their possible identity or purpose. I said that poor Buckfast had taken the worst of the assault and in my estimation was unconscious when he was dropped into the river. I told Warren that I was communicating this intelligence to him out of a sense of duty, and I trusted that he had due authority to start immediate inquiries—but in the strictest confidence. I said if it became public knowledge that I had been attacked and almost murdered, I wouldn't answer for my mother the Queen's health. Such news had been known to induce heart attacks in elderly parents.

He was on pins and needles at this. "Are you inviting me to investigate this dreadful assault myself, Your Royal Highness?"

"Who else should I ask?"

"But I am a soldier by vocation. An engineer. A surveyor. I'm not trained as a detective, sir."

I said, "Come now, you're the most senior policeman in the land."

He had the effrontery to tell me, "The principal reason for my appointment, as I was informed, sir, is to marshal the police to subdue the unruly elements in society."

Seeing red, I told him forcefully, "And I am marshalling you, sir, to find the unruly elements who viciously attacked a member of the Royal Family, and possibly killed his companion. Is that clear?"

He went so rigid that his monocle sprang out of his eye. "Crystal clear, sir."

The Duchess said, "You don't appear to have eaten much, Sir Charles. Would you care for some horseradish sauce on that?"

He said, "No thank you. It would not restore my appetite."

He left soon after.

I thought it judicious at this stage of the evening to announce that I could not remain much longer. Carrie took it in good part and escorted me to her smoking room for a final cigar. She enjoys a smoke as much as I. It was a large room, wainscoted halfway in dark oak and hung with all manner of racing paraphernalia, jockey's silks in the all scarlet, whips, stirrups, framed race cards and portraits of her notable winners—though she has yet to win a classic, the famous Sefton having belonged to her late husband.

As she poured me a cognac, she remarked, "I made an ass of myself earlier—a regular moke."

I said graciously, "I shall remember only how kind you were."

She sighed heavily and said, "I've buried two good husbands and I ought to be satisfied."

I felt unable to comment on that.

She added, "I'm impossibly high-spirited."

I said, "Not at all."

We were silent for a while. Then she said, "Tell me, Bertie, what *was* your purpose in coming here?"

My purpose in coming here? It seemed remote now, and no longer of any importance. "I wanted to talk to you about Archer."

"Poor Fred?" She took out a handkerchief and dabbed her eye. "I don't know if I can bear to talk about Fred."

I said, "In that case, please don't."

She pressed the handkerchief to her nose and blew into

it. "We had an understanding, Fred and I. We each had great losses to bear."

I said insensitively, "He was a heavy gambler." You see, my mind was elsewhere, following Sir Charles Warren on the trail of two assassins.

She said, "I meant bereavements."

"Oh."

She went on, volunteering information that I would earlier have been overjoyed to elicit. "We could have been a great comfort to each other, Fred and I."

"Really?"

"I decided to marry him. Then he shot himself."

I stared down into my cognac, telling myself how appalling it would be even to begin to smile. I managed to say, "Why?"

She frowned. "Why marry him?"

"No. Why did he shoot himself?"

She answered, "Everyone knows. It was the typhoid. It turned his brain." Her eyes widened. "Didn't it?"

I said, "Archer rode your horse, St. Mirin, in the Cambridgeshire."

She asked, "What does that have to do with it?"

I said, "There are stories that he staked his entire career on that race."

"I haven't heard them."

"He is said to have bribed Woodburn to stop the favorite."

She shook her head in disbelief. "Who told you this?"

"Arthur Somerset, the owner's brother."

"The Somersets ought to be brought to court for putting such lies about. Their horse shot its bolt. Why can't they admit it? We were all beaten by a good old stayer with a bit in hand at the finish, Bertie, and I say good luck to the owner."

After this generous tribute, I couldn't resist saying, "Do you know who the owner is?"

"Of The Sailor Prince? Willie Gilbert."

"He's the *registered* owner."

She tensed like a predator picking up a scent. "Are you implying that someone else was behind that damned outsider?"

"Abington Baird—the Squire."

"What?" She dashed her brandy into the fire and hurled the glass across the room. "If that monster fixed the race, I'll kill him. So help me God, I'll throttle him with my bare hands!"

She looked capable of it too.

CHAPTER 12

Carrie Montrose had kindly instructed one of her servants to hail a cab, and a four-wheeler was waiting by the gate when I took leave of her. The cabdriver's bored "Where to, guv?" told me at once that he hadn't been advised of his passenger's identity, which fitted my plan.

"Hoxton, if you please. The Royal Eagle Music Hall."

"Be almost over, time we get there."

"That's of no consequence," I told him forthrightly.

"All right. Keep your 'air on."

He flicked the whip and we trundled off. I didn't mind missing the whole of the bill, so long as I was in time to catch Myrtle Bliss before she left. I had not forgotten, you see, that the Squire had invited Myrtle to Bedford Lodge on the morrow, Sunday, and she had offered, in her quaint, lavender-scented note, to tell me what happened. I'd been inclined to spurn the offer until this evening, when Charlie had returned from Newmarket with the Squire's men in hot pursuit. After that, Myrtle's help became essential to my purpose. Not only would I agree to her proposal; I would persuade her to be more than a mere observer—to act, in effect, as my spy. I meant to have the names of the murderous pair at all costs, and with due respect to Sir Charles Warren and the Metropolitan Police, Myrtle provided my best chance.

Rest assured that I had not underestimated the risk she would be taking. I intended to warn her personally how dangerous were the Squire and his "minders."

The crone on guard at the stage door remembered me— or the sov she'd taken off me on the last occasion—and went so far as to beckon me over as I stepped down. It emerged that one of the performers had asked her to find a cab, a four-wheeler at that. I informed her that mine was not for hire. I'd already instructed the driver to wait for me.

She wasn't pleased. She reviled me with an unrepeatable obscenity, thus ensuring that she got no gratuity this time. I thrust myself past the door and inside. As luck would have it, I met Myrtle on the stairs, burdened with several cages containing her feathered troupe. Spotting me, she put them down, the better to curtsy as I thought, and instead leaned forward, kissed me lightly on the tip of my nose and said, "Lord bless you, Bertie. Just when I needed an extra pair of hands."

I've cut people dead for less, but I was so relieved to see her that I merely observed, "I thought the birds remained here."

"No, love. I finished tonight. Got to move out. Would you be a darling?"

I capitulated. I replied benignly that I was famous for being a darling. My four-wheeler was at her disposal. I carried the cages out to the street and stacked them inside.

Myrtle squeezed my arm and said, "You *are* a darling. There's six more upstairs. And three perches and a trunk."

Oh, yes, I was a darling, and no mistake, but those parrots upstairs hadn't been told. They screeched and fluffed up their feathers and thrust their vicious beaks through the bars when my hand reached for the ring on top of the cage. Only by removing my overcoat and throwing it over each cage before I lifted it did I succeed in getting any cooperation. Then, when the birds were docile and downstairs, the cabbie started complaining. He objected to having his vehicle filled with bird cages. He wanted the parrots to travel outside, on the roof, but Myrtle was reluctant to expose them to the chill night air, a message she articulated in a few choice words that flattened the cabbie like a mangled shirt.

The trunk and perches traveled on top, and the rest of us inside, in earsplitting proximity: six large parrots or cockatoos; sundry parakeets, lovebirds and lories; and two people, one in voluminous skirts and camel's-hump bustle. My face was within inches of a large red-and-green macaw, "a proper old softy" according to his owner, a description I ventured to think didn't apply to his beak as he tried repeatedly to bite me through the bars. He had an obscene black tongue like a spike, and his eye was positively evil. Bertie, I thought, how do you do it? How do you keep copping it like this, when you try so hard to stay out of trouble? We were conveyed to Mile End Road and deposited with our aviary and baggage on the pavement outside the house where Myrtle lodged. I settled with the cabman. After he'd pocketed his tip, he rudely commented, "Far cry from Cheyne Walk, ain't it?"

I sniffed and looked away.

It was close to midnight, yet the street teemed with life—predominantly life of the lowest order. I was presently hemmed in by ragged children and thin-faced women of doubtful occupation curious to look at the parrots, to know if they talked and if I would bring one out and put it on a perch. Myrtle, I should explain, had already gone inside with Cocky. My task was to guard the other birds, who in my opinion were well capable of defending themselves.

Someone remarked that I looked like the Prince of Wales, and I retorted genially that everyone said that. Another woman, over rouged and stinking of patchouli, said if I was the Prince of Wales, she was Mrs. L. (a lady of my acquaintance I prefer not to name), and wriggled her body in a most vulgar, suggestive fashion, going so far as to attempt to embrace me. Fortunately at this juncture Myrtle scythed her way through the crowd and grabbed the woman's hair, shouting to me, "She's got your bleedin' watch and chain," and sure enough, the thieving hussy had, though it would not have been of any use to her as a timepiece, for it was full of Thames water. I grabbed her wrist and recovered it, and she ran off, leaving Myrtle with a handful of black hair.

I took over the portering and by stages removed everything upstairs. By this time, I was becoming increasingly conscious of the river water I had swallowed. I asked for the bathroom and was handed a chamber pot. With a silent prayer that it would be equal to the demand, I put it to use, while Myrtle busied herself with her hat. Once I was comfortable and she presentable, we left the birds in noisy occupation and went out, pausing only to empty the pot at the communal privy in the yard—not a place to linger in.

In the quiet of a private room in a city restaurant where I occasionally treat a companion to supper, I took Myrtle completely into my confidence. Her large brown eyes regarded me steadily as I related my efforts to learn the truth about Archer's strange death, and how I had deputed Charlie Buckfast to keep watch on the Squire. I told her quite candidly how Charlie had broken into Bedford Lodge in search of evidence and surprised two of the Squire's men in bed together. She giggled for some time at this, until I shocked her with news of the ferocious attack in Cheyne Walk.

"He's dead?" she said in disbelief. "Your mate Charlie Buckfast has snuffed it?"

"I'm afraid so. I saw him thrown into the river. He was in no condition to save himself."

"Cripes."

Myrtle didn't indulge in false sentiment. After all, she

had last described Charlie to me as an old poopstick. She had integrity, for all her rough edges.

She asked, "What did they look like, these two?"

"My dear, it wasn't easy to see, but they fitted Charlie's description of the men who followed him from Newmarket. A broad fellow, built like a gorilla, and a taller one, something over six foot, I'd say. They were muffled and wearing long coats."

After a moment's thought, she said, "So what's it all about, Bertie? Two Mary Anns caught in bed? Is that what Charlie was killed for?"

I shook my head. "It doesn't seem likely. I can understand them taking offense. They might have given chase. Even attacked him. But murder—that would be excessive."

"Are you sure it was murder?"

I nodded gravely. "They knew Charlie was out to the world when they pushed him over the Embankment."

She was thinking again, resting her pretty chin on a small, clenched fist. "But they didn't do *you* in. Why didn't they treat you the same as Charlie?"

"I nearly drowned," I pointed out.

She said, "They could have made sure."

"What charitable things you say!"

She laughed and put her hand over mine. "Bertie, you know what I mean. They was after Charlie. They had no quarrel with you. You just got in the way, so they chucked you in and all."

She was a sharp thinker, and probably right. I sighed resignedly. As the second highest in the land, it's somewhat demeaning to admit that you got in the way, so you were chucked in and all, but that, express it how you will, was the likeliest explanation.

The champagne buoyed me up, a good Veuve Clicquot, infinitely kinder to the throat than the poison we'd imbibed on our previous supper engagement. It went down famously with pigeon pie. I was glad of a bite. I hadn't acquitted myself too well at Carrie Montrose's table, after swallowing half the Thames.

Myrtle, too, had a decent appetite, and we called for second helpings. We were seated side by side on a double-ended sofa of the sort thoughtfully provided in private rooms, and the waiter was clearly intrigued that my guest hadn't yet removed her hat, but there was more on our minds than spooning.

In privacy again, I said, broaching the subject with extreme tact, for I know the feminine mind, "There may be another interpretation of these events. It's possible, is it not, that the two men were sent to kill Charlie Buckfast?"

She frowned.

I said, "They could have been acting on instructions."

"Whose instructions?"

"The Squire's." I planted a firm, restraining hand on her arm. "Before you raise the roof, my dear, will you hear what I say? If the Squire got to learn that a man had kept him under observation for a week and actually broken into his house, wouldn't he ask himself what that man was looking for? And mightn't he suspect it was something incriminating? And if so, mightn't he want that man silenced for good?"

Myrtle had turned as white as my shirt. I might have just walked over her grave. She shook her head. "He's a rogue, I grant you, but he's never a murderer. Never."

I said, "He's a blackmailer. And what's more, he thrives on blood and violence. What else is fistfighting?"

"It ain't killing, Bertie."

"Dogfighting is. And cockfighting."

Myrtle gave me a withering look and said, "How many grouse do you shoot in a day?"

I capped that with, "Have another slice of pigeon pie," and she gave a reluctant smile. "To return to the Squire," I said, "if he *did* give orders to two of his roughs to dispose of Charlie Buckfast, and they discovered they had me—a second man—to reckon with as well, isn't it logical that they behaved as they did? They made sure of killing Charlie and left me to take my chance in the water. They hadn't been told to commit a double murder."

She was still unwilling to cast her friend the Squire as a murderer. "Why would he want Charlie killed?"

"I told you. Charlie found out about the blackmail."

"Bertie, the Squire's been called all kinds of things—a bully and a cheat and a public nuisance. What's blackmail? One more thing on his list."

"No."

She was surprised to be challenged. She glared at me defiantly.

I said, "This wasn't one more thing on the list. The Squire may seem like a fellow who respects nothing and nobody, but don't be deceived. There was one man he idolized."

She knew at once. "That jockey—Fred Archer."

"Yes. He took riding lessons from Archer. He adopted his style and learned how to get the best from a horse and how to 'kid' the other jockeys. As a result, he's the best gentleman rider in the country. But it wasn't enough for the Squire. He wanted to be Archer's equal. He wanted a partnership. His dream was to own a racing stable with Archer, but Fred wouldn't hear of it. So what did the Squire do? He devised a plot to entrap Archer. He got him implicated with others in a jockeys' ring, a conspiracy. And the sole purpose of this was to make Fred vulnerable to blackmail."

Myrtle took in a short, audible breath and a tear slid down her cheek. All her defiance had evaporated in the face of my ruthless exposure of the Squire's duplicity.

I said, "Charlie Buckfast overheard talk of a document, a contract: the proof that only Fred's signature was wanted to seal a partnership."

She understood. "That was what Charlie went into Bedford Lodge to find?"

I gave a nod. "Can you imagine how the Squire must have received the news that Charlie had broken in? He'd hate the world to find out that he hounded his hero to death. That's why Charlie had to be silenced."

Myrtle bit her lip. She had gone so rigid that her stays creaked.

I topped up her glass, understanding her distress.

At length, she said bleakly, "What do you want me to do, Bertie?"

Her forlorn expression moved me profoundly. How would I ask her to betray the man who, for all his wicked ways, had plainly claimed a place in her affection? How could I conceivably expose this trusting young woman to such danger?

Only with profound misgivings and the assistance of Veuve Clicquot '78.

You see, as I explained to Myrtle, nothing would have prevented me from undertaking this perilous mission myself, except that I am so damnably well known. It's next to impossible for me to creep along corridors in strange houses without being recognized.

When she had agreed to make a search of the Squire's bedroom and obtain the contract, she said, "It's a queer thing, Bertie. You say the Squire idolized Fred Archer."

"Emphatically."

"And Charlie Buckfast was devoted to him."

"Yes, he did everything for Fred except ride the horses."

"And you're just the same. You can't forget him. You've got this bee in your bonnet about his suicide."

"If you wish to put it that way."

"Then tell me this: What is it about Fred Archer? What made him so special?"

It was a profound question, worthy of a thoughtful answer. I daresay to the more discriminating among my readers that the same question may have crossed your mind as you read these pages. After reflection, I told Myrtle, "It's not easy to explain. In some respects, he was obnoxious. A tyrant on the racecourse, particularly with boy jockeys and less experienced riders. He insisted on weighing out first, to get the prime position at the start. His language in a race would make your hair curl. And he gave his horses no mercy. He frequently drew blood with the whip and the spurs.

"He was a mean beggar too. They called him the Tinman. He'd take the pennies off a dead man's eyes. Yet his gambling was out of control at times. He was proud, unsociable, lacking in humor, and generally unprepossessing. He was a bag of bones, of course. He neglected his health in the cause of racing. He'd neglect anything in the cause of racing, as I'm sure his wife and infant daughter discovered. But in spite of all that, he was a man in a hundred million. The finest jockey who ever lived. Uneducated and illiterate, but a genius. Intelligent, yes. Highly intelligent. After a race he would tell me not only how his own mount fared, but how everyone else performed. And no braver man ever lived—which is why I still can't understand him killing himself."

"It takes a brave man to do that," Myrtle remarked.

"But a braver man would face up to his problems—wouldn't he?"

She didn't reply. She said, "I never met him. Tell me about his eyes."

"His eyes? Yes, they *were* remarkable. They were deep set and heavy lidded and appeared to be looking inward, except when something caught his interest. Then the light leapt from them. They were very expressive then. I won't forget them."

She said, "You can tell a lot from the eyes."

To which I replied, "And I can tell from yours that you're ready for bed."

CHAPTER 13

Yes, thirteen—the unlucky number. When I arrive at a dinner party, I always count the places at the table. If they number thirteen, I call for my coat. In practice this hardly ever happens, because Francis Knollys advises my hostess in advance that thirteen will not be tolerated any more than crossed knives or spilled salt. I won't have my mattress turned on a Friday, either.

These superstitions of mine may sound ludicrous to some, yet there's no denying that Chapter Thirteen contains an unpleasant shock. I mention this for the benefit of readers of a delicate disposition.

But I must not anticipate . . .

I left London for Sandringham on Sunday, 28 November, and put myself in a thunderous mood by purchasing a copy of *Reynolds's News* (why do I punish myself?) to read on the train. You wouldn't think the birth of an innocent child (my dear sister's) a subject for political comment, but then you underestimate the socialist propagandists. "The Queen has now thirty-one grandchildren," observed the writer, "and the people are of the opinion that this is more than a sufficient number of paupers of the royal and expensive sort. A much more joyful thing to the people than the birth of

this boy would have been to hear that his father had fallen
into some sort of useful occupation and was in a position
to provide for the progeny he sends into the world." What
vindictive drivel! Who are they to voice the opinions of the
people any more than I? I screwed up the disgusting rag
and tossed it out of the window and picked up the *British
Medical Journal* instead.

Lest anyone suspect that I have morbid interests, let me
hasten to declare that I am not a regular reader of the
medical press. I happened to have a copy with me that was
more than a week old. Francis Knollys had slipped it into my
attaché case with the suggestion that I would find something
of interest inside, and I had not troubled with it until then.
It turned out to be a comment on Fred Archer's suicide.
Speaking of the alleged typhoid that afflicted the jockey, it
read, "This disease is so associated in the minds not only of
the public, but the medical profession, with prostration and
low, muttering delirium that the fact that acute delirium
with delusions, usually of a suicidal character, sometimes
comes on during the early stage, will be new to many." I
trust that the irony of this piece is not lost on my readers;
more support, if any were needed, that the tragedy was not
medical in origin.

At Sandringham on Monday morning, I commended
Knollys on finding the piece. The trouble he'd taken to bring
it to my attention was, I had decided, an indication on his
part that he now accepted my involvement in the matter,
even if he could not wholeheartedly support it. I asked him
what engagements I had this week. Before he answered, I
added, mindful of Myrtle, ". . . because I propose to spend
Tuesday and Wednesday in London."

There was a pause of the sort that novel writers describe
as pregnant.

He said, "Might I be so bold as to inquire, sir, if that is
an engagement of a private nature?"

"It is, Francis. And it can't be ducked."

"I see." He gave me that look.

"Well, man," I said, "what's the difficulty?"

"Wednesday, sir, is December the first."

"Good thing too. November has been a brute."

He coughed into his hand. "I took the liberty of ordering the usual red roses, sir."

Oh, my hat! I thought. *Alix's birthday.*

I said, with an effort to keep my dignity, "This year I have decided to take Her Royal Highness to London for her birthday."

"But she always likes to spend it here, sir."

"I shall persuade her otherwise."

"As you wish, sir."

"As *she* will wish—when I have explained what I propose."

"Undoubtedly, sir."

I marched to the window and stared out at the frost. "I must admit to some difficulty in choosing a suitable present. Can't just give her the damned roses."

"A choker, sir?"

"You have it, Francis! The good old dog collar." I should explain that Alix has a small blemish on her neck, of which she is inordinately self-conscious, so she contrives to keep it covered. Fashion being so imitative, every well-dressed woman in the land now sports a high collar or choker, and all in consequence of one small brown mark on Alix's neck.

After a short interval while I wrestled with my memory, I said, "Didn't I give her a choker last year?"

"Yes, sir, but you could choose different stones."

I told him to arrange it with Garrard's, our usual jeweler, after consulting his sister Charlotte, who is Woman-of-the-Bedchamber.

At luncheon, I announced to Alix that I proposed taking her to London on her birthday.

She twisted her pearls around her finger, always an

ominous indication. "Aren't I going to have my usual party at Sandringham?"

"Not this year. I'm taking you to the theater."

Her lower lip quivered, and I knew that tears would follow, but I'm glad to report that they were tears of joy. "Bertie, what a dear husband you are, full of surprises! What are we going to see?"

Fortunately, I'd taken the precaution of studying the newspaper. "A new comic opera called *La Béarnaise,* with Miss Florence St. John and Miss Marie Tempest. It's said to be the equal of anything by Offenbach."

"A comic opera. What fun!"

"You're pleased?"

"Indescribably." She hesitated. "Bertie, do you know what would make the evening complete for me?"

"Supper at Romano's?"

"What I should really like would be to take our turtle-doves with us." (This affectionate term is one we use for our daughters, the Princesses Louise, Victoria and Maud.)

"Why, yes," I said as enthusiastically as I was able while thinking how to escape to Mile End Road on Tuesday evening. "It will do them good." (They are shrinking violets, all three, and I can't fathom why, with a papa like me. I'm told they are unkindly known in society gossip as their Royal Shynesses.)

Alix further complicated matters by suggesting we travel to London on Wednesday, but I scotched that with a white lie that solved my difficulty. I said I'd been invited to attend a meeting on Tuesday evening of the Queen's Jubilee Committee for the East End. It would probably drag on until late, but I felt bound to give it my support.

So the five of us, and my little dog Peter, and Knollys and his sister, took the train from Sandringham on Tuesday morning.

In the entrance of Marlborough House stands a stuffed

baboon holding a tray on which the letters are left. This morning the poor thing was laden to its snout with birthday cards. Alix wanted to open them at once, but I insisted that she wait until Wednesday. Nor would I allow her to unwrap any of the parcels heaped against the wall. She's like a child at these times and begged me to allow her to read the addresses and see if she could guess who had sent them. In a moment, she announced, "It isn't fair. The biggest one is for you, Bertie!"

"Are you sure?"

She was holding a cardboard box large enough to contain a framed painting. I frequently receive unsolicited daubs from artists seeking royal patronage. However, from the way Alix was handling this, it didn't weigh as heavily as a picture. I said, "I expect it's for you, really. Someone's made a mistake."

"It says 'personal' on the label."

"Let's unravel the mystery, then." I cut the string and took off the lid.

"Tissue paper," said Alix. "Something special, obviously. Perhaps it *is* for me."

I drew back the wrappings and discovered my evening shirt, freshly laundered. And the suit I had worn when I fell in the Thames, now cleaned, with the torn sleeve invisibly mended.

I muttered, "My laundry."

Alix said in a puzzled voice, "But you don't send your clothes to the laundry." She delved into the wrappings and took out my socks and suspenders. Then my merino wool vest and nether garment. And a solitary glove. All beautifully cleaned. On this evidence, one could recommend Carrie Montrose's laundry to anyone, but at that minute I wished they had lost the lot.

I said, "It must be a practical joke," and my daughters supported me by giggling behind their hands. Alix likes a joke, too, but on this occasion she declined to join in.

I blustered on, "I'd like to know who did this. Charlie Beresford, I shouldn't be surprised."

Alix said in disbelief, "Your clothes, Bertie? Your intimate garments. How could Charlie possibly have acquired them?"

"From Knollys!" I declared in desperation. "Francis! Explain yourself."

But he had vanished. There are no flies on Francis.

I said, "Infernal liberty! I'll take it up with him later. Clever jape, though. Charlie B had better watch out. I'll settle the score when I can think of something fiendish enough." I stuffed everything back and replaced the lid, saying to Alix, "I think it would do no harm to open your presents, dearest. You're bound to get many more tomorrow." As she reached for a parcel, I made as dignified an exit as I could, with the box under my arm.

Of course I said nothing to Francis when I caught up with him, except to make quite sure that a glittering choker was on order.

The day did not improve for me. It emerged that Sir Charles Warren was waiting in an anteroom in his cocked hat. He had "an urgent and confidential matter" to communicate. I asked Francis to step outside and send Warren in.

The commissioner preferred to remain standing. His eyes gleamed as brightly as his medals. "Yesterday evening, Your Royal Highness, we recovered something from the river."

He punctuated his statement with a dramatic pause. I waited for it to end.

He resumed, "When I say 'we,' I mean Thames Division. We found the body of a man answering Captain Buckfast's description."

I'd feared this, of course, but I still felt my skin prickle. I suppose I had hoped for a miracle. I asked, "Truly? Where was the poor fellow found?"

"In Battersea Reach, sir. It was a stroke of luck."

"Luck? That's a rum word to use in the circumstances, Commissioner."

He didn't flicker an eyelid. "I mean, it was lucky that we recovered him, sir. In this cold weather a body tends to sink and stay on the riverbed for weeks before it rises. A bargeman happened to notice the heel of a boot projecting above the water level. Boots don't usually float, so he took out a boat hook and made contact with something larger. He informed Thames Division, and they advised me." Warren added on a note of self-congratulation, "I had already asked to be notified of every corpse recovered from the river."

"Are there so many?"

"Twenty and upward, week in, week out, sir. Most of them are suicides or accidents. The watermen bring them in usually. We pay them a shilling for their trouble."

I said, "Are you certain that this is Captain Buckfast?" Then I added hastily but emphatically, "It would not be appropriate for *me* to identify the body. There might be a constitutional difficulty about my attending a coroner's inquest."

Warren said reassuringly, "That has already been done, sir. I sent for two witnesses, people who knew Buckfast well: a Mr. Harry Sarjent of Newmarket, who was the late Fred Archer's groom and valet, and John Parker, his gardener."

"Sarjent is a capable fellow and a good witness," I said, recalling how he had performed at Archer's inquest and afterward brushed my hat and coat.

"You know him?" said Warren in some surprise.

Resourcefully, I answered, "I read his evidence in *The Times.*"

"Ah."

"So there can be no doubt that this was Captain Buckfast?"

"Regrettably, none, sir. They identified the clothing first. Then they were asked to examine the personal effects. His pocketbook containing several of his visiting cards was still in the jacket, and a badge of the Seventeenth Lancers was attached to his watch chain. Finally, they viewed the body. They both remarked on a strange fact."

"What was that?"

"The man pulled from the Thames was clean-shaven. My information is that Captain Buckfast possessed a particularly fine mustache."

"That is correct."

I believe I mentioned the whiskery exuberance of Sir Charles Warren's own upper lip. In speaking of Buckfast's loss, his hand crept protectively toward it.

I explained, "He recently shaved it off. I should have mentioned it."

"The identifying witnesses were both certain that the dead man was Captain Buckfast, sir, with or without the mustache. And there was clear evidence of the attack that you described. Bruising about the head and shoulders." Sir Charles took a deep, significant breath. "There can be no doubt, sir, that I am dealing with a case of murder."

"No doubt whatsoever, Commissioner."

Warren cleared his throat. "Then with your permission, sir—"

I raised my hand to interrupt. "Before we go any further, Commissioner, I would like to make something very clear to you. You have my permission to pursue this in whatever way you choose, so long as you keep me out of it."

There was an uncomfortable silence.

Warren ended it by saying stiffly, "I was charged with certain responsibilities when I became Commissioner, sir, and the first of these was to prosecute crime. Murder is the worst of all crimes."

I remarked, "I believe you also swore an oath of loyalty."

"To the Sovereign, sir, if you'll forgive me."

I said, "*I* might forgive you, but will the Sovereign, if you provoke a royal scandal? With due respect, Sir Charles, I know that gracious lady rather better than you, and in her view there is one crime even more iniquitous than murder, and that is indiscretion—indiscretion by responsible individuals whose loyalty ought to be unswerving. Do I make my meaning clear?"

There had been a stirring of defiance, but I'd scotched it. One is obliged to, in such situations. Sir Charles Warren was new in the job, and no match for me. That speech is always a winner, whether you're dealing with a protesting husband or a bumptious policeman.

After Warren had marched out, I spent some quiet minutes thinking about poor Charles Buckfast. I doubted whether his death would touch many people, and he was unlikely to receive an obituary notice from *The Times*. On the other hand, he was a Turfite who had never brought disrepute to the sport, and by all accounts he had been a loyal friend to Archer. He had served me loyally too. He wasn't much of a conversationalist, and I wouldn't rate him as the wittiest companion I've known, but he was brave and dependable, qualities not to be underrated in detective work. Notwithstanding the tragedy, you see, I was still thinking as an investigator, implacable in my resolve. This brutal murder wasn't going to stop me; rather, it spurred me on. I owed it to Charlie to bring the case to a successful conclusion.

What next, then?

First, I required another assistant. After all, there are certain investigative duties it would be unthinkable for me to undertake alone. I needed someone of unquestioned loyalty, a good observer, brave and capable of outwitting the Squire and his murderous gang.

Why not a woman? Why not Myrtle Bliss?

In relation to the Squire, Myrtle had certain physical advantages over Buckfast that I've hinted at before. True, she was not much of a hand with a pen, but I didn't require her to write out reports or take evidence. She was very responsive to me, which is a mark of intelligence.

In a sense, she was already on probation for the job. This evening, I would hear what she'd gleaned from her assignation with the Squire on Sunday. If it was of any use, I'd take her on as Buckfast's replacement. I didn't mind paying her the wage she'd get from the music halls.

I took an early dinner and left Alix to an evening of whist with our turtledoves. She urged me not to return too late from my Jubilee Committee meeting. As we sleep in separate rooms (and have for the past fifteen years), I was most unlikely to disturb her, but I assured her that I would escape at the first opportunity because I wanted to be at my brightest on her birthday.

I crossed the street to my club, the Marlborough, and consulted the *Era*, to see where "Miss Bliss and her Feathered Friends" were performing this week. I had a notion that I might visit Myrtle's dressing room, but when I saw where she was engaged, I changed my mind. The Bell Music Hall is situated along St. George's Street, in the dockland area of the East End, a street so notorious as the old Ratcliff Highway that its name was altered in an attempt to whitewash its reputation. A more notorious and dangerous locality could not be imagined.

So I remained in my club for a couple of hours and inevitably got caught in conversation and stayed longer than I intended. When I finally escaped, it was after ten. I hurried down to the rank in Piccadilly and asked the first hansom driver if he could get me to Mile End Road by eleven.

He trotted out that favorite saying of his trade: "That's all right, sir—Archer's up!"

I smiled grimly and said I hoped he was.

I don't mind confessing that for some unfathomed reason that November night in the cab, I felt uneasy. "Archer's up!" must have been said a million times and more to impart confidence. It troubled me. There's something about the arrangement of a hansom, with the driver aloft and out of sight behind you and only the apron over your knees and the horse's rump in front, that can give you a feeling of isolation. With a fog thickening every minute, blotting out the lamplight, your imagination doesn't need much to take a macabre turn.

Progress was slow through the city. It was well after eleven when we got to Mile End Road. I instructed the cabbie to wait while I went upstairs. My knock on Myrtle's door elicited no response. She was not back from the Bell.

I won't prolong the description of what, for me, was a tedious wait for more than forty minutes. I went down to the street and talked to my complaining driver. He told me he went off duty at midnight, so I gave him a half-crown and promised a sovereign at the end of the hire. I was as cold and depressed as he was.

Having come this far, I was in no mood to give up. "Chewsdy about 11" was what Myrtle had written, and dammit, I'd rearranged Alix's birthday to make the appointment.

When I heard the chimes of midnight, I told the cabbie to take me directly to the Bell.

This is the hour when the lodging houses have taken their quota, and unfortunates and ne'er-do-wells by the thousands wander the streets of the East End looking for staircases and doorways where they can huddle down for the night. Foreign seamen stagger out of the dancing rooms and public houses. It is the worst time for a young woman to be walking home, yet I doubted whether Myrtle could find—or afford—a cab.

To search for her in the fog was out of the question, so we made haste through Whitechapel, turned south across Commercial Road and Cable Street (all sinks of iniquity), and into St. George's Street, where my heart sank. The Bell was already in darkness when we halted outside. I climbed out and crossed the pavement to the front. The doors were bolted, and several ragged families, cadaverous men and women with babies in arms, had already taken up residence against them. A creature of hideous description attempted to importune me.

I looked for the stage door, in hope that some of the artistes might still be leaving by that means. The door was closed, and the entrance filled by a huge man—probably a stevedore—who told me forcibly to be off, because that was his "doss."

I returned to my cab and discovered the driver in animated conversation with a youth of markedly better appearance than the other denizens of this locality. It appeared that this uppish young fellow proposed to hire my vehicle. I stepped forward to disabuse him of the intention and discovered that he was the assistant manager (probably the barman, in reality) of the Bell and had just locked up for the night.

I asked when Miss Bliss had left, and he ventured the opinion that she must have departed at least an hour ago. No one was still inside.

I asked if he had actually seen her leave, and he had not. I said she had not come home, which led him to assume I was her father, which I found rather tiresome.

Quite off the cuff, I concocted a most ingenious story. I said I was a veterinary doctor and I'd been treating one of Myrtle's parrots. This evening it had died, and I feared that the cause was psittacosis, which can affect humans, sometimes with fatal results (this useful information I had learned from my dear mama, who keeps an aviary at Windsor and won't go near the parrots). It was a matter of the utmost urgency that I should examine the other birds.

Really, of course, I wanted to gain admittance to Myrtle's dressing room to see whether she had left me another of her lavender-scented notes. She couldn't possibly have forgotten our arrangement.

Upon receiving an assurance that he could share my hansom if he let me in, the young man took out his keys and made a determined move toward the family encamped at the front doors. They let us through. He said he would show me Myrtle's dressing room, which he didn't propose to enter himself, in view of the risk to his health. He found a couple lanterns and led me through the auditorium to a door at the side of the stage. The dressing rooms were to our right. Mrytle's, I was informed, was the last one, and would I kindly make my own way back to the front of the building when I had finished?

I stepped to the door, opened it and shone my lantern inside. Two or three of the birds were picked out, sleepy, silent on their perches. Cocky rocked from one claw to the other and stared at the light, flexing his yellow crest.

I moved the lantern lower and had a momentary shock as the beam flashed back at me from the mirror over the dressing table.

This all happened within a few seconds, yet I recall it vividly as a series of impressions that might have taken minutes.

I thought dully, Cocky shouldn't be here. She always takes him home.

Then I saw Myrtle's corpse on the rug in front of me. There was blood. There was a hole in the side of her head.

I thought, I've got to get out. I can't be found here. Whatever this means, it's no place for me.

If that demonstrates a want of compassion, so be it. The compassion came later. In the shock of discovery, you think only of practicalities.

I backed out, and as the lantern beam flickered across the room, a voice said, "Hello, Bertie."

There was no one there.

Cocky repeated, "Hello, Bertie. God bless the Prince of Wales."

Myrtle's letter: "Hes got a new trick to shew you."

A new trick be damned. He'd give my name to the police. I would have to take Cocky with me.

CHAPTER 14

Having persisted with me to this point, you know that I don't shirk the facts of life when they are necessary to my narrative, and now you know that I treat the fact of death with the same candor.

I thought of issuing an instruction to the printer to mark the previous chapter with a black edge as a token of respect, and also as a warning to the unwary. After much heart searching I abandoned the idea. I have the greatest difficulty in bringing myself to read anything surrounded with a black edge, so how could I ask my readers to face what I could not?

Forgive me. After a death has occurred, one's instinct is to talk about anything but the dreadful fact itself. I'm coming to it now.

I am at a loss to find words adequate to the horror of that grim November night. Don't imagine that my life of privilege has spared me from bereavement. I am not unaccustomed to the death of close friends and members of my family. I know the process: the sense of shock, overtaken by numbness, turning to grief as the mind begins to accept what has happened. After that, despair may set in, or even loss of faith.

Myrtle's violent death affected me in other ways. I was

gripped by horrid sensations. I was appalled, afraid, and worse, I was convinced that I was responsible.

Responsible? you ask.

Allow me to explain. The killing of Charlie Buckfast had taught me how dangerous it was to tangle with the Squire and his gang. I was shocked beyond words at the viciousness of that attack. I was deeply distressed about Charlie, and I regretted sending him to Bedford Lodge. I'd miscalculated badly. On the other hand, I didn't feel directly responsible for his death. No one could have foreseen that we were dealing with murderers.

Myrtle's death was squarely on my conscience. True, I'd alerted her to the dangers. I'd told her that Charlie had been killed. But I'd still recruited her as my spy, knowing she was willing to take the risk. She had been blessed, or fated, with the confidence of the young. She had been generous hearted and unafraid, and I'd taken advantage of her cheerful acquiescence with this dreadful consequence.

Let us return to that room of death. As I related, immediately after the discovery, my reaction was to flee from the scene.

Cocky said for the sixth or seventh time, "Hello, Bertie," and I knew I must attend to him first. I put down the lantern and transferred him to a cage. When I grasped him, he gave a screech, assuming, I suppose, that my purpose was strangulation. He submitted quite readily to being pushed through the wire door and was silent thereafter.

It was out of the question to escape by the way I had entered. The cabman and the assistant manager would be waiting at the front of the building. As yet, they had no suspicion of my identity. To the cabbie, I was just a "fare" he had picked up in Piccadilly; to the young fellow, an animal doctor. After what I'd just seen, it was vitally important that they remained in ignorance. However, I was in no state to keep up the pretense, and I was damned sure Cocky would give me away if they heard him.

I climbed out of a window in the property room by means of a conjurer's card table. My feet located a convenient cask in the yard outside and I remembered to reach for the parrot cage before descending to *terra firma*.

My ulster was heavily stained with some sort of grease from the window frame, and I ripped the bottom of one trouser leg, which was all to the good when I got out among the ragtag and bobtail of St. George's Street. Do you know, I believe I have Cocky to thank for saving me from being attacked and robbed? With the parrot cage and my beard, you see, I passed for a seaman. I received numerous invitations from tarts who called me sailor, but the thieves and garotters let me pass on the assumption that a seafaring man is likely to put up a fight.

Without much idea of direction, I stepped briskly ahead, alert for the sudden attack from behind. Groups of roughs were standing at many of the corners. Without being too obvious about it, I quickened my step and crossed to the other side whenever I saw such a gathering, and, I'm ashamed to say, I did the same when I spotted a constable's helmet. However, the thought did not escape me that we owe a great debt to our gallant police, nightly patrolling these festering thoroughfares.

The scene stretched ahead, it seemed unendingly, tenements looming on either side, passageways cluttered with what might have been rubbish heaps until one heard a baby cry or a man mouth an obscenity. Doors were thrust open without warning, and bodies would stagger across my path in a shaft of light. Still the street women pestered me with offers that turned to taunts and curses as I stepped aside and hurried past.

My entire future was reduced to reaching the next lamppost in safety.

I marched on as rapidly as my steps would take me and at last discerned a slight improvement in the dress and behavior of people I passed. The street widened. Then, praise be, I recognized Tower Hill—not usually an auspicious locality for one of the blood royal—but a haven to me that night, for there, to my profound relief, I succeeded in stopping a cab. He wanted extra, of course. Had he known, I felt ready to offer him half the kingdom. He put me down in the Mall, and I returned to Marlborough House about one 1:45 A.M.

Knollys must have heard me, for he came down in dressing gown and carpet slippers as I was calming my nerves with a dram prior to retiring. Without asking, he poured one for himself.

He said, "This is bloody early for you." We don't mince words in the small hours, Francis and I.

I nodded.

He said, "Your trousers are torn. How did you do that—climbing out of a window?"

"It's really no concern of yours."

That should have been enough. However, when Francis is inquisitive, he finds it hard to stop. "The husband came home unexpectedly, then?" He takes it as read that I devote my nights to adulterous adventures.

I ignored the question.

He persisted, "It's before two."

I said, "So far as you're concerned, Francis, this is before midnight."

He finally felt the frost in the air, for he paused before informing me on an appeasing note, "Her Royal Highness retired at eleven."

"In that case, I was back by a quarter past."

There was another interval while he took stock.

He resumed, with due formality, "The choker is wrapped and on your desk, sir. There is a card. It wants only your inscription."

Alix's birthday. After this evening's excursion into hell, how could I bring myself to think about a birthday?

I undertook to write something in the morning.

Knollys asked me what was under my coat (which I had taken off and draped over the parrot cage).

There was no possibility of denial, so I answered casually, "A talking cockatoo."

He commented, "What a splendid idea, if I may say so."

"Really?" I said, bemused.

"As a birthday present."

He was right. It was a capital idea, and I was pleased to take credit for it in the morning. Have I told you that Alix adores animals and birds to a quite ridiculous degree? One afternoon on our voyage up the Nile some years ago, she was reclining on a chair in a shaded area of the deck when she felt something cold up her skirt, nuzzling her knee. It was the nose of a black ram, which had slipped its tether in the kitchen quarters and wandered out of bounds. Instead of taking fright, Alix was enchanted. She offered the beast a sugar lump and sent for more. When she learned that she'd made a pet of tomorrow's dinner, she was horrified. That sheep traveled all the way back to Sandringham with us and lived for some years after.

So you can understand why Cocky was such a success as a birthday present. She took him out and allowed him to perch on her arm. When he said, "God bless the Prince of Wales," Alix whooped with delight. She convinced herself that I'd bought the bird weeks ago and had been giving him secret elocution lessons. She took this as evidence of my devotion and went quite watery eyed as she told me so. I decided not to enlighten her that Cocky could also ride a tricycle, walk a tightrope and snatch cigarettes from the mouths of theatergoers.

As for the jeweled choker, she didn't give it a second look.

During the morning, there were several callers, much to

my agitation, for I fully expected the cocked hat and mono-cle to appear around the door at any second. I'd convinced myself that my cabman or the young fellow from the Bell had recognized me and named me as the likely murderer. As the last person to visit the scene of the crime before the body was discovered, I would have plenty of explaining to do. However, the visitors without exception had come to greet Alix, and when Oliver Montagu arrived for lunch, I knew I would have some precious time to myself. (Oliver is hopelessly in love with Alix, and has been for about twenty years. The affection is mutual, and I allow it, knowing well that Alix has never conceded the ultimate favor and never will. I think she's forgotten how.)

In the quiet of my study, I agonized over my predica-ment. By now, someone, some cleaner or janitor, must surely have looked into that room of death and called the police. A description would presently be issued of the bearded, well-spoken and handsome gentleman with an intriguing trace of Germany in his accent who had fabricated a story to gain admission to the room. Theories would abound: that he had arranged a secret rendezvous with his victim; or that he had killed her earlier in the evening and was returning to the scene of his crime, as all murderers are said to do, if only to cover their tracks.

You may think that as a potential suspect, I would have an advantage over a commoner. The contrary is true. If the Prince of Wales shaved off his beard to avoid detection, every newspaper in the land would make a sensation of it. I would find it impossible to disappear into a crowd, or secretly take a passage to France. I was a sitting duck.

Knollys came in toward noon. His worried countenance was no comfort at all.

"What is it?" I asked.

"A difficulty, sir . . ."

My heart raced.

"... and I am most reluctant to mention it on this happy day."

I said, "Don't stand on ceremony with me, Francis. Is someone outside?"

"Well, yes."

"Is it Sir Charles Warren?"

He frowned. "No, sir. It is Sir Frederic Leighton."

"Fred Leighton?" I couldn't begin to think what would bring the president of the Royal Academy to see me without making an appointment. He was a dinner-party acquaintance who had more than once turned his talent to supervising the decorations for a fancy dress ball we gave: a useful fellow to know but without much sense of fun—hardly one of the Marlborough House set. "What does he want?"

"It appears that criticisms have been voiced in certain quarters of the Academy sir, and he wishes to bring them to your attention before they become public."

"Criticisms of what, precisely?"

Knollys coughed.

I glared at him. "Of me?"

He swayed back and lowered his eyes.

"Of what am I accused?" I asked.

"Of favoritism, I gather, sir."

"Favoritism? In what connection, for God's sake?"

"The Wellington statue."

Imagine! I was in imminent danger of being hauled off to Scotland Yard to answer questions about a murder, and Fred Leighton wanted to talk to me about the Wellington statue. As if I hadn't sacrificed enough of my time already on that tedious committee.

"Begging your pardon, sir, Sir Frederick insists he has a duty to impart this information to you." Knollys was so patiently unhappy that I began to feel sorry for him.

"To keep me in the picture, in other words," I quipped, and felt a shade more affable. "Very well. Tell him he can make a lightning sketch, Francis."

As I expected, the whole thing was the silliest nonsense. Artists are supposed to have a sense of proportion, which of course they completely lack. It emerged that certain dissidents in the R.A. were complaining because the Wellington statue competition had been awarded to Edgar Boehm. They said his plaster model was inferior to several others submitted, and it had come to their ears that I, as chairman, had championed Boehm and influenced the decision.

Holding myself in check, I asked Leighton why a chairman should not state his views, and he said there was a suspicion (which he did not share, of course) that my support of Boehm was more a matter of pro-German bias than artistic judgment.

I rocked with laughter at this, and it quite took the wind out of Leighton's sails. I told him truthfully that Boehm's nationality hadn't influenced me in the slightest. As a matter of fact, he wasn't a German at all. He was a Viennese who had become a naturalized Englishman over twenty years ago. I suggested that Leighton impart this information to his petty-minded members. As he was going through the door, I gave him a Hanoverian boot up the backside by telling him that paint and politics don't mix.

I felt better for that encounter. It helped me through lunch. I ribbed Oliver Montagu once or twice, and I was kindness itself to Alix, even managing to feign surprise when she told me how Cocky had stolen Oliver's cigarette.

Some fitful rays of sunshine broke through in the afternoon, encouraging me to take my dog Peter for a walk in the grounds while Alix drank tea with her swain. As the hours went by, and Sir Charles Warren failed to appear, I began seriously to entertain the hope that I'd not been reported to Scotland Yard. Instead, my thoughts took a more constructive turn. I considered what was to be done about Mr. Abington Baird, the Squire.

The thought of him caused me to clench my teeth and

give a jerk to Peter's lead, so that the innocent animal reared up unexpectedly on its hind legs. The Squire was a killer by association, if not with his own hands. For reasons that are too obvious to repeat, I couldn't tell everything to the police, which left me with a heavy responsibility.

Do you appreciate my difficulty?

I asked myself whether, unaided, I was capable of taking on the Squire and his murderous gang.

Of course not.

If I enlisted help, who could I trust?

The Marlborough House set? Emphatically not.

The Freemasons? I am, of course, the Most Worshipful Grand Master of England, and my fellow Masons are pledged to support me. The brotherhood would be more discreet than the likes of Charlie Beresford and Podge Somerset. Unfortunately, the second most eminent Mason in London happens to be Sir Charles Warren.

Not the Freemasons.

I was compelled to act alone. But how? And what was to be done?

There was nothing else for it: I must see the Squire in person. I required something more than circumstantial evidence that he had hounded poor Archer to death and ordered the killing of Charlie and Myrtle. He was an incurable braggart, so I was damned sure I'd have no difficulty persuading him to talk. My object would be to obtain a confession, a signed statement of his guilt, together with the names of his accomplices. I'd send it to Warren, and the case would be concluded without any reference to me.

Was this a pipe dream, or was I capable of making it happen?

That evening, we went to the theater as arranged, and I believe Alix and our daughters enjoyed the operetta. I remember little of it, for I was plotting and scheming more inventively than anything that happened on the stage.

My reasoning went like this: I was determined to extract a full confession from the Squire for the deaths of Archer, Charlie Buckfast and Myrtle. Clearly, it would be folly for me to go to Bedford Lodge. It would be folly of another sort to summon him to Marlborough House or Sandringham. So the confrontation had to be on neutral ground. And he had to be persuaded or induced to come there without his henchmen. First, I thought of the Jockey Club, but there are too many sharp ears there. The meeting place had to be private.

Neutral ground, where he'd feel secure.

Before the National Anthem was played for the second time, I'd chosen it.

With that off my mind, I gave the rest of the night to Alix. As soon as we were home, we challenged Knollys and his sister to skittles and trounced them three times over. Then it was blindman's buff with the Princesses, followed by General Post, followed by a riotous game of hide-and-seek all over the house. For a woman of forty-two, my dear wife has exceptional energy. She prefers rough games, when everyone shouts at the tops of their voices, to playing cards, when she can't hear the calls. I'm sure she went to bed exhausted and happy, and that pleased me, for I'm very attached to her.

The following morning, I set my plan in motion. When Knollys came in with my list of engagements, I told him I had another to fit in.

"What is that, sir?"

"I want to see the Great Christopher."

"Mr. Sykes, sir? That might be difficult. I've had to make some adjustments already, to free you this afternoon."

I said, "I'm not concerned about this afternoon, Francis. I want him here as soon as possible."

"Yes, sir."

I took my time trimming a cigar. "What's the difficulty, then? What's upsetting my afternoon?"

CHAPTER 15

Two items on different pages of *The Times* caught my attention that same morning. Among the announcements of recent deaths I found the name Buckfast, "Captain Charles of Jermyn Street, formerly of the Seventeenth Lancers." No information was revealed about the circumstances of Charlie's passing. It was simply worded "... suddenly, in London, on 27th November." *Suddenly* was no exaggeration, poor fellow. The funeral was to take place privately at Highgate on Friday morning. I jotted a memorandum to Knollys to be sure to order a wreath.

The second item was a report tucked away at the end of the column of police intelligence:

MYSTERIOUS DEATH OF A MUSIC HALL ARTISTE

The body of a young woman well known as a music hall performer was discovered in a dressing room of the Bell, St. George's Street, East London, yesterday morning. She had been shot in the head. She was identified as Miss Myrtle Bliss, aged twenty-three, a bird trainer. The Whitechapel Police have announced that they wish to interview a man who gained admission to the hall after it closed on Monday evening. He is described as aged about fifty, of foreign extraction, short and portly in appearance, bearded, and wearing a brown ulster and Homburg hat.

My first reaction was to snort at the description. Then, having seen in cold print that I was in effect a wanted man, I took a different view. The gross distortions could work to my advantage. They were certain to confuse the public, which I was confident didn't think of its future King as foreign in extraction, or fifty, or the other libelous things. The only accurate information was the hat. Even my ulster is more gray than brown. Pity the Whitechapel police, and pity all fat foreigners over fifty!

Actually, there was something that troubled me more than the police, and that was the summons from Windsor. If my mother the Queen had heard of my adventures in Chelsea and the East End, I'd be better off behind bars with a ball and chain attached to my leg.

For distraction, I started some paperwork. The field for the Prince of Wales Steeplechase at Sandown Park wanted my undivided study. An animal called Hornpipe took my fancy. On the memo to Knollys I added, "£25—Hornpipe, 1:30, Sandown." A distracting thought came to me: What if Knollys took this as the message to be attached to Charlie Buckfast's wreath? I daresay as a racing man, Charlie might have appreciated the sentiment.

Christopher Sykes was announced before I'd made my choice for the two o'clock. Let's give credit to the Great Xtopher: he answered the summons and was over from Hill Street inside the hour, dipping his vast head toward me like a buffalo at the water hole.

"Splendid!" I greeted him. "I was hoping you'd be in London. Do sit down and stop staring at your shoes, Christopher. There's nothing offensive on them, is there?"

Perching himself on the extreme edge of an upright chair, he said, "Your Royal Highness—"

"Before you go any further," I interposed, "we've known each other long enough to dispense with that. I'm looking for some help."

"Whatever you require, sir."

"You'd better hear about it first. I'd like you to throw another of your house parties at Brantingham Thorpe."

Brantingham is Sykes's pile in Yorkshire, a Jacobean manor house near Beverley, the town he represents in Parliament. It's convenient for Doncaster racecourse, so we always get up a party in September.

He winced with the honor of it. "Another house party, sir. What a capital thought! Do you have the New Year in mind?"

"The weekend after this."

He swallowed and tried to stay calm. "So soon?"

"Unavoidably," I said. "People will be delighted to come, I'm sure."

"Yes, indeed." He had twisted his long legs into an extraordinary shape that reminded me of barley sugar. "Then I had better attend to the invitations at once. Do you have any particular guests in mind, sir?"

"Your sister-in-law Jessica, for one."

"Jessica?" The legs tried for another twist and failed. "I expect she would come . . . if invited." Now he was sucking his cheeks like a saint undergoing martyrdom. "You know her reputation, sir. She's considered fast."

"Yes," I said tolerantly. "She has some fast friends as well. Have a discreet word with her, Christopher. Ask her to recommend half a dozen of the giddiest girls in London."

He dropped his hat.

As he bent to retrieve it, I explained, "I want this house party to be a romp, a veritable romp. Oceans of fizz, of course. Log fires in all the rooms. Colored lights. A German band. A performing bear."

He straightened and blinked. "A bear at Brantingham, sir?"

I made an expansive gesture. "Well, an Irish fiddler, if you like. Or a sword swallower. Anything to jolly up the ladies."

Sykes looked ready to ask for the last rites.

I said, "Have you got a bellyache?"

He shook his head.

"Chilblains, sciatica or piles?"

"No, sir."

"Well, then, what's the trouble?"

He gulped and said, "All these active young women, and just you and me?"

He's extremely obtuse on occasion. I said, "Most of Jessica's friends are married, aren't they? Let them bring their husbands. That won't cramp their style if they're the sporting girls I take them for. Besides, there are one or two others I want you to invite."

"Personal guests, sir?"

I smiled. "Depends how personal you want to make it, Christopher. There's a charming little creature by the name of Lady Florence Dixie I'd like you to meet. Over rouged by some standards, but full of dash. She has a pet jaguar which she takes for walks in Kensington Gardens."

He had the grace to say feebly, "How exotic."

"Invite her, then."

"Oh, I didn't mean—"

"And there's one more guest I must have on the list."

"Mrs. Langtry?" ventured Sykes.

I gave him a glare. "Heavens, no. She's in America. Besides, I wouldn't let Lillie anywhere near a house party like this. I'm referring to a gentleman—Mr. Abington Baird, the Squire."

Sykes stiffened like a rabbit at the sound of gunfire.

I said, "I understand your apprehension, Christopher. He's an odious fellow."

"Infamous," whispered Sykes.

"Christopher, I'll put my cards on the table. I need to have a meeting with the Squire, man-to-man. A meeting of the utmost importance. I don't exaggerate when I say that it's a matter of life and death. Brantingham Thorpe is to be the setting for that meeting."

"But the other guests? All those excitable ladies?"

"The bait, so to speak."

"Bait?" repeated Sykes, as if he didn't understand the word.

"The Squire is an absolute Lothario."

"Oh."

"When you issue the invitations, don't mention that I'm coming. Don't breathe a word to anyone. Tell the Squire that some of the most adventurous ladies in London are desirous of meeting him, and make it clear that the invitation is for him alone. We don't want his pugilistic friends aiming punches at your Ming vases."

By this time, Sykes was too far gone to worry about his vases. I dismissed him gently, and he glided out like a sleepwalker.

Reader, you may sympathize with Sykes. I do, myself, when he is absent. I have the greatest difficulty in explaining why the sight of the fellow turns me into such an ogre. It's utterly against my nature, as you must have divined by now. Anyway, you might think there was some sort of justice at work later that day when I traveled to Windsor for my audience with the Queen. I was in a state of trepidation close to panic. The boot was on the other foot—and my dear mama has a kick like a mule.

A carriage was waiting in the yard at Windsor station. During the drive I rehearsed my speech for the defense. Give nothing away, I had decided. Don't get boxed in by detail. Steer the discussion toward the general issue of one's role as the Heir Apparent.

It was a closed carriage, so I spoke aloud, addressing the empty seat opposite, reminding it that the best years of my life would be wasted if I continued to be excluded from affairs of state. Ten years ago, my brother Leopold, rest his soul, was handed the Queen's Cabinet key. At the age of twenty-two he was permitted to open the secret dispatch boxes. Here was I, at forty-six, the future King, still denied that privilege. Was I so irresponsible, so neglectful of my duties? Had I mismanaged any of the twopenny-halfpenny committees I had been deemed worthy of chairing?

On second thought, this sounded too much like a complaint. One needed to make it more assertive. I am in the prime of my life, Mama. I am capable, healthy and energetic. I shall not be wanting when I am called upon to begin the great task ahead. Of course I wouldn't wish it to be one day sooner than the Almighty in His wisdom decrees, but you will not need reminding that you are now in the fiftieth year of your reign. Is it not time that I shouldered some of the burdens of State that you have borne so ably all these years?

That was better.

I must have been venting hot air, for the carriage window had steamed over. I cleared a peephole and saw trees. Too many trees. This wasn't the drive to Windsor Castle.

I was being brought to Frogmore, to the Mausoleum.

Bertie, I thought, this does not augur well.

It was twenty-five years since the death of my father, Prince Albert. Twenty-five years to the month. In the family, we speak of December 14 as "Mausoleum Day," when we congregate annually to pay our respects, but Mama is to be found at the "dear resting place" as often as you or I take the dog for a walk. On any occasion or anniversary of the slightest significance, she will find time to visit there. On the day before our wedding, Alix and I were taken into the shrine for Mama to link our hands and tell us that Papa gave us his blessing. I mistakenly took this as a sign that I was forgiven for past misdemeanors. I'm afraid she will always blame me for Papa's last illness, even though Dr. Jenner blamed the drains at Windsor. (Without wishing to belabor a story familiar to many, I should explain that my father felt obliged when feeling greatly out of sorts to visit me at Cambridge to admonish me for bringing disgrace on the family with an actress who was introduced to my bed in the Curragh Camp as a jest by brother officers of the Grenadier Guards; this at a time when my parents were pressing me to become betrothed to Alix. Papa's cold developed into typhoid, and Mama, in her distressed state, refused to send for me, so I was only enabled to come to my father's deathbed when my sister Alice sent a telegram without Mama's knowledge.)

My maternal grandmother, the late Duchess of Kent, has her own mausoleum at Frogmore. She had died earlier the same year, which undoubtedly compounded my mother's grief. There had been a rift between them for years, which I need not go into here, but Mama felt the bereavement keenly. She refused to leave Frogmore and the room where her mother died. She accused me of being heartless and selfish for writing to her on mourning notepaper with insufficiently wide black edging. When I tried to comfort her in person, she said I showed insufficient grief. She said I lacked the brains to feel emotion. All in all, you will understand why Frogmore is not my first choice for a tête-à-tête with Mama.

We drew up at the Mausoleum, which is about as cheerful in conception as taste will allow, for my mother wanted a living memorial rather than a *Sterbezimmer,* a death chamber. The stonework is light in color and the interior is ornately decorated, with profuse gilding that catches the light from many arched windows, though in December the main source of illumination is the gas.

Inside, the chill gripped me and I remembered all those December vigils beside the tomb, looking at my brothers and sisters in prayer, wondering which of us would go down with pneumonia first.

Just inside the entrance, an Indian servant gave me a shock when he moved out of the shadows, bowing and making a gesture toward the inner chamber. I stepped forward, my shoes making such a fearful clatter on the marble floor that I didn't hear my mother the Queen greet me. However, I saw her in the gaslight, a small veiled figure beside one of the four sculptured angels who guard Papa's tomb.

I just said, "Mama, dear." It didn't seem fitting to add, as I generally do, ". . . what a pleasure!"

She regarded me for a moment through her veil and sighed heavily. Her mood evidently matched her widow's weeds.

I remembered to say, "Dear Alix sends her love."

Mama is fond of Alix. She asked, "Did she have her birthday?"

I don't know what answer this was meant to evince. If it was negative, poor Alix would be dead. I said as heartily as circumstances allowed, "Never a better one."

"I expect she received the small present I sent."

"My word, yes!" I had no idea what it had been. "So very acceptable! She uses it constantly."

"Bertie, you are being deceitful again. Let us pray."

So we got on our knees and Mama led us in prayer. We prayed for Papa and all departed souls. We prayed for the Church and Parliament and the armed forces, the farmers and the fishermen, my brothers and sisters and all the family. We prayed for our servants and our pets. Then we prayed for truth to enter our hearts.

"Amen," said Mama at last; then, in the same breath, turning to face me, "She uses it constantly! I sent her a dog basket for the Pekingese. Now, Bertie, I want to speak frankly to you."

I asked, "May we get up first? My knees have gone numb."

So we promenaded around the tomb. She said, "It is necessary for me to speak to you about a person."

I should explain that in Mama's vocabulary, a person is not a person at all as you or I would understand it, but an undesirable, a reprobate, a monster of iniquity. I rapidly reviewed the persons I had encountered in the last week or so: Myrtle, the Squire, Carrie Montrose. Any of these would qualify for Mama's censure.

I asked as casually as I was able, "Do you mean somebody of my acquaintance?"

"Certainly."

"A lady?" An unproductive question, I realized as soon as I asked it, for a person might be female, but she could never be a lady.

"Certainly not."

There was an interval while we walked and said nothing. Oddly, Mama appeared reluctant to pursue the subject, now that she had started it.

"A titled person?" I inquired.

She made a sound in her throat, a stifled laugh that carried no joy and humor. Irony, perhaps. She said bitterly, "It wouldn't surprise me if that's next."

Now I was all at sea. I said, "I'm afraid I don't know who you mean."

"Mr. Boehm."

"Boehm the sculptor? Edgar Boehm?"

"Who else?"

The relief! I almost did a dance of triumph around my father's tomb. I said, "Does this have something to do with the Wellington Statue Committee?"

"Isn't that evident?"

"And our choice of Edgar as the winning sculptor? Is there a difficulty?"

She cried out with such force that the black ostrich feathers quivered on her hat. "You call him by his Christian name, as if he's an intimate! I can scarcely bring myself to speak of this person at all."

I was baffled. Edgar Boehm was an old friend of the family. Papa, himself, had sat for him and approved the bronze busts he had made. His sculptures of several of us had appeared in the Royal Academy Exhibition. I so liked the 1872 equestrian statue of me as Colonel of the Tenth Hussars that I invited him to make a bust of the Princess Maud, which he charmingly entitled "Little Harry," our family name for her. In 1878, he created a figure of me on horseback described in the catalog as colossal. I presented it to the City of Bombay in celebration of my visit to India. He'd even sculptured my mother the Queen in marble.

I said, "Forgive me. I had no idea he had given offense to you."

She said, "Not only to me. To his fellow artists. I am informed that an approach was made to you yesterday morning."

The Queen is possessed of sensitive antennae. She might appear to be shut away from the world, but she has her ways of gathering information. As a detective, I was a mere beginner beside her.

I admitted, "Sir Frederic Leighton came to see me on the matter, yes. There is apparently some feeling in the Academy that I influenced the committee unduly."

"Did he ask you to alter the decision?"

"He didn't put it so plainly as that."

"Did you make any promises?"

"Not exactly promises," I prevaricated. "However, in view of your feelings on the matter, I shall reconvene the committee as soon as possible. It's not too late for second thoughts. We rejected some very acceptable designs."

To my dismay, she stopped, shook her fist and said, "Imbecile!"

Telling myself to stay calm, I said, "Mama, I've just explained. I can get the decision rescinded."

She said, "I *don't want* it rescinded! Leighton is a mischief maker who ought to be stripped of his title. The decision must stand. Boehm is the winning sculptor. Is that understood?"

It was noted, but by no means understood.

We made another circuit of the tomb before she would say any more. Then she sighed again and added, "I can understand your silence. The fact of the matter is that something occurred in the past, something that now enables Mr. Boehm to insist that we favor him."

"Ah."

"Your committee made the correct decision. We cannot allow that nincompoop Leighton to question it."

I dug deep into my memory, to Balmoral in the summer of 1870. A family crisis. I had been summoned to talk some sense into my sister Louise, who had fallen in love with a commoner: a personable thirty-five-year-old sculptor by the name of Erasmus Boehm. He changed it later to Edgar, which had a more English ring to it. Louise was twenty-two at the time, a talented artist and very suggestible. The romance had started innocently enough. The Queen had invited Boehm to Balmoral to make a sculpture of John Brown, the gillie to whom she was foolishly attached. Boehm had moved in with his mallet and chisel for three months. He was attracted to Louise and was soon giving her lessons in clay modeling and, I gather, much else besides. One morning Mama decided to see what progress had been made on the statue of Brown. She found Louise alone in the studio with Boehm.

In the pandemonium that followed, Louise declared her undying love for the sculptor. The Queen for once was speechless, so I was called in to read the riot act while Mama diverted her fury into finding a suitable husband for this wayward daughter. Boehm couldn't possibly marry into the family; he was a Royal Academician, and that was the only thing royal about him. I'll say this for him: considering his situation, he conducted himself with dignity and charm, or I'd never have continued to commission his works.

Louise was married to the Marquess of Lorne the following March. I'm afraid it's an unhappy match. They are childless and lead virtually separate lives. Under Boehm's unflagging tuition, Louise has become a very proficient sculptor.

I presumed that the entire episode must have been forgotten and forgiven by Mama, for she certainly sat for Boehm two or three years after. Personally, I find a lot to admire in the fellow. Whether he actually rogers my sister I can't tell you, but at least he has the manners to keep it to himself.

Or—a disquieting thought came to me—had he used it to gain advancement?

I asked my mother directly, "Does this have to do with that episode at Balmoral, the year Boehm made the statue of Brown?"

She said bitterly, "Do you need to ask?"

I said, "So is he willing to threaten a lady's reputation to gain advancement? That's deplorable!"

"Detestable!" muttered my mother.

I said, "But I had the impression that he was quite devoted to Louise."

She lifted the veil and stared at me with her pale blue eyes. "It has nothing to do with Louise. Absolutely nothing." She jerked down the veil and walked on, out of the room containing my father's tomb.

I followed, mystified.

Outside in the anteroom, she paused briefly beside the plaque she had insisted be installed there to the memory of John Brown, the insinuating, coarse-mannered Highlander I've already mentioned.

Nothing was said, and the Queen walked out of the Mausoleum, but I was no longer mystified. It wasn't my sister's reputation that was under threat as a result of Boehm's sojourn at Balmoral in 1870, but my mother's.

CHAPTER 16

In a private room at the Marlborough Club on Friday evening, 3 December, I spent several hours with Christopher Sykes planning the house party at Brantingham Thorpe. I learned that the invitations had already gone out; a small orchestra had been engaged; and the domestic staff at Brantingham was preparing the rooms and the menus. As ever, the great Christopher had spared no effort, for all his misgivings.

What, then, was left to occupy us for so long in the Marlborough Club? It was, of course, the *raison d'être* of the party: the ensnaring of the Squire. If Sykes is unequaled as an organizer of parties, I may modestly claim a fair reputation as a hunter. One day in Nepal I shot six tigers, two of them man-eaters. I have bagged the fastest land animal in the world, the cheetah; and the largest, the elephant. In Bavaria, I was once in a party of ten guns that beat all records by shooting over twenty thousand partridges in ten days. I am the first to admit, however, that when the hunter pulls his trigger, it is only the final act in a process involving a small army of gamekeepers, beaters and loaders: hence the absolute necessity of planning. And hence our deliberations in the Marlborough Club.

So I approached the task as a hunter, taking account of the feral instincts of my quarry. The Squire was more dangerous than the tiger, more stealthy than the leopard. I suppose if one took into account the nature of the killings, he was akin to the vulture, relying on others to make the attack, but it would be foolhardy to fit him into any category. He was certainly capable of killing me if I gave him the opportunity.

I remained in London until Tuesday the seventh, diligently attending to my official duties while preparing for the dangerous encounter to come. A pleasing ceremony was enacted at Marlborough House that morning when Prince Komatsu of Japan, representing the Emperor, conferred on me the Insignia of the Imperial Japanese Order of the Chrysanthemum. Alix, who is as ignorant about Japan as she is about ceremony, couldn't understand why they hadn't chosen some more suitable flower, like the daffodil (for Wales, you see?). I told her they picked the chrysanthemum for me because it was large, round and shaggy, which shows that my humor hadn't deserted me under the strain.

Late in the afternoon, we left the metropolis to be the guests of the Danish minister and his wife, Madame de Falbe, at their splendid seat at Luton Hoo. I looked forward to some good shooting and Alix to jabbering in Danish to her heart's content. I'd already arranged to absent myself from the party on Saturday. Affairs of state, I'd told my host. Alix was sure to have something sarcastic to say in Danish about my affairs of state, but this time she would be mistaken.

And now, by the power of the pen, I'm going to transport us to Brantingham Thorpe on the evening of 11 December. Take it from me, the railway journey from Luton to York on a Saturday afternoon doesn't bear description.

My arrival was enshrouded in secrecy. Fortunately, I'm quite an old hand at entering houses by way of the mews or the servants' door. Muffled to the eyebrows, I stepped from the station fly straight through the woodyard into the kitchen, where a trusted butler with a candlestick showed me up the back stairs, through a baize curtain to the wing where Sykes accommodated his guests.

We had arranged that I should occupy the Beverley Room, an oak-paneled bedroom of modest proportions with, I was satisfied to discover, a blazing log fire and, even more welcoming, a table set for supper: toast and anchovies, oysters with brown bread and butter, chicken breasts and baked ham, quails' eggs, frog's thighs in jelly, a variety of cheeses and a large bowl of gooseberry fool. After the butler had poured me some Chablis I dismissed him and set to, for I was famished.

Some appreciable time passed before I was conscious of anything but the needs of the inner man. When I was round to the port and cigars, my ears picked up the strains of the orchestra from downstairs. An eightsome reel. By this time the house party was going full bat, and the most sociable fellow in the house was closeted upstairs! It was enough to make a parson swear.

I knew precisely what was happening. The guests, including our quarry, the Squire, had arrived much earlier than I. An afternoon around the piano had given the ladies, in their tea gowns, an opportunity to parade their talents, and the gentlemen to assess them. The flirtations and light behavior had begun in earnest over dinner, when Lady Jessica and her winsome friends had appeared in alluring décolletage. After five or six courses and wines, the ladies had retired to refresh their scent and prepare themselves for the excitements in prospect, while the gentlemen plotted their conquests over brandies and large cigars.

Reader, as I was chiefly responsible for establishing the weekend house party as a vogue in society, I had better explain the rules of conduct. You must understand that the main object is fun and games of an adult (not to say adulterous) character, so infinite care is taken over the invitations.

The discerning host makes sure that his guests are sportively inclined, attractive and amusing, and upon this the success of the weekend depends. No less in importance is the allocation of bedrooms. Husbands and wives are not expected to sleep together. Everyone is allotted a single room. Spouses are then enabled to follow their fancies independently, provided of course that the wife has previously satisfied convention by bearing her husband a male child. Wives without sons are off-limits to gentlemen of honor, as are unmarried girls. If a liaison is well known, the fortunate couple may be provided with rooms in reasonable proximity. Otherwise, as in this case, it is a fair field and no favor.

As for me, this night had something less delectable in prospect. I would remain in the Beverley Room awaiting the moment when the Squire would spring the trap.

Downstairs, I heard Sykes shout, "If you please, ladies and gentlemen, if you please!" As master of ceremonies, he was endeavoring to intersperse the program of dancing with after dinner games. The high-spirited crowd we'd invited would not be much subdued by its po-faced host. Charades and Dumb Crambo would rapidly give way to games like Sardines, involving hiding, romps and forfeits. Forfeits galore! There's something in the English character that relishes embarrassment, either to oneself or others. That's why the majority of parlor games are designed for the express purpose of extracting forfeits.

As always, the climax of the evening would be "crying the forfeits." Everyone compelled to pay a forfeit hands to the host some personal article, such as an item of jewelry, a key or a watch. Some who have collected several forfeits are obliged to deposit more than one item. These possessions are redeemed when the forfeits are completed to everyone's satisfaction.

The forfeits are cried by two of the guests. One, known as the forfeit master, is seated, with the articles in his lap.

The other (generally a lady) is blindfolded and must kneel before the first, who picks an object and holds it aloft, crying, "Here is a thing, and a very pretty thing. What shall be done by the owner of this very pretty thing?" The blindfolded lady asks, "Is it a lady's or a gentleman's?" She then names an appropriate forfeit, and the hapless owner performs the undignified task. A boisterous party can result in singular frolics.

I've gone to some trouble to explain how it works because I proposed to use the crying of the forfeits to implement my plan. I was relying on Sykes to set the whole thing in motion. During the evening he would closely observe the Squire to see which lady aroused his passions most. When he was certain, he would slip out of the room and take out a silver chain and locket provided by me. Inside the locket would be a slip of paper inscribed with these words: "The Beverley Room tonight, handsome Squire. I will be waiting impatiently." Sykes would append a forged signature—that of the lady admired by the Squire.

Do you see the trap? The Squire is called upon by Sykes to be the forfeit master. The trinkets, including the locket containing the note, are heaped in his lap. Naturally, when he holds up the locket, nobody will claim it. Intrigued, the Squire will open it and read the message.

So I had to be patient. If patience is said to be the beggar's virtue, is it so remarkable that a prince should be without it? I hate inactivity, and I didn't expect my visitor for at least a couple of hours. Sykes had providently arranged for a stack of magazines and newspapers to be left out, and I settled down to pass the time with these, closing my ears to the sounds of high jinks downstairs.

I picked up *The Sporting Life*, grateful that someone understood my taste in reading. I studied the results from Sandown Park. No winners from yesterday—not even a place. Steeplechasing doesn't have the same appeal as the flat for me.

There are enough imponderables in a flat handicap, without putting in jumps as well.

An item about Archer's will caught my eye. A rather surprising item. His estate amounted to £60,000—a sizable fortune by most standards, but distinctly less than anyone had predicted, except Charlie Buckfast. The smallest estimate that I'd seen in the press was the figure of £100,000 in *Reynolds's Newspaper* and some had put it as high as half a million. The principal beneficiary was Archer's infant daughter, Nellie Rose, who was now in the care of her grandparents. Eight other relatives and friends received legacies.

Unable to concentrate any longer on the papers, I smoked two or three cigars, musing on Archer and the tragedies that had beset him. Even after his passing, death had claimed more victims, as if still exacting payment for his genius. Who was to say that the price had yet been paid?

I shivered, and it wasn't because I felt a draft.

My morbid thoughts were banished by a shriek from downstairs, followed by wicked laughter. In the intervals between dances, Sykes was still manfully attempting to direct the parlor games. Judging by the hysterical response of certain of the ladies, he was either having a brilliant success or a ludicrous failure. How tempted I was to surprise them all! Frankly, Lady Florence Dixie was wasted on Sykes. She's a bubbly, mischievous minx, and I've never found an opportunity to plumb the depths of her mischief. Once she formed a quadrille at Blenheim with Bay Middleton and another pair who included Gladys de Grey (then Lady Lonsdale). She took one look at the elegant Gladys and piped, "Why can't I be as tall as you?" and sprang high in the air like an acrobat.

Sometime after midnight, the music stopped. For me, the evening was about to begin. I tossed my cigar butt into the fire and got up from the armchair, listening keenly. I took a few deep breaths, bracing myself for a set-to with the Squire. My skin prickled and my hands shook a little when I clenched them. One doesn't get much hand-to-hand combat in Court circles. At least, I thought, I'll have surprise on my side.

Presently I heard a sound below my window. I drew back the curtain a fraction and saw the band loading their instruments into a van. The task took about ten minutes. They whipped up the horse and left.

Next, much giggling on the stairs and the swish of skirts as the ladies came to bed. I crept across the room to listen. When their voices grew more distinct, I heard one say plaintively, "He's divine. But he'll never know where I am."

A reassuring voice told her, "Daisy, darling, he's only got to find his way along here. It's really quite light in the moonlight."

"And so is Daisy!" remarked another, to screams of laughter.

A relative silence ensued for up to an hour before the party in the smoking room broke up and heavier steps trod the stairs. The stronger sex are tight-lipped at such times. I heard a few murmurs of, "Good night, old boy." Doors were closed and that was all.

Good taste decreed a further interval of at least half an hour before the first noctambulation. Like everyone else, I daresay, I opened my door a fraction and waited for the creak of a board. I turned down the light to the merest blue flicker.

I had taken up a position to the left of the door, with the intention of grabbing the Squire the moment he entered. I'm not very adept at wrestling, but I was confident of handling a fellow who tips the scales at under ten stone. Besides, the indispensable Sykes was located just across the corridor, ready to come to my assistance as soon as I gave the shout.

I exercised commendable patience in the next twenty minutes or so. Eventually I was conscious of a movement somewhere nearby.

I strained to listen.

The first tiptoed steps came along the corridor, rapidly, supremely confident where they were going. I pressed myself to the wall. The steps came level with the Beverley Room—and failed even to pause. I heard a soft click as a door opened and closed, followed by a muffled greeting, then silence again.

After a tense hiatus, someone else made a move, padding determinedly in my direction.

I held my breath.

He actually stopped outside my door. He was so close that I could hear his breathing. I heard him sniff. He was taking an unconscionable time to come in. I could barely restrain myself from flinging open the door and snatching him inside.

Then—would you believe?—he crept away!

It's true—the footsteps retreated along the corridor.

For all the tea in China—why?

The door of the Beverley Room was labeled plainly enough, and he'd had no trouble seeing it, because, as the ladies had remarked, the corridor was aglow with moonlight. A shaft extended through the gap in the door and across the carpet. My eye followed it back to the door, and that was what caused me to notice something on the floorboards. First I thought it was some creeping thing, but common sense told me that the Brantingham Thorpe cockroaches couldn't be quite so large.

I stooped and picked it up.

My locket and chain. He'd chucked it down in the doorway. I felt like a woman spurned.

What the devil had gone wrong? This was utterly, maddeningly out of character. The Squire had no business behaving like this. He was about as coy as Casanova.

An ugly suspicion uncoiled itself: Had Christopher Sykes botched the plan in some way?

I unfastened the locket and took out the slip of paper and read the message. It was certainly the invitation I had written. And, just as I'd directed, a signature had been added: "Jessica."

I couldn't fault Sykes. He'd done precisely as I'd ordered, even though it had meant admitting that his own sister-in-law was the Squire's choice for a bedmate.

So I had nobody to blame. The plan had failed, and I couldn't fathom why.

Then I turned over the piece of paper and saw a message written on the reverse: "You should give up cigars—they don't become a lady."

The Squire had smelled the fumes.

All these elaborate preparations, all the thought I'd put into this weekend, and my plan had foundered because I can't resist a smoke.

I called softly for Sykes, and he rushed in, armed with a poker. I told him it wasn't required and explained why. I am bound to say that he appeared more relieved than angered.

"Better sleep on it, sir," he suggested. "We'll think of something else in the morning."

I said, "Stop talking like my old nanny, Sykes. I mean to settle this tonight."

"Tonight?" He looked even more troubled than usual.

"At once."

"But what can you do, sir? He'll be on the alert now."

I said grimly, "He'll be on the first train back to Newmarket if we don't detain him."

I asked Sykes for the name of the Squire's bedroom. Then I sent him to station himself with his poker at the foot of the stairs in case there was a chase. I proposed to step into the lion's den.

The room was called York, and it was situated on the same floor as mine, around two turns of the corridor. You'll have to take my word for it that an Indian scout could not have crept through the house more stealthily than I did. I might have been walking on eggs. Yet I'd defy anyone to master the loose boards in Brantingham Thorpe. When I felt the ominous movement under my shoe, it made more of a rasp than a creak. I tensed.

An enticing murmur of feminine origin responded from a door left ajar. I refused to be distracted.

I hesitated at the first turn, and it was a good thing I did, because a figure in a dressing gown was moving quite rapidly toward me. He had too much girth to be the Squire. He was making such a beeline that I guessed the bathroom at the end of the corridor was his destination. Haven't we all been so afflicted soon after going to bed?

I stepped back fast, through that open door from which the murmur had emanated, pulling it almost shut.

The lady's voice asked at once, "Is that you?"

I answered, "No."

She said generously, "I don't mind."

The loose board outside gave a startling screech, and to my consternation, the door opened. The fellow in the dressing gown walked straight past me toward the bed.

The lady in the bed asked in an interested voice, "Are there two of you?"

I said, "Yes, and this one is leaving." Which I did.

My second noctambulation was conducted with more purpose. I abandoned all stealth, stepped out boldly and located the York Room. The door was closed, so after putting my ear against it and hearing nothing, I tried the handle. It turned readily enough, but the door wouldn't yield. I was locked out—or the Squire was locked in. I rapped and got no response.

What wretched luck!

I knocked more firmly, knowing in my sinking heart that the Squire wouldn't respond, whatever I tried. I didn't want the whole of the house turning out to complain at the disturbance, so I reluctantly returned to the Beverley Room.

I let myself in and was reaching for the port when my collar was gripped from behind and jerked upward, practically choking me.

I must have made quite a racket, because my assailant said in a voice I didn't recognize, the coarse, throaty growl of an uneducated man, "Stow it, Teddy, or I'll shove your face through the wall."

Being a prudent man, I stowed it, and for my cooperation I was flung onto the bed. I cracked my head against the wooden headboard and saw a fireworks display worthy of the Crystal Palace.

CHAPTER 17

Through the pain, I said, "Do you know who I am?"

My assailant put a face of unexampled brutality within a couple of inches of mine and said, "Yes, Your Worship. You're the Prince of Wales. And I'm Charlie Mitchell, the Champion of England. You got a title and so have I. The difference is, I had to fight for mine."

This is impossible, my beleaguered brain told me. The Squire was told to come alone.

Mitchell, you'll recall, was the Squire's chief henchman, the most famous prizefighter in England. This notorious pugilist had been smuggled into Brantingham Thorpe to deal with me. He had been to America in 1883 to try conclusions with John L. Sullivan, the world champion. Swarthy in appearance and clean-shaven, without a glimmer of intelligence to animate his menacing features, he reminded me strongly of my odious brother-in-law, the Marquess of Lome.

Bertie, I said to myself, unless you're nimble witted you're about to go the way of Buckfast and Myrtle.

I asked him good-naturedly, "Do you want money?"

Mitchell replied with a sneer, "You can make me a Knight of the Garter if you want." With that he forced what I prefer to believe was an unused handkerchief into my mouth to serve as a gag and grabbed my own silk scarf from the coat hook on the door and pressed it across my face, tugging my head upward to tie a knot behind. His hands felt like well-scuffed shoes. He pushed me onto my front and bound my wrists. Then he warned me superfluously, "Don't give no bother, right? We're going downstairs."

He's planning to murder me in the grounds, I decided. It's less likely to disturb the people in the house and he can make his escape more easily.

He gripped my left arm by the biceps and swung me off the bed and toward the door. His strength was terrible to contemplate.

There was one chance of salvation, and I dared not put much hope on it. Christopher Sykes was waiting at the foot of the stairs with a foot-long poker. Even from his vast height, Sykes would need to wield the poker with prodigious strength and speed to fell Charlie Mitchell with one blow. As sure as the Creed, he wouldn't get a second try. But if I were alert and agile, it might enable me to escape.

Unfortunately, it did not, for instead of turning toward the main stairs, Mitchell steered me to the left, and by now every bedroom door was closed. We passed the Squire's without pausing, turned right, through the baize door and down the servants' stairs to the kitchen, which was deserted except for a couple of cats.

Mitchell unbolted the door and marched me across a cobbled yard, past the stables. A clear sky gave us strong moonlight and penetrating cold. Bareheaded and without so much as an overcoat, I was horribly reminded that royal executions always seemed to happen during the most inclement time of the year.

Across the yard was a high, gray building with a tiled roof already glittering with frost. The coach house, I decided, and this was confirmed when Mitchel kicked open a door and pushed me inside. Coach house or slaughter house?

There were four or five vehicles in front of me, and beyond them one with its lamps lighted. I didn't have much time to study my surroundings because a figure in a topper and greatcoat stepped out of the radiance and swaggered toward us. The insolent grin framed by sandy-colored muttonchops was really no comfort, although I hadn't expected the Squire to be in at the death.

He whisked off the hat and swung it in front of him in an insolent, exaggerated bow. Addressing Mitchell, he said, "Charles, my dear fellow, there's no need to hold on to the Prince like a punt pole. We're not likely to lose him now. And take that scarf off his face. He looks like a bank robber. It's enough to get us all into trouble."

Mitchell untied me and removed the gag. I spluttered as the air entered my throat again.

"God save us, Your Royal Highness, I don't like the sound of that," commented the Squire. "You'll be catching your death if we don't look after you. Why don't you step into my private brougham? There's a blanket inside that you can put around your shoulders."

I wasn't fooled by his show of concern, but I was so relieved to be offered anything less than a bullet through the head that I didn't think twice about acting on the suggestion. I climbed into the coach (you're right, it was the one with lighted lamps, but that didn't seem significant at the time), grabbed the blanket and wrapped myself in it.

The Squire came in after me, took the seat opposite and shut the door. The light entering the window picked out the dissipation in his face, though I knew him to be barely twenty-five. His rubbery lips were held in a permanent sneer and his eyes were so pouchy that he might have been sparring with Mitchell.

"Now we're alone, Your Royal Highness," he said, "I'll speak out. I'm bloody insulted."

It was some comfort that he proposed to speak at all. My

best chance of a reprieve was to keep reminding him who I was, so I said, "I'll thank you to show some respect."

"A fat lot of respect you showed me," he returned, "trying to pull a threepenny-novel trick like the message in the locket."

I looked away. I wasn't obliged to listen to his ranting.

But out of curiosity I did. He continued, "Your toadying friend Sykes obviously didn't throw the house party for his own amusement. I knew you'd be here, and I knew why. It's about Myrtle, isn't it?"

Astonished that he had the gall to raise the subject, I said, "Yes. Since we're speaking out, Mr. Baird, I want to know why you killed her."

He gave me a stare I can only describe as maniacal. "I killed her? You're accusing *me* of killing Myrtle?"

"You or your pack of jackals."

He protested in a rush of words that didn't impress me at all, "No one talks to me like that. No one. She was my girl, my guest at Bedford Lodge. A peach of a girl. I wouldn't hurt a hair on her head."

"Your henchmen did."

"That's a vile suggestion!"

"It was a vile crime," said I. "They also attacked and killed Captain Buckfast. Before you deny it, I was there. They threw me in the Thames—me, the Heir Apparent—and I might very well have drowned with him."

With about as much concern as a fishmonger feels for a lobster, he said, "Are you telling me that you were there when Buckfast was killed?"

"Can I put it more plainly?" He still appeared to doubt me, so I added, "Didn't your two thugs tell you?"

He was silent for some seconds. I wouldn't go so far as to say I'd delivered a knockout punch, but I might have winded him.

Outside, Mitchell had unbolted the large doors at the end of the building, and someone else led in a pair of grays.

The Squire began again on a more conciliatory note, "I'm trying to make sense of this. What reason would I or my friends have for killing Buckfast and attacking you?"

Some bluff on his part was to be expected, and I didn't have much patience with it. I said, "This show of innocence doesn't impress me much, Baird."

"You see?" he said. "You accuse me, and you can't explain why."

"Of course I can explain why!" I told him angrily. "We were too close to the truth about your dealings with Fred Archer."

"Dealings? What dealings?"

By now, the force of the argument had taken hold of me, "Buckfast spent a week in Newmarket collecting evidence. He broke into Bedford Lodge—"

He repeated rudely, "What dealings?"

I glared and said, "The blackmail that drove him to shoot himself."

"Blackmail!" he said, doing his best to sound outraged.

"You corrupted Archer with bribes, and then threatened him with exposure."

"I did not. Fred never took a bribe in his life."

How ironic that I, who had started out believing Archer was incorruptible, should find myself recounting his sins to this loathsome humbug. I said, "He was regularly pulling races and you paid him to do it. He was in your pocket, to quote your own words."

"Who told you I used those words?"

"Buckfast. He heard you bragging all over Newmarket."

"Then he lied."

"Why should Buckfast lie to me? As a matter of fact," I added, voicing a suspicion I'd been saving for this encounter, "I now understand why the running of the Cambridgeshire was so peculiar. You and Archer rooked everyone."

"There was nothing fishy about the Cambridgeshire,"

he insisted. "I kept my horse's form from the bookies, that's all."

"Really? How many jockeys are capable of beating Archer in a close finish? Two or three at their best? Cannon, perhaps, and Wood. Who was on your animal—Albert White? Come now. *Albert White!* He wouldn't live with Archer in a fair-run finish. Fred obviously let him get up. And what happened to Carlton, the favorite? It finished nowhere. Why? Because you bribed its jockey, Woodburn."

He said defiantly, "I paid Woodburn nothing."

"If it wasn't you, it was Archer who handed over the money. You had Archer on a string. You were all ready to take him on as a partner and bleed his reputation white."

He said, "There's no evidence for any of this."

I said, "But there is. That's why Buckfast broke into Bedford Lodge."

"When was this?"

"Two weeks ago last night. The night you went to the dogfight at the Greyhound."

My grasp of the facts was manifestly beginning to trouble him. He said tamely, "We're often at the Greyhound."

I said, "He got into your room and surprised two of your men . . ."

"In my bedroom?"

". . . in a state of nature and in a proximity that was anything but natural."

He snorted his disbelief.

I said, "The same men followed Buckfast to London on Saturday and made that murderous attack."

He asked me to describe them, which was a change from all the denials, and some indication that I'd impressed him. When I'd given as good a description as I was able, he said in a more subdued manner, "If there's a grain of truth in this, I'll see those men hanged. I don't know who you mean, but I'll question every one of my associates."

"Don't shift the blame, Mr. Baird," I told him sternly. "I still hold you accountable for three deaths."

"Three?"

"Archer, Buckfast and Miss Bliss."

"You're talking rubbish," he rasped. "By Jesus, you're wrong from beginning to end and I'll prove it." He thrust open the carriage door and called, "Get those bloody horses between the shafts and drive away."

CHAPTER 18

That ride through the night in the Squire's brougham was an experience I wouldn't care to repeat. We careered up the drive of Brantingham Thorpe as if pursued by wolves. I fully expected us to throw a wheel at any minute. No such premonitions afflicted Charlie Mitchell, on the box beside the coachman shouting to him repeatedly to whip up the horses.

Inside, so buffeted that only with difficulty could I remain on the seat, I inquired where we were going so late and at such speed. The Squire refused to tell me. He had retreated into a churlish silence, which angered me greatly. If anyone had cause to feel aggrieved, it was myself.

We veered left at the main road with a tremendous grating of iron on grit, and an alarming possibility presented itself. I knew of nothing in this direction except the north bank of the River Humber. My fortunate escape from drowning in the Thames was all too vivid in my recollection. On that occasion, I'd saved myself with a few rapid strokes of the dog paddle, but the Humber is up to two miles across in places. If they proposed to make a better job of annihilating me this time, the vast, deserted reach to the south of Brantingham Thorpe would be ideal for their purpose. My body might never be found.

How I regretted speaking out so forthrightly about the Squire's guilt! I've never been noted for guarding my tongue. Time and again it has got me into hot water. Hot or cold, I can't abide the stuff.

Bertie, I thought, this cannot be tolerated. If ever the silver-tongued charm of the Saxe-Coburgs had a challenge, this is it. So I suppressed my jitters and summoned up a fraternal smile. "Mr. Baird," I said civilly, "whatever our differences, we both respected Fred Archer as the greatest jockey who ever lived."

He ignored me.

Doggedly I continued, "That is why I chose to interest myself in the mystery of his suicide."

He stared through me.

I added in the same conciliatory vein, "However, I am coming around to the view that it might be sensible to dismiss the whole unfortunate matter from my mind."

Do you know what this more than generous offer elicited from the Squire? Nothing, not so much as a raised eyebrow. The man was impervious to charm or compromise, and I refused to grovel until it was absolutely necessary.

I lapsed into silence again and endeavored to control my anger by applying my mind to other things. What would an experienced detective be doing now? Studying the scene from the window to learn where he was being taken.

I peered out. My view gave me precious little information. I could see no water yet, and I reckoned at the furious rate we were traveling that we ought to have reached the Humber by this time. Presently a sharp turn to the left gave me a slight pretext for optimism. The steadier rumble of the wheels suggested we were on a trunk road. We might, after all, be traveling east, toward the town of Hull.

It transpired that we were not. My sense of direction had failed me utterly, for we were approaching Beverley. I knew it was Beverley, because in the moonlight I saw the familiar outline of the twin towers at the west front of the Minster. When I say "familiar," I should own that I've never worshiped in the Minster; I usually pass it on my way to the racecourse. It is on open ground to the south of the town.

We drove farther in and stopped by the market cross, whereupon Mitchell got down for a consultation. He asked which street we wanted, and I leaned forward to listen. I heard nothing of value because the Squire simply swore at him and ordered him to change places. Mitchell needed no second bidding. When he climbed in, I saw that the front of his overcoat had acquired a thick covering of frost.

Our destination proved to be a terraced house in a narrow street off the marketplace. Automatically, I made ready to get out as the carriage stopped. Mitchell growled and wagged his finger at me, and I subsided again. The Squire marched over to the door of the house and knocked. I wondered what reception he'd get at this hour, for I'd heard a clock striking three as we came through the town.

Almost at once, a window opened upstairs. Inconveniently, I couldn't hear what was said. After a brief exchange, the Squire came over to the brougham, opened the door and ordered me out.

The purpose of all this exercised me greatly, and my brain grappled with some horrid possibilities. If I wasn't to be drowned this time, perhaps my fate was to be struck on the head and buried in the backyard. Or did they intend to stuff me into a tin trunk and bury me at sea?

As I crossed the cobbles with the Squire, he said, "I haven't told him who you are."

"The ignorance is mutual," I answered.

But I *did* recognize the face when the door was opened by a diminutive, rat-faced young fellow in a nightshirt. He was probably under twenty years old. His features were pinched by sleep and I couldn't see much of his eyes, but

I knew him. I'd seen him often. The deuce of it was that I couldn't think where, or who he was.

The Squire told him brusquely, "This won't take long. Where can we talk?"

"In the back room, Mr. Baird, so long as you keep your voices down."

I was still unable to place him. The voice came in a throaty rasp that wasn't familiar. I have no ear at all for accents.

He led us—that is to say, myself, the Squire and Mitchell—through a damp-smelling passage to a small room where the embers of a fire glowed faintly. A linnet in a cage twittered at our host when he lighted an oil lamp. The flame showed us a few sparse furnishings. I claimed a wooden armchair nearest the dying fire, and the others found stools on either side of a small, square table covered with oilcloth.

In the better light, I stared at the youth I have called our host, searching for the clue that would tell me where I'd seen him. My first impression of him as "rat-faced" was, perhaps, uncharitable, but if you had seen his beady eyes, sharp nose and protruding teeth, you would undoubtedly have reached a conclusion not very different from mine. Curiously, for all his lack of stature, I had an idea that I was accustomed to looking up at him.

This I found puzzling, for people are meant to look up at *me*. I'm invariably elevated above the public on some form of dais or rostrum. Even at the races, I stand on a carriage for a better view.

The races.

"Got it!" I blurted out. "You're a jockey!"

He raised his hands in alarm and said huskily, "Stash it, mate. My landlady's asleep upstairs."

The Squire nodded to me and said, "It's Woodburn."

"Woodburn—of course!"

The scene at Newmarket surfaced in my memory. I saw the field charging up the hill again, sharpening into focus in my glasses. Woodburn was the rider in blue, with white diamonds, on Carlton, the favorite, and he was leading the gallop, with Melton and St. Mirin tucked in behind. He had nothing to give when they challenged. He was a terrible disappointment to the crowd.

There was the sound of someone—presumably Woodburn's landlady—shifting in bed upstairs. The jockey put a finger to his lips and pointed at the ceiling.

The Squire ignored him. He had decided at last to explain the purpose of this bizarre meeting. "Woodburn does winter work up here with Tom Green, the Beverley trainer who looks after some of my horses. I'm giving you the opportunity to question him, Your Royal Highness."

I was so overwhelmed that this was indeed Woodburn the jockey, and not (so far as I was aware) an assassin or a disposer of corpses, that for a moment I couldn't think what I wanted to ask him about.

The Squire prompted me. "About Fred Archer," he added.

"Archer, yes." I nodded vigorously. What I needed now was a strong drink to marshal my thoughts. Unthinkingly, I turned to young Woodburn and asked, "Would you have such a thing as a cognac?"

Woodburn screwed up his face and demanded of the Squire, "Is this one of your famous practical jokes, Mr. Baird? I mean, am I really supposed to take this old geezer for the Prince of Wales?"

The Squire answered tersely, "It's no joke."

"You can't deny that there's a likeness," Woodburn blundered on inanely, although I suppose he couldn't be blamed for persisting in his error. A few minutes ago he'd been soundly asleep. I think if my mother the Queen had been there beside me in her coronation robes he still wouldn't have believed it.

To me, the Squire said irritably, "Get on with it, blast you."

No doubt, sensitive reader, you are appalled that anyone could address me so. You may imagine my feelings. For the present, I contained them, for I had collected my wits. I realized I had been handed a perfect opportunity to test the truth of the Squire's claim that neither he, nor Archer, had paid a bribe to Woodburn. I was confident that he would get his comeuppance very shortly.

Addressing Woodburn, I said, "I want some honest answers from you, my lad. I want to get to the bottom of the Cambridgeshire result."

Woodburn looked extremely alarmed, as I had expected. He said, "The Cambridgeshire?" Turning to the Squire, he asked, "What is this, Mr. Baird—a stewards' inquiry?"

I answered grimly, "It's a great deal more than that. You rode Carlton, the favorite, and it ran like a selling-plater. I want to know why."

He squirmed on his stool. "Even a good colt has a bad run sometimes."

Ignoring that evasion, I plunged in and asked, "Is it true that you took a bribe from this gentleman?"

Woodburn blinked and looked at the Squire and then at me as if I'd impugned the Archbishop of Canterbury. "From Mr. Baird? Never."

At this, the Squire thrust out his fat lower lip in triumph, and I reflected how futile an exercise this was. Of course, Woodburn would stand by the Squire if they were both in league.

"From Archer, then?" I suggested.

"Fred Archer?"

"Don't try me, Woodburn."

He said, "Fred was offered the ride on Carlton, and he turned it down."

"You haven't answered my question."

The Squire sprang to his defense. "But he has. If Fred turned down the ride, he must have known St. Mirin was a better colt."

"Not necessarily," I said. "There was a trial before the Cambridgeshire, and Carlton beat St. Mirin easily. What do you say to that, Woodburn?"

The jockey nervously wetted his lips. "Fred wanted the ride on Carlton, but he was under an obligation, sir."

I noted the *sir*. I was making an impression. "An obligation. To whom?"

"St. Mirin's owner, the Duchess of Montrose. She's a very forceful lady."

"I'm aware of that."

"I was over in Ireland with Fred for the Curragh October Meeting, and I was there when he opened a telegram. It said: 'My horse runs in the Cambridgeshire. I count on you to ride it. Montrose.' For Fred it meant getting his weight down to eight stone six. That's terrible wasting for a man of his size."

I said, "You're still avoiding my question. Did you or did you not take a bribe from Archer?"

A look appeared in Woodburn's eyes that I find difficult to describe. There was embarrassment there, which I expected, and defiance. And there was something I didn't expect: fear, amounting almost to panic.

The Squire must have noted it, too, for he took this as the cue to indulge in some blatant leading of the witness. "For God's sake! Fred was straight as a die. Answer the bloody question, man!"

"I can't," said Woodburn. "I dare not."

"Why?"

To everyone's amazement and confusion, Woodburn said, "He could be listening."

After a breathless interval I inquired, "Who exactly do you mean?"

"Fred."

There was another stunned pause.

Trying to sound reasonable, Woodburn explained, "I'm not really a believer in such things, but when people I know—honest, reliable people—tell me they've seen it as clear as daylight, I can't ignore them, can I?"

"Seen what?" demanded the Squire.

"His ghost."

"Strewth!" said Mitchell.

Woodburn added quickly, "They say it's an unquiet spirit. Fred won't stay in his grave."

"Absurd!" I said, wishing I carried more conviction. You see, I'm constantly being told by mama about psychic phenomena, voices and apparitions, and some of it rubs off, try as you might to take a rational view.

The Squire said, "There was something about this in the paper. He rides around Newmarket on a spectral horse."

"In that case," I said resourcefully, "he won't appear in Beverley. Ghosts only ever haunt one place."

"That's a fact," said Mitchell, though what claims he had as an expert on the supernatural, I cannot think.

I said, "You can tell us the truth, Woodburn. Did you take a bribe?"

The Squire got up from his stool and placed an encouraging hand on the young jockey's shoulder. He said, "You don't even have to speak to answer the question. Just shake your head."

"Or give a nod if the answer is yes," I said with a glare at the Squire.

The rodent features twitched. Woodburn was a very agitated young man.

I said, "You threw away the race, didn't you?"

He dipped his head in confirmation.

"And Archer paid you to do it?"

Another nod.

This was too much for the Squire to stomach. He grasped Woodburn by the nightshirt and picked him off the stool. "What the devil are you saying, you little toad—that the greatest jockey who ever lived was a cheat? Look me in the eye and say it."

"It's true," whispered Woodburn. "As I live and die, it's true, Mr. Baird."

The Squire suddenly went very pale.

Charlie Mitchell, understanding only that the little toad had given offense, stood up and prepared to crush him, but the Squire gestured to him to remain seated.

A flame of triumph leapt up in me. I had proved my case. Instead of the back room of a humble terraced house in Beverley, this might have been the Central Criminal Court at the Old Bailey. I was ready to take my place among the great forensic lawyers.

It was but a small leap from there to the judge's bench. I told Woodburn gravely, "You have said enough to bring a premature end to your career as a jockey, but it need not be repeated outside these walls if you confess the details fully and frankly. Do you understand?"

"Yes, sir." He fingered the collar of his nightshirt. His hands were trembling.

"How much were you paid?"

"Two hundred, sir."

"To stop Carlton?"

"Yes, sir."

"And when precisely did Archer hand you the bribe?"

"He didn't, sir."

"What?"

"Fred didn't pay me. Captain Buckfast did."

"Buckfast?" I heard my own voice pipe ridiculously high.

"He was acting for Fred," said Woodburn, aware that he had some rapid explaining to do. "Fred couldn't do anything without someone watching. People never took their eyes off Fred, so the captain conducted his business for him. He approached me on the first day of the Houghton meeting. He handed over half the money on the day before the Cambridgeshire and the rest on the morning after."

"So you had no dealings directly with Archer?" said the Squire.

"That was the way Fred preferred it, sir."

I believe the Squire winkled out some more from Woodburn about the money and how it was left in a cigar box in a four-wheeler engaged to wait for him at the end of the day's racing, but my concentration was broken. I was thunderstruck at the suggestion that Charlie Buckfast, my assistant, an officer and a gentleman, had not only colluded in the bribery but also actively promoted it, and mentioned nothing of it to me. It was unthinkable. And deplorable. A vicious slander on a dead man.

I wondered whether Woodburn and the Squire had cooked up the story between them. I was tempted to believe this was so, yet I was compelled to admit that Woodburn's account contradicted the Squire's. According to the Squire, Archer was practically a saint, incapable of anything so underhanded as bribery. Woodburn's statement that Archer was corrupt had shocked the Squire profoundly. Take my word for it; I can tell when a man flies into a temper. His outburst had unquestionably been genuine.

What was I to make of it? I could only assume that Woodburn was unhinged. The possibility had crossed my mind when he had started talking about Archer's ghost, though it has to be said that wiser and more eminent heads than his have entertained such notions. Yet the story about Charlie Buckfast was preposterous. Mad.

I didn't believe a word of it.

Shortly after, we drove back to Brantingham Thorpe. For most of the ride we were silent. Only as we turned into the drive did the Squire ask, "Are you satisfied?"

"Not in the least," I told him candidly.

"Will you still pursue it?"

"To the end, Mr. Baird. To the very end."

He grinned brazenly. "In that case, I'll see you there . . . if you survive."

CHAPTER 19

There were no early risers in Brantingham Thorpe on the Sunday morning. Lady Jessica and her set were not so frisky on an icy December morning when the fires of every sort had ceased to flicker. Breakfast was not even contemplated. The mere thought of renewing social contact over porridge and smoked haddock must have been like a prospect of hell to those nightshirted rovers of the previous night. So I was enabled to slip away at mid-morning, unnoticed by anyone except Sykes, who decently arranged to have me driven to York, where the stationmaster, good man, called up a special train.

I resumed my investigation on the following Tuesday afternoon, 14 December. I traveled down to Newmarket and put up at my private suite in the Jockey Club. I was convinced that my detective quest would be brought to a triumphant conclusion in the town we Turfites know as Headquarters, and so it was, as you shall see.

After a hearty dinner, I passed an instructive evening with Captain James Machell, the fount of all wisdom concerning the Heath and its personalities. Machell is a mournful-looking cove, with a caustic turn of phrase, and he's made many enemies over the years, but I've always found him stimulating company, and as a judge of a horse he's second to none. He'll always be linked in racing memories with Hermit's Derby, in 1867. A week before the race Hermit broke a blood vessel at Newmarket. Henry Chaplin, the owner, wanted to pull out, but Machell patched up the colt and insisted that it should run and personally backed it to win £3,000. It got up sensationally at 1,000-15. What's more, when Hermit was put to stud, he sired many outstanding horses, among them two Derby winners and one whose name will be familiar: St. Mirin.

This evening the captain was in spanking form, recounting the latest incident in his unending feud with his neighbor in Newmarket, Carrie Montrose, whom he styled as "that superannuated scarlet woman." Carrie, it emerged, was back from London with a young man of twenty-two, whom she had "roused at dawn from his exhausted slumbers for a ride across the Limekilns." After a night with Carrie the young man was in no condition for a gallop. His hack had bolted and thrown its rider and interfered with Machell's string and there was such a barney between Carrie and the captain that nobody noticed that the young man had broken his leg.

Our conversation moved inexorably to Archer, and Machell told me that before their misunderstanding Fred had actually consulted him upon the advisability of marriage to Carrie Montrose. He had wanted to know whether it would make him a duke. Poor deluded Archer! I was convulsed with laughter at this.

From there it was an easy transition to the tall stories that were circulating of Archer's apparition being seen in Newmarket. Greatly to my amazement, Machell announced that he had seen it himself. I wouldn't have bet a brass farthing on that wily old cynic seeing a ghost, yet he was serious. "I can't get over the poor fellow's death," he told me. "We had a falling out, I regret to say, shortly before he shot himself. He told me to back something in the Seller at Newmarket and it was beaten a head by Wood. Then I heard from a lady friend in the stand that Archer had told her to put her money on Wood. I'd had a dreadful week and I was foolish enough to believe her. When I met Fred in the paddock, I cut him. Turned my back on the fellow who rode more winners for me than any other. On the word of a garrulous woman. How I wish I could turn back the clock! It was the last time I saw him . . . alive."

I said with due seriousness, "But you believe you've seen him in spirit form?"

"Last Friday night, sir. I was lying awake—and I'll swear on the Good Book that I was wide awake—when I saw Archer standing beside my bed. He was in his jockey's rig, though I can't tell you whose colors they were. I watched him for a few minutes, and I don't know whether I spoke or not. After a time, he put out his hand and patted me gently on the shoulder, and the action, strange to say, so soothed me that I went to sleep and have slept all right ever since."

I asked how much he'd drunk the previous evening, but he wouldn't be budged. He was certain that Archer's spirit was abroad in Newmarket, attending to unfinished business. Late one evening, a policeman had observed a strange luminous glow in Falmouth House, which had been empty and locked since the inquest. When he had investigated, nobody was inside. Moreover, several of the locals claimed to have seen the ghost on the Heath after midnight, racing over the Cambridgeshire course. Poor Fred was assumed to be still trying to win the race he had never managed to win when he was alive, though, as I pointed out, with no visible opposition it was a walkover, and the great jockey wouldn't have cared for that.

I retired late, and the skeptical reader will be satisfied to hear that I received no visitor during the night, mortal or immortal.

Next morning I started on what was to prove the crucial

stage of my investigation. I first visited Heath House, the training establishment where Archer had been apprenticed to the redoubtable Mat Dawson at the age of eleven. The present manager was Mat's nephew, George, whom I had come to see because he was an executor of Archer's will. My purpose: to discover whether there was evidence in the accounts to support Woodburn's story of a bribe of £200.

I was received with due courtesy (a pleasant change after my experiences in Beverley) and shown into the drawing room, which was a veritable museum of the Turf, with Archer prominently represented in two oil paintings and an equine statuette by Edgar Boehm, the sculptor and blackmailer to the Queen. The first punch of the festive season had been prepared for me, and I formed the impression that young Dawson was expecting social conversation. If so, I disappointed him. I pressed my inquiries without preamble.

"I wish I could help, sir," he responded to my question, "and you are welcome to examine the accounts, such as they are."

"That doesn't sound too promising."

"Truth to tell, it's extremely difficult to pin down particular items of spending. Fred made most of his transactions in cash. He was betting heavily toward the end of his life, and he withdrew the money in hefty amounts of up to a thousand at the beginning of each month."

"That doesn't sound like the Tinman," I commented.

"He earned a fortune and spent it, sir, whatever his reputation for penny-pinching. The ledgers confirm it. Would you care to examine them now?"

Accountancy is as foreign as Timbuctoo to me, so I told him precisely what I was searching for. He ran a finger down one of the columns. Just as I feared, it was impossible to trace the £200 allegedly paid to Woodburn. "Were these accounts kept by Captain Buckfast?" I asked.

"Yes, sir."

"Are they correct?"

"They balance, if that's what you mean, sir."

"But you were saying that up to a thousand a month in cash was withdrawn."

"The entries are here, sir, if you care to look."

"So it's possible that the two hundred pounds we are looking for was actually paid to Mr. Woodburn and didn't appear in the books."

He thought it proper to come to Charlie's defense. "I'm sure Captain Buckfast did all in his power to convince Fred of the need to be more businesslike, but he was hamstrung. For Fred, racing was the only thing that counted after his wife, Helen, died."

"Not quite the only thing," I observed.

"What do you mean, sir?"

"I mean, a thousand a month. Where did it all go—on women?"

The directness of my question shocked him. The family's reputation had to be defended. "Emphatically not, sir. I'm afraid he must have been gambling more heavily than any of us realized."

"And losing?"

"I can't think where else it went." Dawson closed the book.

This wasn't the time to air my theories. I said, "There's another matter I wish to raise. When you were going through Archer's papers, did you come across any documents or drafts of documents suggesting a possible financial arrangement with another party?"

"What do you have in mind, sir?"

"A marriage settlement, perhaps?"

I didn't have the gratification of another shocked response. He asked quite calmly, "Does this relate to the rumor that Fred was planning to marry a certain Dowager Duchess?"

"It could—if there's any evidence."

"I haven't seen it, sir."

Not much point in pressing him further on that subject. "Possibly you came across something else: some indication of a partnership that was mooted with Mr. George Alexander Baird."

"The Squire?" He looked a sight more shocked at a connection with the Squire than with Carrie Montrose. "The gentleman has a sulfurous reputation, I hear."

"Not without foundation," I informed him.

"I can't recall seeing anything about this in the personal papers."

"Possibly not," I said, and added firmly, "I should like to look through them myself."

"I'm sure we can arrange it. They're in a writing desk in Fred's old home, Falmouth House."

"I know the place."

"Yes, sir. I'm afraid it's locked and shuttered at present. We were worried about souvenir hunters."

"Do you have the key?"

"His valet has it: a man by the name of Sarjent."

I remembered Sarjent, the tall young man who'd given evidence at the inquest and afterward made a good job of brushing my hat and overcoat.

"Where can I find him?"

"He should be over there this afternoon, sir. He attends to the horses."

He offered to drive me back to the Jockey Club, but I elected to walk the short distance. It was a crisp December morning, and I don't often have the opportunity to exercise on public roads, so I made the most of my opportunity, missing only my dog Peter for company.

After a reviving lunch I set off on foot again, this time in the direction of Falmouth House. In a matter of minutes, along the Ely Road I spotted the gabled front to my left about three quarters of a mile out of the town. Recalling my previous visit to the house and all that had happened since, I found it difficult to credit that only five weeks had passed.

I walked up the gravel drive toward the unhappy house with its drawn curtains, wondering if it would ever be occupied again. I wouldn't care to live in it myself.

I was making my way around the side and through the kitchen garden toward the stable when a shout of "Oi!" caused me to stop.

He was only a gardener who had emerged from around the wall, and I was prepared to overlook his want of manners, but for some unfathomable reason the sight of him rang alarm bells in my head. He wasn't particularly grotesque. His features meant nothing to me. I could only suppose that his physique and bearing—the disproportionate breadth of his shoulders on a squat body—reminded me of someone obnoxious from my past. I've met so many obnoxious people that this wasn't much help, except that few of them, if any, were gardeners.

He called out, "What do you want?" His voice was so uncouth that I was certain I'd have recognized it if I'd heard it before, but it made no connection in my memory.

I asked for Sarjent, and he pointed me to the building I had been approaching before he stopped me.

It was a four-stalled stable containing a couple of hunters, a carriage horse and Archer's gray hack. A voice hailed me from the saddle room and I found Sarjent the valet there, reclining in a chair balanced on its back legs, smoking a cigar, his long legs draped over the bench on which the harness was meant to be polished.

At my entrance, he practically fell off the chair. Unlike the gardener, he knew me at once, so I capitalized on his state of fright by remarking, "Is this how you serve your ex-master now?"

He dropped the cigar and crushed it with his heel, in the

same movement coming to attention like a guardsman. He had the height for the guards, too.

Sniffing the fumes, I inquired, "How can a man of your class afford to smoke Havanas? Did you filch it from the house?"

This stung him into a response. He protested forcibly, "I wouldn't touch Mr. Archer's things. I bought them myself from the tobacconist in the High Street. You can ask him if you want."

I'd been quite favorably impressed by him on our previous meeting. I said cuttingly, "If you wish to address me, kindly have the good manners to do it properly. I've spoken to Mr. Dawson, the executor, and now I'd like to see inside the house."

"Certainly, Your Majesty."

"*Sir* will suffice."

As we crossed the kitchen garden, I looked for the oaf who had first bellowed at me, but he hadn't remained in view. I asked Sarjent, "The gardener I saw, how long was he in Mr. Archer's employ?"

"Parker, sir? Five or six years at least."

"What will happen to him now?"

"He's buying a public house in Cambridge, sir."

"I hope he doesn't shout at the customers."

The experience of entering Archer's darkened house after the stories I'd heard unnerved me somewhat. It smelled musty. A grandfather clock stood silent in the hall. Sarjent showed me into the drawing room where the inquest had been held. He pulled aside the curtains and opened the writing desk for me.

"Would you prefer to be left alone, sir?"

In a haunted house? Perish the thought!

"No," I said as casually as I was able, "you may remain. Have you found a new position yet?"

"I'm proposing to take a year off, sir, to visit my brother in New Zealand."

"You have saved some money, then?"

"Yes, sir."

"Mr. Archer was generous to his staff?"

"I always found him so, sir."

I applied myself to the task of searching through the papers, which were in a fearful mess. I remarked on it to Sarjent, and he said, "They were tidy until yesterday, sir."

"What happened yesterday?"

"Mr. Baird went through them."

I gave him an appalled stare. "The Squire? What was *he* doing here?"

"Looking for something that belonged to him, as I understand it, sir."

"The devil he was!" said I. "Did he find it?"

"I've no idea, sir."

I was manifestly wasting my time if the Squire had got here first. I thrust the papers back into the box and closed it. "Can any Tom, Dick and Harry come in here and search through Archer's private papers?"

It was a rhetorical question, and he had the sense not to answer, though I thought I detected the beginning of a smile at the corners of his mouth.

Determined to put this visit to some advantage, I asked, "How well did you know Captain Buckfast?"

"He was often at the house, sir. He looked after Mr. Archer's correspondence and that."

"So he had occasion to speak to you?"

"He paid us our wages."

"I believe you were asked by the police to identify his body."

"Someone from the house had to do it, sir. The Captain had no family that we ever heard of. So Parker and I performed the melancholy duty."

"Parker the gardener?" I made an attempt to lighten the conversation, which looks callous written down but wasn't intended to be. "A bit of a change from pruning and weeding. Have you heard anything from the police since then?"

"Some detectives were here yesterday, sir."

"Have they interviewed Mr. Abington Baird?"

"This morning, I heard, sir. He was taken into town to answer questions from a titled gentleman who came down special from Scotland Yard."

I don't mind admitting that I took a certain malicious pleasure at the notion of Sir Charles Warren catching up with the Squire.

There was one more important matter to deal with. I remarked, "Doubtless you've heard of the stories that Archer's ghost has been seen."

Sarjent said, "I don't believe them, sir," but I'd observed a muscle at the side of his jaw quivering at the question. That's the sort of thing a detective of my caliber doesn't miss.

"You've noticed nothing here?" I pressed. "There was a report of lights being seen at night."

"I'm never here at night, sir."

"Is anybody?"

"The place is empty and locked up."

"Good thing too," I commented. "It's eerie enough by daylight. I declare it's colder inside than out. Like a tomb. I suppose you wouldn't know where Archer kept his whiskey bottle?"

Sarjent was off like a ticket-of-leaver.

The whiskey was simply a pretext on my part. The few moments I had alone in the room enabled me to cross to the window and unfasten the latch so that it would be possible to open it from outside. When Sarjent returned, I had resumed my position in front of the fireplace.

Warmer and wiser, I returned to the Jockey Club.

But whither next?

First, a hot bath.

Reader, I invite you to join me.

CHAPTER 20

Ah, the blissful moment of immersion when the goose pimples go under. I'm a firm believer in the bathtub's restorative powers. Indeed I'd go further. A leisurely soaking clarifies the mind. It may even result in an inspiration. One of the few things worth remembering from an education in the classics is the story of Archimedes. I've forgotten precisely what it was he discovered in his bath, but the truth of the experience reaches down the ages. You relax in the tub, letting the water creep exquisitely over your belly. Suddenly inspiration strikes.

Would you care to try it? I won't insist that you read this chapter in the bath (though it won't come amiss if you are careful to keep the book dry). I won't insist that you read it at all unless you are interested in unmasking the murderess, or murderer, or murderers (to give nothing away except precedence to the fair sex).

What follows is the process of reasoning that led me to cry "Eureka!" when I seized on the truth of the mystery. Kindly understand that I offer this from serious motives and I trust that you will accept it in the same spirit. I have no intention of treating three dreadful deaths as a parlor game. It pleases me to hope that the science of criminology will ultimately profit from my experiences as a detective.

Let us lie back, literally or figuratively, according to circumstance, and consider the essential facts of the case as I did that crucial afternoon in my bathroom in the Jockey Club.

Three people have died violently (I told myself). Fred Archer, by his own hand; Charlie Buckfast, beaten unconscious and drowned by two masked men; and Myrtle Bliss, shot through the head by an unknown intruder.

The deaths of Buckfast and Myrtle occurred after they agreed to help me investigate Archer's suicide. Therefore it appears that the key to the mystery is Archer's death. Find the reason for that, and I may well discover why the others were murdered.

Are we comfortable with that? Shall I run in a little more hot water?

The verdict of the inquest that Archer's mind was unhinged by typhoid must be extremely dubious. It rests on flimsy medical evidence. I'm no doctor, but I speak from personal experience of the disease, and I have the support of the *British Medical Journal* that "the fact that acute delirium with delusions, usually of a suicidal character, sometimes comes on during the early stage, will be new to many." Personally I doubt whether the poor fellow was suffering anything worse than a feverish chill induced by wearing insufficient clothes on the racecourse. There was no announcement that typhoid was suspected until he died, and on that day his temperature was normal, he was able to hold rational conversations and in the words of several witnesses, including his own doctor, he was better. It seems likely that the doctors settled on typhoid for the sake of Archer's family and his reputation. They wished to exclude the possibility that he killed himself coldly and sanely.

Let us take the more likely supposition that Archer's mind was sound, and his suicide deliberate. What could have provoked such a desperate act?

The most obvious cause of suicide is despair. Archer's

life had twice been blighted by death in the last three years: first, the baby son who lived only a few hours in January 1884; and then, in November of the same year, his wife, Helen Rose, after giving birth to their daughter. The death of a child in infancy is distressing but by no means unusual, as Alix and I can testify. The loss of a wife in childbirth is not uncommon, either, though harder to bear, I am sure. Everyone agrees that Archer was deeply affected. To occupy and distract him after the tragedy, he visited America with Charlie Buckfast for company. When he returned, his appetite for racing was undiminished. As a jockey, he was better than ever, winning four of the five classics in 1885. This year he added his fifth Derby and his sixth St. Leger. Two years passed since his wife's death, so the worst was behind him. He had a two-year-old daughter to live for, and the prospect of many more years as champion jockey.

No, I can't believe that he shot himself out of grief.

On the contrary, he was considering getting married again. Carrie Montrose admitted to me that she had "decided to marry him." He must have given it serious thought because he asked Captain Machell if marriage to a duchess would make him a duke. Fred was twenty-nine years of age; Carrie Montrose, sixty-eight. She is, however, a surpassingly energetic sixty-eight and extremely rich, the owner of the largest stud of thoroughbreds in the kingdom.

Better turn off the hot water now, because we've got to the Cambridgeshire, and that's sure to raise the temperature no end.

Archer rode Carrie's horse, St. Mirin, in the big race and let the world know that he expected to win. According to young Woodburn, a bribe was paid to stop the favorite and leave St. Mirin to take the palm. The plan was foiled when St. Mirin was beaten on the post by an outsider.

My inquiries revealed that the *de facto* owner of the winning horse was the Squire, and that's enough to make anyone smell a rat. The probability that he is implicated in these crimes is inescapable.

Let's consider the three fatalities. Two weeks after the Cambrigeshire, Archer shot himself after uttering those mysterious last words, "Are they coming?" This apparently meaningless question was cited at the inquest as evidence of delirium. I disagree. The patient was better. He was talking rationally to his friends during the morning. According to his sister, his manner was quite normal up to the moment of the fatal incident.

Those dying words cannot be ignored. They may well hold the key to the mystery.

While we're still with Archer I'd like to dispose of another canard. I've heard it suggested that his suicide was due in some obscure way to the constant efforts he was obliged to make to reduce his weight. Certainly he was below weight for a man his size, but so are countless other jockeys. As professional sportsmen they accept the obligations of the job. Lack of food may have made him irritable, but it is most unlikely to have unhinged his mind.

Where else shall I look for an explanation? Was it financial? He was spending heavily in the last months of his life, making large withdrawals of cash, allegedly for betting. He left a smaller estate than was generally anticipated, except by Charlie Buckfast, who managed Archer's business affairs and correctly estimated that the figure would be as low as £60,000. When all's said and done, sixty thou is more than most men earn in a lifetime. Where's the sense in shooting yourself if you've still got a fortune to your name?

The second fatality we must consider was the murder of Charlie Buckfast, which came perilously close to being a double murder.

You'll recall that I sent Charlie to Newmarket to keep watch on the Squire. When he got back, he told me that he'd overheard the Squire speak of pressing Archer into a partnership. Acting on this information, he'd broken into Bedford Lodge to look for evidence. The two men he surprised had followed him to London. Two men answering to the same description made their murderous attack on Charlie and myself outside Carrie Montrose's house. Charlie was beaten unconscious and thrown into the Thames and his body was later recovered and identified. I was lucky to escape with my life. As a result, my suspicions of the Squire amounted almost to certainty of his guilt.

And the Squire is linked with the third death, that of Myrtle Bliss.

Myrtle was the Squire's latest plaything. On the night of the Cambridgeshire, he went to London and celebrated his win with her. Buckfast and I subsequently visited the music hall where she was performing. I was still pursuing my investigations when the Squire interrupted us in Myrtle's room in Mile End Road. Later, she wrote offering to assist me. After Charlie's untimely death, I saw her a second time and accepted her offer for help. She went to Newmarket as the Squire's guest, and as my observer. I arranged to meet her in London the following week. To my horror, I discovered her dead in her dressing room.

Tragically bereft of my two assistants, I have since pursued my inquiries in isolation. Naturally, I concentrated on the Squire, because all the evidence suggests that the murders were carried out on his orders. Extract a confession from him, I decided, and he'll readily identify the thugs who carried out his bloody work.

Unfortunately, he outflanked me at Brantingham Thorpe. What is more, he produced Woodburn, and the whole case was turned on its head. I was at first reluctant to believe Woodburn's story that he had accepted a bribe to stop the favorite. If, as he admitted, he was open to bribery, what was to stop the Squire from bribing him to tell me a pack of lies?

Yet Woodburn's admission pleased nobody. The Squire had previously insisted to me that Archer was honest. He didn't expect to hear from Woodburn that a bribe of £200 had been paid to stop the favorite. And I didn't expect to hear that Charlie Buckfast had handed over the money.

Is it conceivable that Woodburn was telling the truth? His confession was like a wink from a bishop's wife: so unlikely that I'd be a fool to ignore it. What are the implications?

For one thing, it means that the Cambridgeshire result must have shocked Archer more than any of us realized, for he had acted dishonestly to guarantee a win for St. Mirin, only to be beaten by a 25-1 outsider. Why take such a risk at the peak of his fame? Was it because his gambling had taken such a grip that he put it before his reputation? Or was it because he heard wedding bells? Was it to please St. Mirin's owner, Carrie Montrose?

Another thing Woodburn's story means, if true, is that Charlie Buckfast held his information back when he and I talked of the Cambridgeshire, and this I find difficult to swallow. True, I had no cause to ask him about an illegal transaction, for I didn't remotely entertain such a notion. But in all our discussions, he never hinted at the possibility.

If Woodburn was lying about the bribery, I can't fathom why. He had nothing to gain by admitting it. He could have denied it, spoken the words that the Squire had wanted to hear and kept his own reputation clean.

Bertie, I think as I straighten my legs and push myself upright, there's something fundamentally wrong with all this. A false assumption somewhere.

And then I shout, "Eureka!"

Do I hear you shout the same, dear reader? Will you commit yourself? Have you reached your conclusion yet?

In that case, let us reach for a towel and climb out, for I almost hear poor Archer's dying words.

"Are they coming?"

CHAPTER 21

Before taking my bath, I had instructed my valet to put out a choice of evening wear that may surprise you: that is to say, the Norfolk jacket, knickerbockers and leggings I generally wear for shooting. It didn't surprise Massie, my valet. He is a dour Highlander who has looked after my wardrobe for so long that he is incapable of being surprised by anything. After high tea in my rooms, I left the Jockey Club soon after dark, having donned an overcoat and deer-stalker cap. I believe in dressing to suit the occasion, and this occasion was a ghost hunt.

I had resolved to lay the ghost of Frederick James Archer.

According to the tales being bandied about in the Jockey Club, Archer's restless spirit was quite liable to materialize at one's bedside, but inconveniently couldn't be commanded to make an appearance, so if you wanted a sighting, you were advised to go out on the heath by night and wait for the drumming of spectral hooves. I had a better plan. I was going to call on the late Mr. Archer at his home in Falmouth House, where I had last seen him lying in his coffin, and where the local policeman had reported seeing that "luminous glow."

In my overcoat pocket was the small silver revolver I

had acquired from Dougall, my gunsmith, a few years ago at a time when the anarchists were doing their damnedest to bag all the royalty in Europe. No, I don't need telling that a bullet would pass clean through a legitimate ghost; I still felt the need of a loaded revolver, and you may draw your own conclusions from that.

The crisp evening air was a splendid antidote to morbid thoughts. "Ghoulies and ghosties and long-leggedy beasties and things that go bump in the night" hold more terrors indoors, in the shadows cast across a sitting room by a log fire, than out in the lamplight of Newmarket High Street—or so I told myself. In front of the Rutland Arms at the eastern end the waits were giving a brassy rendering of "The First Noel." If anything was creeping up on me, it was the festive season. The shops were full of Christmas cards, and I hadn't addressed a single one as yet. Did you know that the custom of sending the wretched things was started by my dear papa of blessed memory? He still has the most insidious ways of troubling my conscience.

I put the lights of Newmarket behind me and marched intrepidly up the Ely road in the direction of Falmouth House. I'd chosen to foot it because I didn't want carriage wheels announcing my arrival. Ten minutes along that deserted road my confident mood was dented a little by a sign pointing the way to Phantom House. What on earth possesses people to choose such a grisly name for their place of abode? Almost immediately I disturbed a pheasant roosting in the hedgerow, and I don't know which of us gave the louder screech. Worse, I dropped my hip flask and spilled good whiskey on the road.

The house that Archer had built came into view across open ground on my left, the opposite side of the road from the Bedford Lodge estate. Moonlight gleamed on the white barge boards under the gables with an intensity that didn't help my state of mind. However, I drained the dregs of my flask and passed through the gate, whereupon my boots on the gravel sounded like the changing of the guard, so I stepped off the drive at once and took the silent route across the lawn tennis court toward the south side of the house.

If there was anything of a supernatural character inside, it wasn't declaring its presence yet. The curtains were drawn at all the windows, and no radiance showed from within, whether of spectral origin or by courtesy of the gas company.

Emboldened, I approached the drawing room window that I had earlier unfastened, took a grip on the lower frame and eased it up a fraction to satisfy myself that it would still move. It responded readily, so I pushed it up fully, put a leg over the sill and climbed in.

Without wishing to brag, I can state confidently that I have as much experience of creeping around country houses at night as any housebreaker you could name. I picked my way through that, room without disturbing a single ornament. At the door I turned the handle and retained my grip on it until I'd confirmed that the hall was unoccupied.

Where do you start looking for a ghost? Upstairs or down? In the attic or the cellar? I chose the latter.

I can usually be relied upon to remember where the champagne is kept. You never know when these God-given talents will be needed. The cellar door was located in the scullery. In the kitchen I was pleased to discover a candle on the dresser. A smoker is never without his matches, so I put a flame to the wick, opened the cellar door and started down the stone steps with the light flickering fitfully in the draft.

A few steps down, the flame died. I felt for another match and prepared to strike it. Then I paused.

Precisely why, I cannot explain, but I became convinced that I was not alone in the cellar. I can't say that I heard anything, or apprehended it with any of my faculties, unless one believes in a sixth sense.

Better remain in the dark, I thought. Why reveal myself to

whoever or whatever is down there? I returned the matches to my pocket, set down the candle and withdrew my revolver. At the same time I pressed my back against the wall and listened.

Nothing.

I waited perhaps half a minute before feeling my way down two more steps, staring into a prospect as black as the Earl of Hell's riding boots.

Then something moved in the depth of the cellar. A slight, but perceptible, sound.

I said at once, "Who's there?"

No answer. Possibly I'd heard a rat; possibly not. With the stealth of one who has tracked the leopard in his time, I crept down the remaining steps to the floor. I probed the darkness with my free hand, feeling for the nearest wine rack. Having located it, I edged along the length of the rack with my fingertips touching the bottles. I wanted to get right away from the place where I'd spoken those two words.

From what I could recall of my previous visit to the cellar with Charlie Buckfast, the racks were in seven parallel rows extending at least sixty feet from end to end. Moreover, there were barrels and other containers stacked along the sides.

I reached the last bottle of the row. My hand probed the darkness and made no contact, but my foot struck against something that scraped the stone floor inconveniently loudly.

I ducked low and held my breath.

The thing I had kicked had sounded remarkably like a piece of crockery, a plate or a saucer, an unlikely object to find on the floor of Archer's wine cellar, which had impressed me as tidy to the point of fussiness when I had last seen it. Even more unlikely was the loaf of bread that my free hand came to rest on: unmistakably a loaf, fresh, crusty and recently cut. The sliced end was soft and springy to the touch.

I had no opportunity to dwell on the significance of this discovery because something was happening at the far end of the cellar. From my position I could make out a faint radiance that threw the joists overhead into relief. It flickered and faded and then intensified.

Oh, Gemini! It was moving toward me between the racks!

If there was a moment when my nerve was put to the test, this was it. I crouched and waited, gripping my gun. I didn't have a clear view. I caught glimpses in the intervals between the bottles. The radiance became brighter, flitting along the row as if it had no substance.

The thing was almost upon me when I fired a shot.

It was meant for a warning shot, and it startled me if nothing else, for I succeeded in shattering several bottles of Archer's champagne, creating a regular fountain of froth and glass.

The light sheered away, revealing to me that its source was nothing more supernatural than a common bull's-eye lantern.

Whoever was holding the lantern took to his heels with a clatter of shoe leather that was most unsuggestive of the spirit world. I set off in pursuit, for he was clearly making for the door. I shouted to him to stop, but he raced up the steps, pausing only to hurl the lantern in my direction before he went through the door and slammed it. Then I heard the key being turned.

I groped my way up the steps and hurled myself at the door, succeeding in confirming how solidly the house had been constructed. My entire physique was numbed by the impact. There was a moment when the air was blue before I thought of using the revolver. I stood back and fired twice at the lock and then gave it an almighty kick that burst through the mortise.

Now where was my quarry? The moonlit interior of the kitchen was as bright as day to my eyes after the cellar. Ahead, the door to the hall swung back on its hinge, informing me that someone had just gone through. I gave chase, caught a glimpse of a running figure, fired a shot over his head and by a happy accident brought down a stag's stuffed head that was mounted over the front door. The fellow instinctively stopped in his tracks as it dropped toward him. Another yard and he certainly would have been brained.

The shock petrified him. He could barely raise his hands when I ordered him to turn around and face me. He was suddenly very pathetic. He was only a pint-sized fellow.

When he saw who I was, he cried out, "God Almighty!"

He was the Squire.

I can't begin to describe how enraged I became at the sight of him. My temper is notorious, but my feelings exceeded anything in my experience. I don't know how I prevented myself from emptying the chambers of my revolver into him.

He was terrified that I would do it. He blathered cravenly for an interval while I contrived to find words adequate to this moment. I had better explain the reason for my outrage, or you may have leapt to the wrong conclusion. The Squire wasn't the murderer. I'd stake Marlborough House to a tenement that he wasn't the murderer. He was a spoiler, a saboteur, a congenital nuisance who had given me a fright, wasted precious time and in all probability allowed the real killer to escape.

Finally I demanded, "What the devil are you doing here?"

"Trying to find out the truth about Archer . . . Your Royal Highness."

"How did you get in?"

"Through the front door. I made an impression of the key when I borrowed it yesterday." He started bleating out some sort of justification: "I'm being persecuted by the police, you know. Sir Charles Warren wants to pin everything on me. The murders, Archer's suicide. What sort of monster do they think I am?

I said, "That's a matter of supreme indifference to me, Baird."

He said, "For pity's sake, sir, I came in here to trap the murderer."

"That much I'm willing to believe," I commented. "There was someone in the cellar, and not many hours ago."

"You found the bread?"

I said with contempt for such a crude assumption, "I had already deduced it." I let him brood on that while I contrived a way of salvaging something from this debacle. If nothing else, I'm used to being in tight corners. And getting out of them. "Against all the evidence, I'm going to have to trust you, Baird," I resumed. "I know where to find the murderer."

"You do?" he whispered.

". . . but I require your help."

"I give it, sir. Unreservedly. Which way do we go?"

"I shall go there alone."

"Is that safe?"

"Far from it, but there are other things to attend to, and I shall have to rely on you."

"Rest assured, sir."

What lip! Imagine anyone resting assured upon the Squire's reliability. However, I had no other choice.

He asked, "Where is it? Where will you go?"

"To Sefton Lodge," I answered. "The residence of the Dowager Duchess of Montrose."

CHAPTER 22

So . . . Carrie Montrose.

My decision to visit the lady and confront her with the truth may strike certain clever readers of mine as obvious and overdue; if you are among them, I doff my deerstalker to you and caution you not to be too complacent. The story isn't over yet.

The plodding majority (God bless you) will want to know what the deuce I was up to. If so, kindly read on.

Sefton Lodge is on the Bury Road, a gray mansion in spacious grounds on the edge of the Heath, across the road from Bedford Lodge, the Squire's headquarters. Next door is a church built by the Duchess as a mausoleum to William Stirling-Crawfurd, her second husband. She buried Craw in Cannes in 1883, and two years later had him disinterred and shipped all the way back to Newmarket to be her neighbor, which was commended in the sporting press as evidence of almost unexampled devotion (the other example being the Blue Room at Windsor, where my late papa's clothes are still laid out each evening with hot water and a fresh towel, twenty-five years after he passed on). The church, by the way, is known as St. Agnes, that being Carrie's middle name.

To save precious time after sending the Squire on his way, I left the road at the first opportunity and hiked across the Severals. The moon was on the wane, yet full enough to throw a pale luminosity over the frosted gallops. It was treacherous going, and I was glad to reach the Bury Road. When Sefton Lodge loomed into view on the right, there were lights at all the windows.

My knock was answered by the same housemaid who had cried "Jerusalem!" when I came dripping from the Thames at Cheyne Walk. I wondered if her knowledge of the Scriptures extended to anything else, but the reception I got this time was disappointing, to say the least. She gave me a cursory glance, turned and called over her shoulder, "It's all right, ma'am—it isn't him."

I can take spontaneous outbursts of awe from servants, but I'm damned if I'll let them ignore me, so I stepped closer to the light, removed my hat and told her cuttingly, "It will oblige me if you now inform your mistress that it *is* him."

She said, "Holy jumping mother of Moses!" and fled.

Unwilling to freeze on the doorstep, I stepped across the threshold into a marble-tiled, oak-paneled hall with a crystal chandelier above me and a staircase ahead. Almost at once Carrie Montrose appeared at the head of the stairs in a black costume glittering with jet. I'd expected to surprise her, but I hadn't pictured it as a scene from a melodrama. She was uncommonly agitated, muttering and making extravagant gestures with her arms. She started swaying so dangerously that I expected her to fall. Instinctively, I moved to the foot of the stairs and stretched out my arms to her.

She clutched the banister rail and called down to me, "Bertie, any night but this!"

I told her with quiet authority, "Duchess, I am waiting to be received."

She shook her head. "It isn't convenient."

I was stung into a sharp rebuke: "Don't be idiotic. Nobody speaks to me like that. I command you to step downstairs at once, or I shall come up to you."

She rolled her eyes most oddly and said, "That's music to my ears, darling—but it cannot be tonight!"

I said with ice, "You misunderstand me. I have come here to question you."

"The answer must be no."

I put my foot on the first stair and she caught her breath in alarm and said, "Don't!"

"Will you come down, then?"

"Impossible."

"Duchess," I said with an effort to be reasonable against all the odds, "you have no choice."

After some hesitation she asked, "Will you give me a moment?"

"If it is brief."

"Kindly wait in the drawing room, then."

I stepped into a room of gracious proportions decorated in pink, with oval panels depicting hunting scenes. Spy cartoons of jockeys were ranged over the fireplace, Archer predictably at the center. To one side was the *Vanity Fair* cartoon by Lib of Newmarket in 1885, with all the elite of the Turf grouped around a figure, supposedly me, though a poor likeness in my opinion. Carrie was depicted to the right of me in her post boy hat and sealskin coat, and above us all was Archer, mounted, I think, on Ormonde.

While I was still identifying the figures, Carrie's voice, close behind me, boomed as if through a speaking trumpet, "I shall stand here in the open doorway."

I turned and asked, "Who else are you expecting?"

"Who else?" Without answering the question she put her hand to her hair and made a great performance of rearranging the russet curls that hung over her ears. The spectacle of Carrie Montrose flustered was novel in my experience.

She was like a wasp at a window. She said, "What are you suggesting?"

"Come now, you heard what the maid said when she opened the door to me."

"Ah." She clasped her hands to her throat. "Bertie, I'm in a terrible state."

"That is obvious, Duchess." I gave her a penetrating look. "Is this, by any chance, connected with Archer?"

She nodded about six times. "He's been seen, you know—seen by reliable witnesses. Lord Rossmore. And Machell. Machell is a pigheaded person with no manners at all, but he's nobody's fool."

I said with contempt, "You don't believe in ghosts, do you?"

In response, she started reciting in a voice of doom some doggerel that I remembered having seen in the *Newmarket Journal:*

> *"Across the heath, along the course,*
> *'Tis said that now on phantom horse,*
> *The greatest jockey of our days,*
> *Rides nightly in the moonlight's rays."*

I commented, leaving no doubt that I was unimpressed, "I always took you for a down-to-earth sort."

She said dramatically, "If Fred is manifesting himself in Newmarket, he'll come to me. Sooner or later he'll come. When you knocked, I thought it was he."

"He won't need to knock," I pointed out. "He can float through the wall."

She said, "Don't mock the dead, Bertie."

I told her reassuringly, "There's no need to be afraid of ghosts."

"I'm not afraid!" she piped on a note of high indignation. "I want to catch the blighter and ask him why he jilted me."

She was serious too. "Since you're so anxious to see him," I said with calculation, "why not go out on the heath? He may be riding there now."

Carrie shook her head. "I can't leave the house." She pointed her finger at the ceiling, at the same time twisting her features into a look of tortured significance.

Recalling Machell's story of the young man with a broken leg, I remarked in a carrying voice, "I was sorry to hear about the accident to your guest."

She said offhandedly, "Gilbert? He's in no pain. They gave him morphine and he'll sleep for hours."

The remark confirmed what I fully expected to hear: that the cause of her agitated manner had an altogether different origin. I said, "When we last met, I asked you about the Cambridgeshire; in particular, the rumor that Archer paid a bribe to Woodburn. You denied it emphatically."

She said in a distracted voice, "Did I?"

I continued, "Last weekend, I spoke to Woodburn. To my surprise, he confessed that the rumor is true. He said he was paid two hundred pounds by Captain Buckfast."

Carrie passed no comment.

I wasn't standing for evasions. I said, "Duchess, I'm bound to ask whether you are able to confirm this shameful transaction."

Her response to this topped everything, for she nodded emphatically and at the same time said, "Of course I can't confirm it. I knew nothing about a bribe."

"So you deny it?"

She answered, "Emphatically," and at the same time shook her head!

This was strongly reminiscent of that old parlor game called the Rule of Contrary, when the players are given instructions and expected to perform the very opposite action. However, Carrie and I were playing a more dangerous game, and the forfeit could even be death. I said in as steady a voice as I could sustain, "People have been murdered, Duchess. Are you, or are you not, prepared to help me?"

She nodded her head three times and said, "I'm unable to throw any light on the matter. Haven't I made that clear?"

I said, "If you won't speak to me, I'm afraid I shall have to ask the police to question you."

This, as I had expected, alarmed her even more, for she vigorously shook her head and flapped her hands to discourage me.

The reason for the dumb show was by now abundantly clear to me. I lifted my eyebrows inquiringly and pointed at the ceiling, and Carrie responded by enthusiastic nods of the head.

I glanced at the ormolu clock on the mantel. I was sensitive to her message that she wanted me to remain, whatever she'd said to the contrary. Of course I had no intention of leaving yet. I just hoped to God I could rely on the Squire to play his part in the plan.

I said, "Won't you come away from the door and be seated? I don't insist that you stand in my presence. Ladies look better on chairs."

Carrie gave me a piercing look and answered, "That will not be possible." Without pausing for breath she launched into a diatribe about the position of women in society and her lifelong fight to assert her independence. Apparently she wore plaid trousers for hunting in the 1840s, years before Mrs. Bloomer's fashion was taken up. What this had to do with the matter I had come to investigate was far from clear, but I was content to let her continue as long as possible.

What happened next will strain your credulity, I am certain. As I live and die, it is true. At some stage, I stopped listening to Carrie. The idea of ladies in trousers doesn't appeal to me in the least, and my ears had picked up another sound. I wasn't sure whether it was autosuggestion, and I strained to listen more acutely, because it seemed to me that I'd heard the drumming of hooves on turf, and it came from the direction of the heath.

Carrie heard it, too, for she interrupted the oration and asked, "What was that?"

"Something in the fire," I told her to avert the jitters.

She said, "It sounded like a rider to me."

"You're imagining it. Please go on. Did you say tartan trousers? How very diverting!"

Although she resumed, she might have saved her breath, for I didn't listen to another word of it. My heart had doubled its beat and I had to hold down my knees to stop them from shaking. Archer was out there galloping his phantom steed. He had gone by once, and now he was returning.

Carrie stopped. We could both hear the beating hooves now, and they were coming closer, closer. The rhythm slowed from a gallop, to a canter, to a trot.

We stared at each other.

A scream rang through the house. Carrie's maid came clattering from the servants' quarters.

"God save us, ma'am, it's him—the ghost! I know it's him!"

"Be quiet, girl!" Carrie rebuked her. "His Royal Highness will deal with it."

His Royal Highness was already behind the sofa. I had no quarrel with Archer; in fact, we'd got on tolerably well, but now that he was dead, I wasn't insisting on a reunion.

The maid whimpered, "He's in the garden."

To my considerable surprise, Carrie took this as encouragement. She gave the order, "Turn off the gas and draw back the curtains."

I was closest to the chandelier and I didn't mind plunging us into darkness if we were less visible from outside, but I wasn't so rash as to pull back the curtains. Carrie marched across the room and did that herself with one powerful sweep of the arm.

She said in a flat, trancelike voice, "There he is. He's wearing my colors and he's on St. Mirin."

Thinking she was mad, I ventured close enough to the window to check the truth of her statement, whereupon I learned what it means when the flesh creeps. Mine crept like an army of tortoises on the march.

Not thirty yards away on the frost-covered lawn, pale in the moonlight, was a mounted jockey I recognized as Archer. The style, the seat, was his alone, long legs almost straight in the stirrups, so that the feet were visible below the body of his mount; the rounded shoulders and the way of wearing the cap so that the peak jutted upward from his forehead.

Horse and rider were motionless and staring at the house.

"Lord be merciful unto me, a sinner," whispered the maid.

Carrie announced, "I'm going to him."

"No, ma'am!" the maid appealed to her. "Ma'am, it isn't safe!"

But Carrie was off like a lamplighter. For a heavyweight, she moved at exceptional speed across the room and into the hall. I heard the front door being opened before I started to follow. I wouldn't have put a foot outside the door alone, but when Carrie moved off to square her account with the ghost, I discovered that curiosity is the best antidote for a blue funk.

She hadn't even stopped to snatch up a coat. She charged across the hoarfrost in her evening gown, shouting, "Fred Archer, I want a word with you!"

Let's give credit to the horse; spectral it may have been, but the sight of the Dowager Duchess of Montrose bearing down on it must have been terrifying. It stood its ground until she was within a dozen yards, and then it reared slightly, whinnied and trotted away toward an evergreen plantation at the edge of the lawn, its rider allowing the retreat, yet turning his head to see if he was being pursued, which he was.

"Fred, I want to know why!" shouted Carrie.

As far as I was concerned, she was speaking for both of us. I padded after them, all fear dispersed—that is, until they turned behind the evergreens and I heard a scream from Carrie that rooted me in my tracks.

It was a full-bellowed shriek that stopped halfway through, choked off as if she had fainted.

Then I heard a voice say, "Someone pick the lady up, for heaven's sake."

There were people behind the holly bush.

I assumed they were people and not ghosts. I was less certain when a hat bobbed above the level of the foliage: a cocked hat of the sort worn by the late Duke of Wellington. For a petrifying instant I thought the Iron Duke had materialized to add his support to the haunting, doubtless to register a complaint about his damned statue. Then I saw the glint of a monocle, and I remembered Sir Charles Warren.

"You're perfectly safe now, Your Royal Highness," the commissioner told me as I stepped around the holly.

I stared at the spectacle behind the evergreen plantation. Three policemen in shirts and braces were on their knees attempting to revive Carrie Montrose, who was wrapped in their jackets. Another dozen or more with truncheons drawn were watching the house. And the "ghost" of Archer had dismounted and was tying the horse to a tree. He it was who had caused the Duchess to swoon, for he was not Fred Archer, but her archenemy, the Squire.

"You!" I said.

The Squire gave an insufferable smirk. "Did I take you in as well, sir? Not a bad likeness was it? I learned my riding from Fred and my build is similar, so I can give a fair imitation. The horse is a ringer for St. Mirin too."

I snorted my contempt and asked what on earth had justified such a pantomime. It certainly wasn't in my instructions.

He explained, "I alerted the police and brought them

here as you ordered, sir. We surrounded the house and waited for a signal from you, but none came."

I said frigidly, "I didn't say I'd give one."

The Squire went on as if he were speaking for Sir Charles Warren and all the police, "As time went on, we became increasingly concerned for your safety. We couldn't send in the police while you were at risk, so we decided to draw you and the Duchess out of the house by some means. Nothing less than Archer's ghost would bring out the Duchess, so I devised this pantomime, as you describe it, and Sir Charles fell in with it. Saved both your lives, probably."

"The devil you did," said I. "We'll probably die of pneumonia."

At this juncture, Warren hissed in my ear, "Do you mind bending down, sir?"

"What?" I was starting to doubt my sanity, or theirs.

"We're about to storm the house," Warren explained.

"To arrest the murderer," said the Squire with damnable smugness, as if some of the credit belonged to him.

Willy-nilly, I found myself cooperating with Warren's request, sinking out of sight like a broadsided galleon.

"How many are in the house now to your knowledge, sir?" Warren inquired.

"To my knowledge? Three. The maid and a young man whose name is Gilbert. He has a broken leg and is sedated."

"And the third?"

"The murderer. I didn't see him. He was upstairs, I gathered from the Duchess."

There was a moan from Carrie. She was regaining consciousness. She said, "I'm innocent. He forced his way in and threatened to murder Gilbert. He was holding a gun at Gilbert's head."

"He still is, Your Grace," said Warren, causing the Duchess to relapse into unconsciousness.

Warren took out a whistle and blew it, and everyone

except Carrie stood up and charged across the lawn toward the house. Policemen sprang up from behind walls and hedges all over the garden. A couple of shots were fired. I couldn't tell where they came from. I was keeping my head down.

I found myself in a crowd of policemen waiting by a window, which was presently pushed open by the Squire. "It's all right," he assured us. "He's still upstairs."

Fifteen or more of us clambered over the sill into the drawing room. Warren was already there by the door, directing his men. "Those with guns, step forward," he ordered, and several did.

Someone said to me, "You've got a shooter." He was right. I'd withdrawn it from my pocket as we raced toward the house.

"He's the Prince of Wales, mate," said someone else.

"He can pull a trigger," said the first.

His simple logic galvanized me. This was my moment, and I'd almost allowed it to go by default. The police would not have been here unless I had summoned them. My investigation was about to be brought to a triumphant conclusion, and by Jove I would take charge of it myself.

I ordered Warren to stand aside. He gaped, swallowed and obeyed.

I wish some painter of heroic subjects had been there to record the scene. Standing squarely at the head of the posse, I pointed my gun up the stairs. In a strong, clear voice I addressed my adversary, the killer I had cornered at last. "This is the Prince of Wales. I have twenty armed men down here. Put down your weapon and come downstairs with your arms raised."

We all watched the top of the stairs.

"Be sensible, man," Warren called up. He couldn't bear to keep his mouth shut and leave it to me.

A movement was audible upstairs, a chair being scraped

back and something thudding on the floor. Footsteps crossed the landing.

"Keep the arms high," I ordered.

A figure appeared in view. One arm was held high. The other was limp at his side. If you thought all the ghosts in Newmarket had been laid to rest, you were mistaken.

We were looking at Charlie Buckfast.

CHAPTER 23

An awesome silence prevailed as Buckfast descended the stairs without a word and was handcuffed.

I heard the Squire whisper, "He should be dead." A moment later he added with more voice, "Dammit, his body was pulled out of the Thames. It was dressed in his clothes. It was identified."

"By his accomplices," I pointed out, making it plain that I thought any fool would have deduced as much. "Messrs. Sarjent and Parker, the valet and gardener at Falmouth House. I suggest you send someone to arrest them, Sir Charles."

"Sarjent and Parker—at once, sir!" responded the commissioner. He rounded on the luckless senior policeman in Newmarket and said, "Inspector, haven't you attended to this already?"

"Very suspicious characters," commented the Squire, transparently trying to recoup some respect. "Didn't care for them at all."

Of course he impressed no one.

"I suggest you take your prisoner away and ask him some pertinent questions," I advised Sir Charles. Everyone except me seemed incapable of thought or action; bemused, I suppose, by the sensational turn of events. Even Buckfast was staring at me as if I had turned into the genie of the lamp.

Sir Charles said, "Emphatically, Your Royal Highness." Then he cleared his throat, turned extremely pink and asked me in a subdued voice, "Would you care to accompany us to the station, sir?"

I gave him the Saxe-Coburg stare. "That wouldn't be seemly, Commissioner."

"I merely suggested it for selfish reasons: for the benefit of your indispensable advice, sir," he said, groveling.

The wretched fellow hadn't the faintest idea what to say to Buckfast.

I said, "Captain Buckfast, are you ready to do the honorable thing?"

"And confess?" said Buckfast. He drew back his shoulders in what amounted—unintentionally, I have no doubt—to a mockery of the regiment he had once served with distinction. "Yes, sir. I'll make a clean breast of it."

"To the commissioner?"

"Certainly."

I turned to Sir Charles Warren. "That being the case, Commissioner, I shall return to the Jockey Club for supper. If I feel so inclined, I may call at the police station at a later hour."

About 1 A.M., restored to my equable self by good Scotch broth, ptarmigan pie, broad beans and bacon, plum pudding and champagne, I was admitted to the interview room, a narrow, functional chamber with barred windows, whitewashed walls and a stone floor. I sat opposite the murderer Buckfast, with only a desk between us and one puny constable on duty.

The murderer Buckfast. It has a strange ring, hasn't it? The credit for his arrest and detention was mine alone, but I had mixed feelings about meeting him. Believe me, I could think of more agreeable ways of passing the small hours of the night. I knew most of what he was likely to tell me, anyway.

However, there were a few minor points to be cleared up, and as you know by now, I'm a stickler for detail.

First I took a cool look at the fellow. Not much over a month ago, I'd appointed him as my assistant. He looked little different from the upright ex-officer, discreet, dependable, who had made such a suitable impression then. The only noticeable difference was the absence of that splendid cavalry officer's mustache, and I couldn't blame him for that.

I refrained from greeting him. The vicious murder of Myrtle was strong in my thoughts.

"I haven't read your statement. I gather that you made a full confession."

He declined to look me in the eye, but he still observed the correct mode of address. "Yes, sir."

"I'm more interested in your motives than what you did. What possessed you?"

A sigh, possibly from remorse, possibly from sheer exhaustion. "I got into deep water, sir."

I was about to remark that he wasn't the only one when it became obvious that he was speaking metaphorically.

"I took advantage of my friendship with Archer. He invited me to manage his business affairs because he was so busy riding and traveling, and it rapidly became obvious to me that he was illiterate and incapable of keeping track of what I was doing. I appropriated his money and put it to my own use."

I said with distaste, "Embezzlement."

"Of monumental proportions, sir. I milked his funds systematically."

"That was deplorable."

"When did you suspect me, sir?"

"Well, it was obvious something decidedly fishy must have been happening when the will was published," I told him. "He should have been worth more than sixty thou."

"He was, to me," Buckfast remarked as coolly as if he

were discussing a dabble in the stock market. I was seeing a fresh side of his character.

"Unfortunately for you," I remarked, "someone else developed an interest in him. A matrimonial interest."

"The Duchess of Montrose."

"The indefatigable Duchess."

He grimaced. "And no oil painting, either. You'd think it was a grotesque mismatch. I did, at any rate, but I underestimated the Duchess. Fred was a lonely man after the death of his wife. He lost interest in everything except racing, and of course, he kept meeting Carrie Montrose on the Limekilns and at the racecourse. He raced her horses, and she paid him more generously than any other owner. She flattered him by taking his advice. She was about the only woman he saw except his sister-in-law. One day he told me that Carrie had offered to marry him. He asked me what I thought. I took it as a jest before I realized that he actually wanted my opinion."

"Which placed you in a dilemma."

"Right, sir. If he married the Duchess, questions were going to be asked about his finances. She'd soon be going through the books asking for explanations. My first impulse was to do everything in my power to dissuade Fred. Yet when I weighed it up, it was as sure as fate that sooner or later the Duchess would claim the victory. Her force of personality far outweighed Archer's. So I decided on a different approach. I would throw in my lot with the Duchess."

"Press her claim as Archer's bride," I said, making apparent my disgust.

He nodded. "I would act, in effect, as a marriage broker."

"For financial gain."

"More for self-protection, sir. A chance to put something back in the kitty. I told Carrie that it was Archer's greatest ambition to win the Cambridgeshire. If she could provide him with a winning mount, I reckoned he would agree to marry her. I remember her eyes lit up like a sixteen-year-old with a Valentine. She told me that her colt, St. Mirin, stood a capital chance of winning if Archer was up. Actually I knew that Carlton had the beating of it, but I had a plan, a way of getting out of the fearful mess I was in, and pleasing Archer and the Duchess. I would place a huge bet on St. Mirin—"

"And pay Woodburn a bribe to stop Carlton," I said.

"You found out the truth about that?" said Buckfast with a frown.

"In pursuit of my inquiries," I murmured casually. Perhaps I flatter myself, but I think he was impressed.

He continued, "If Woodburn held off, I was certain that St. Mirin would win, and I would recoup enough to patch up the accounts before I handed them over to the Duchess."

"You meant to quit?"

"Oh, yes, sir. I couldn't abide Carrie Montrose. However, I didn't show it. I talked to her like a younger brother and encouraged her to draw up a draft settlement of marriage. I promised to make sure that Archer rode St. Mirin and sealed the union with his first win in the Cambridgeshire."

"You didn't tell the Duchess about bribing Woodburn?"

"Lord, no, sir. She believed her colt could win fairly and squarely."

"What did you tell Archer?"

"Nothing—except that I had a tip that Carlton was coughing and might be forced to pull out. It worked famously up to a point."

I permitted myself a faint smile. "The point when The Sailor Prince got his nose in front."

"Yes, sir. A disaster for us all."

"Except the Squire."

"Blast him."

Coming from a man who had admitted to murder, the expletive sounded peculiarly tame.

Buckfast resumed, "I was in desperate trouble after the

race. Everything fell about my ears. I'd lost another thousand of Archer's money. The Duchess went berserk and sold St. Mirin. She blamed everyone but Archer. She was still resolved to marry him and expected me to work the miracle. Fred was cut up at losing the race. He'd starved himself to make the weight, and he caught a chill soon after. Days passed before I could talk to him on the matter. After that weekend of fever, he rallied."

"Ah, so we come to the day he shot himself?"

"Yes, sir. That's on my conscience, too, though I never intended it, believe me."

"You spoke to him alone that morning?"

"Yes."

"He was able to hold a conversation?"

"Perfectly able. He was fully in control."

"What did you tell him?"

"Everything. I admitted that I'd paid the bribe and told Woodburn it was on Archer's orders. I confessed that I'd embezzled the accounts for over two years and that his funds were dreadfully depleted. I let him know that the Duchess expected to marry him. That, I suggested, would be his salvation."

"What a salvation! How did he take it?"

"He was shocked, naturally."

"Ready to horsewhip you, I should think."

Buckfast cleared his throat in a way that signaled another confession. "Actually I didn't give him much of an opportunity. I told him he had no choice but to marry the Duchess."

"Why?"

"Because if he refused, I would inform the stewards that I'd paid a bribe to Woodburn on his orders. It wouldn't be true, but Woodburn believed it and I was damned sure I could persuade the Duchess to throw in her weight if she knew the stakes. Archer was no fool. He understood the effect of that. He'd be warned off the Turf. His career, his reason for living, would be finished. Even if he refuted the charges, some of the mud would stick. His reputation for absolute integrity would be at an end."

"Charlie," I said. "You killed him."

"He had a choice," Buckfast responded impassively. "He could have married the Duchess and agreed to part with my services and no questions asked. In fact, he did agree. I said I would go to the Duchess and tell her the good news. In a short while, we'd return with a marriage settlement for him to sign."

"He consented to this? You're certain?"

"Absolutely. I went straight off to inform the Duchess."

"Which accounts for his enigmatic last words, 'Are they coming?'" I said. "You and Carrie Montrose. *'Are they coming?'* He meant you two."

Buckfast continued with his story, uninterested in my observation. "They said at the inquest that Fred was out of his mind when he shot himself. Quite wrong. It was deliberate. I miscalculated. He wasn't willing to marry the Duchess."

Said without a trace of remorse or compassion! Listening to Buckfast, I understood what sets a murderer apart from other men. It's the logic that recognizes no human feelings.

I said, "You must have been alarmed when you learned that I wished to attend the inquest."

He thought for a moment. "I wasn't worried until you confided to me that you disbelieved the verdict."

A telling remark. I pricked up when he made it. "Ah. With justification, eh?"

"Yes, sir."

"Especially when I told you I proposed to investigate. Not only that, but I wanted you as my assistant! Inconvenient, to say the least."

He had the infernal cheek to comment, "The inconvenience was minor, sir. On the whole, I regarded it as an advantage. I was enabled to lay a false trail. Fortunately for me, you suspected the Squire almost from the beginning, and I encouraged it. I didn't want you going to Woodburn or Carrie Montrose. So I was delighted to be asked to spy on the Squire."

I didn't allow him to rile me. I said evenly, "And did you? Did you carry out my orders?"

"Of course not. I went to Newmarket, but I didn't go near the Squire or Bedford Lodge. I spent the time planning my disappearance."

"Are you telling me that the things you reported the Squire as saying about a partnership with Archer were inventions of yours?"

"Largely, sir. The Squire did once make such a suggestion, but Fred wouldn't hear of it. That was two years ago."

"Good Lord. And the incident at Bedford Lodge—when you broke in and found the two men together?"

"Pure imagination. It fitted in with my plan."

"The plan to make it appear to the world that you were murdered?"

"Yes."

He paused, I suppose, to let me take in the significance of what he had told me. I must have looked slightly dazed. I felt like a fistfighter caught by a low punch.

Figuratively speaking, I stepped out to the scratch again and said, "You'd better tell me what really happened that night on the Embankment."

"First," he said, "I'd like to tell you why it was necessary. You told me before I went to Newmarket that you planned to visit the Duchess. *'Cherchez la femme,'* you said."

"I remember."

"That was the worst thing you could have told me. If you and Carrie got together, she was certain to tell you how she nearly married Archer, and soon enough you'd hear about my part in promoting it."

"As it happens, I didn't. I suppose the lady was too proud to give you any credit."

"I wasn't to know that," he said wistfully. "I had to assume the worst, and the worst was that you'd carry on probing until you got to the truth about the embezzlement. It carries a sentence of fourteen years' penal servitude. I couldn't think of any way to stop you."

"I'm very persistent, true."

"So I decided to do a flit. The obvious thing. When I started to plan it, I saw that my best chance was to give the impression that I was dead. Dead, I thought? Better still to be murdered."

"Why? I don't follow the reasoning."

"I pictured it from your point of view, sir. A murder would pull you up with a jerk. Murder isn't the sort of thing the Heir Apparent ought to get involved in. It's a matter for the police. I was confident that you'd drop the inquiry like a hot potato."

"You deceived yourself, then."

"Obviously."

"So you laid your plans in Newmarket?"

"Yes. I needed two men to pose as the Squire's henchmen."

"Sarjent and Parker. They're under arrest. They were picked up this evening in Exning."

Buckfast showed no concern whatsoever. "I knew them well from my two years at Falmouth House. It was my job to hand out the wages, and I knew how much the money meant to those two. They would do anything for more of the ready. Archer's death had put them out of work. As soon as the estate was wound up, they would be finished. I offered them fifty sovereigns apiece to carry out a mock attack."

"They were the brutes who assaulted us on the Embankment."

I had deduced this much earlier, you will appreciate,

dear reader. Perhaps you recall my remarking upon the unpleasant feeling I'd had on seeing the gardener's stocky, apelike appearance. Sarjent, too, with his height, matched the physique of the masked man on the Embankment. I gestured to Buckfast to continue.

"I also offered them another fifty to identify the body."

"But whose body?"

"Some unfortunate who was fished from the Thames the same week. Three or four are taken from the river every day, usually by watermen who are paid a shilling by the police to deliver them to Wapping. I went down to Blackfriars and made inquiries in one of the waterside pubs and offered a pound for a clean-shaven male corpse. Next day I had the choice of four. I picked the one nearest to my age and build, took him upriver a mile or so in a small boat, stripped him and dressed him in my clothes and then returned him to the water. A drowned man doesn't much resemble the living version after several days' immersion. But just to be certain, when he was found, and inquiries were made in Newmarket, Sarjent and Parker came forward to identify the body."

"Why wasn't one of your relatives asked to do it?"

"I have no close relatives. The Archer family was too distressed about Fred to perform such a morbid duty, so Sarjent's offer was gratefully taken up."

"What about your arm—your war wound?"

"It wasn't mentioned. Thames Division knew nothing about me. They regarded the clothes and my wallet and other possessions as proof positive. The identification was a mere formality."

Personally, I'd found the description of this gruesome procedure quite nauseating, but Buckfast had related it as calmly as if it were a stroll up the Strand.

I asked, "What happened after you were thrown into the river? You *were* thrown in, weren't you?"

"Yes, sir. It was quite shallow there."

"Shallow?"

"Low tide. Shallow enough for me to wade to the landing platform."

"Good Lord. I thought it was deeper than that."

He gave an unsympathetic shrug. "I watched you thrashing about."

"Where were you?"

"In the water at the far end of the landing platform. I waited until you were out and hammering on the Duchess's door and then I clambered out and rejoined my confederates." He paused. "That should have been the end of Charlie Buckfast."

I waited, allowing him to tell me the rest in his own way.

He said in a more somber voice, "Sir, I regret killing Myrtle. I've already confessed, and I deserve to hang for it. Sir Charles Warren was somewhat taken aback when I brought the matter up. He must have heard that a girl had been shot in a music hall, but I'm sure he had no suspicion that her death was linked with what happened here. I expect you want to know how I could bring myself to commit such a ghastly crime." Buckfast sighed, and it sounded like a genuine expression of self-disgust. "I believed at the time that Myrtle was certain to ruin my plan. Do you remember showing me the letter she wrote you?"

I had an unpleasant intimation that he was trying to implicate me, so I didn't respond.

He said as if to mollify me, "I'm not trying to shift the blame, sir. It was Myrtle's misfortune that you happened to show me her letter. You told me you intended to accept her offer. You still wanted proof of the Squire's dealings with Archer. When I heard that, I was devastated. Not only would she discover that my story of a partnership was a fabrication, but she'd learn that I hadn't been anywhere near the Squire all that week, and I certainly didn't break into Bedford Lodge." He looked away, as if unable to bear my reproach. "That weekend passed slowly for me. My plan had worked like clockwork, and yet Myrtle was capable of ruining it. If you learned that I'd deceived you, I was afraid that you'd go on until you stumbled on the truth."

"Stumbled?" I said, outraged, but he wasn't listening.

He said, "I kept thinking of fourteen years for embezzlement, plus God knows how many more they would give me for conspiracy to attack the Prince of Wales. On Monday evening I took the underground railway to Aldgate and walked through the East End to the music hall where Myrtle was appearing. I found her dressing room. I silenced her with my service revolver."

I shivered. The room felt several degrees colder.

Presently I asked him, "Why did you return to Newmarket?"

"To make my escape. Sarjent knows one of the Yarmouth fishing skippers who was prepared to take me aboard on his next trip and put in at one of the Dutch ports. I decided to lay up meanwhile in the cellar at Falmouth House. Sarjent had the key, you see. The house was empty and locked, and I was undisturbed until yesterday, when the Squire insisted on coming in and nosing about. He came down to the cellar and I had to make a rapid exit. He's very astute, isn't he? I gather that he put two and two together and knew that I was still alive. This happened in broad daylight. Where could I go?"

I ignored his remarks about the Squire, which were obviously said out of malice toward me. Buckfast's manner was insufferable, even allowing that he was a vicious murderer. Answering his question in a tone that left him in no doubt of my contempt, I said, "You went to Sefton Lodge."

"Yes," he said. "I had nowhere to hide, and the Duchess owed me a favor. I'd gone to no end of trouble to try to get Archer hitched to her." The ghost of a smile appeared at the edges of his mouth. "She had a proper fright when she saw me. Hysterics. When you came to the house, I was upstairs holding my gun to the head of her latest paramour. I didn't know that the Squire was outside with the police."

The Squire again. I said curtly, "The Squire acted on my instructions."

He gave me an insolent look that I shall long remember and said, "You needn't worry, sir. If you're thinking about the trial, your reputation is safe with me."

I was amazed at his effrontery. What did he imagine—that an English judge would permit my name to be bandied about in a murder trial?

I said, "I don't require any favors from you, Buckfast. They won't be necessary."

"True, sir."

How true, I failed to appreciate at the time, or after, until I heard the news a few days later that he was dead. He had managed to use his shirt to hang himself in his cell at Cambridge Jail. To the last, he was unpredictable.

And now, my loyal companion through these pages, it is time to conclude my humble narrative and place it under lock and key. What did you think of my investigation? I daresay I was guilty of blunders here and there, and you may be tempted to conclude that there are better detectives than I. Far be it from me to try to convince you otherwise. I shan't fish for compliments. I simply thank you, patient reader, for persisting to the end, as I did, in the pursuit of truth and justice. Thanks entirely to my efforts, a murderer and his confederates were apprehended. Stout work, Bertie! There: I said it for you.

A Note from the Editor

The reader will have drawn his own conclusion about the authenticity of this narrative. It must be extremely doubtful whether "Bertie," either as Prince of Wales or King Edward VII, ever found the time or inclination to write a book. He is known to have left instructions that after his death his personal papers and correspondence should be burned, and Sir Francis Knollys, loyal to the last, carried out the task. Whether a document in a "secure metal box" was ever entrusted to the Public Record Office by the King or Knollys has not been established. The manuscript published here for the first time must therefore be treated with circumspection.

Many of the personalities who peopled these pages are, however, known to have existed, and the reader may be interested to know what became of them subsequently.

Caroline Agnes Graham, Duchess of Montrose, married for the third time in 1888, when she was seventy. Her husband, Marcus Henry Milner, was twenty-four. Her horses were run in Milner's name until 1893, when there appears to have been a rift. She died the following year, at age seventy-six.

The Honorable Christopher Sykes went steadily through his fortune entertaining the Prince. One day his sister-in-law

Jessica went to Marlborough House and informed HRH that the Great Xtopher was on the point of bankruptcy. She persuaded the Prince to clear the most pressing debts. When Sykes died in 1898, Bertie attended the funeral at Brantingham Thorpe. Poor Sykes was a source of mirth even at his funeral when, after many attempts and much stifled amusement behind handkerchiefs, it was admitted that his coffin was too long to fit the grave.

George Alexander Baird, the Squire, led life to the full for another seven years before dying in New Orleans at the age of thirty-one, of a combination of malaria, pneumonia and dissipation. He had many successes as a rider and as an owner. In 1887, he infuriated the Turf establishment by declining to lead in his horse, Merry Hampton, after it won the Derby. In 1888, he took Charlie Mitchell to France to fight John L. Sullivan for the heavyweight crown for the second time. After thirty-nine rounds, it was declared a draw.

Sir Charles Warren, Commissioner of the Metropolitan Police, doggedly held office for another two years, despite mounting concern at his incompetence. In 1887, he massed four thousand police and six hundred guardsmen with loaded muskets and bayonets to deal with a demonstration by the unemployed in Trafalgar Square on what became known as Bloody Sunday. He finally resigned in 1888, after mismanaging the Jack the Ripper investigation.

Sir Joseph Edgar Boehm, the sculptor, continued to enjoy the patronage of Queen Victoria and her family. He was created a Baronet in 1889. He died in disputed circumstances the following year. According to the gossip of the celebrated courtesan Catherine Walters (known as Skittles), noted in the diary of Wilfrid Scawen Blunt, Boehm died of a hemorrhage while in the arms of the Princess Louise. The public was informed that death had occurred while he was moving a heavy statue. He was honored with interment in Westminster Abbey.

Frederick James Archer's unhappy spirit is still said to haunt Newmarket. Occasionally when a horse inexplicably swerves or stumbles on the racecourse, Archer's ghost is held responsible by some.

Cocky, a white cockatoo, was kept by Queen Alexandra for many years and outlived everyone mentioned in these pages. After the Queen's death in 1925, Cocky is believed to have been presented to the London Zoo, where it presided over the parrot house until the mid-1930s, with a notice on its perch stating that it was dangerous. Occasionally when Cocky's keeper fed it a large grape, it would mutter, "God bless the Prince of Wales."

Continue reading for a preview of

Bertie and the Seven Bodies

CHAPTER 1

Splendid! You have opened my book. You are curious about the mystery of the seven bodies and my part in it. If I am mistaken, forgive me. I bid you good day. Kindly close the book and turn to some memoirs of a less sensational character. I recommend *Leaves from the Journal of Our Life in the Highlands*, by my dear mother, Her Majesty, Queen Victoria.

If I am correct in my deduction, bravo! Let us plunge together into the plot. It began innocently enough one spring morning in the year 1890.

"So! You have resolved to go back to nature, Alix," I announced with the air of one who has uncovered an intimate secret.

My pretty wife, the Princess of Wales, shot me a startled look. She was seated at the window in her sitting room at Sandringham. "What did you say, Bertie?"

"You are going back to nature. I perceive that you have finally decided to shed your steel appendage."

She frowned. "Is this a riddle?"

"I mean your bustle, of course."

"Bertie!"

"You can't deny it. This afternoon you wrote to your dressmaker informing her that you propose to wear the new narrow skirts in future."

She was openmouthed with amazement.

Not without satisfaction, I said, "If you want to know how I made this discovery, I deduced it."

"Deduced it?"

"I observed what I saw before me and applied the scientific principles of . . . deduction." I paused, to let the word linger in the air for a moment. Then I directed my gaze across the room. "Upon your writing desk is a candle. The wick is blackened, but the candle is not much used. On a bright afternoon such as this, why should anyone light a candle except to melt sealing wax? I deduce that you wrote a letter. How simple when it is explained!"

Alix said, "There is more to explain than that."

"Quite so. On the floor to your left is an open copy of yesterday's *Illustrated London News* from which you have removed a page. The torn edge is clearly visible and so are the words '*Opposite: the new straight skirt as designed by Monsieur Worth.*' So the chain of reasoning is complete. You saw the picture of the latest fashion from Paris and resolved forthwith to tear it from the magazine and send it to your dressmaker."

She rocked with laughter. "Oh, Bertie!"

"Do my methods amuse you?"

"You couldn't be more mistaken. I haven't the slightest desire to wear straight skirts. They make me look like a beanpole. And I haven't written a single letter all day. I was sewing. At some stage I dropped my thimble. I couldn't see it anywhere on the floor so I lit the candle to look under the writing desk. Some candle grease unfortunately dripped onto the carpet, so I ripped a sheet from the magazine to clean it up before it hardened."

"Alexandra, are you poking fun at me?"

"If you don't believe me, look in the wastepaper basket."

I looked, saw that she was right and emitted a bellow of annoyance.

Alix contemplated her fingernails. "Bertie dear, do you think it is wise to persist in this notion that you can be a detective?

The question nettled me, I admit. I responded sharply, "Dammit, one small oversight and I'm branded as a failure. If I'd looked in the wretched wastepaper basket my chain of reasoning would have been different, altogether different. I'm forever being told to find intelligent pursuits and when I do I can't rely on my own wife for encouragement." I turned on my heel and marched out.

ALIX KNOWS THAT MY TEMPER is short and so is its duration. By the next post I received an invitation that altogether restored my humor. A grand *battue* at Desborough in October. Desborough—what a prospect! After Sandringham and Holkham, there's no better shooting in the kingdom. Nine hundred acres in Buckinghamshire. Moreover Desborough Hall is one of the great houses of England, with Tudor banqueting hall, ballroom, gun room, chapel and ninety-odd bedrooms.

"I can't resist it," I told Alix over dinner. "I shall accept."

"Who does the invitation come from?" she enquired.

"Lady Amelia Drummond."

She shifted her head to see around the floral arrangement. "An invitation to shoot from a lady?"

"The widow of Freddie Drummond. Haven't you met her?" I heaved a long sigh to signal sympathy for our prospective hostess. "Perhaps you don't recall? She's easily forgotten, poor soul, rather plain in looks, but making superhuman efforts to keep Desborough on the social map. One feels obliged to show support."

"When did Lord Drummond pass away?"

"Last winter, in tragic circumstances. He was gored by a bull."

"How horrid!"

"Yes, he was a frightful mess, they said. He lingered for six weeks, covered in bandages. Then one morning he sat up, uttered something rather vulgar and breathed his last."

"I didn't catch that. What did he mutter?" Sometimes dear Alix trades on her deafness.

"I think it was 'Oh, bother.'"

"I don't call *that* vulgar. I've heard far worse from Cocky." Cocky is Alix's pet cockatoo. She gave me a searching look and then took a spoonful of Scotch broth. In a few moments she casually enquired, "About what age would Lady Drummond be, Bertie?"

I hedged. "You could look her up in Debrett. I'm not much of a judge."

"Younger than me?"

"Possibly."

"Under thirty-five?"

"Alix, I haven't the faintest idea. Is it important?"

"Conceivably."

LATER THAT AFTERNOON SHE CORNERED me at my writing desk. From somewhere in the clutter of her rooms she had unearthed a copy of *The Tatler* with a studio portrait of Lady Amelia, a ravishing dark-haired beauty in a ball gown cut perilously low. "Bertie, I don't know how you could describe her as plain."

I replied somewhat obliquely, "Where do you keep these old magazines? It smells so musty it must be ten years old at least."

"I looked her up in Debrett, as you suggested. She is still only twenty-seven."

I shut the magazine and handed it back to her. "I suppose you're going to try and stop my sport—just because the invitation comes from a young widow of tolerably good looks."

My dear wife gave me an indulgent smile. "Not at all.

When have I ever stood in your way? Of course you shall have your shoot. And I shall come too and offer some sisterly sympathy to Lady Drummond."

"*You* intend to come?"

She smiled faintly this time. "One feels obliged to show support."

And so the visit was set in motion. Francis Knollys, my private secretary, wrote to advise our hostess of my requirements: a suite comprising bedrooms for each of us, dressing rooms and sitting room. Also accommodation for our retinue of equerries, ladies-in-waiting, footmen, valets, loaders, coachmen, grooms and a member of the Household Police, whose duty it is to guard us from anarchists. Then the guest list had to be approved, a crucial matter as it ultimately turned out. Of sixteen names submitted, I struck out three immediately. If one is planning an agreeable week in the country, one doesn't want to rub shoulders with people who have given offense in the past. Nor, if one wishes to shoot, is one obliged to stand comparison with *all* the best guns in the country.

We were left with thirteen names.

"Would you like me to join the party, sir?" Knollys knows my superstitious nature and volunteered at once.

"No," I informed him. "We have more than enough men in this party. We must cross out someone else. Who have we got? Eight gentlemen and five ladies. The balance is fraught with disaster. Who is this reverend fellow, Humphrey Paget? He doesn't sound like a shooting man."

"The family chaplain, sir."

"Ah."

"He buried the late Lord Drummond."

"The best day's work he ever did, from what I remember of Freddie. Better not object to a man of the cloth, I suppose. Who else have we got?"

"Marcus Pelham, Lady Drummond's brother. I presume he's there to perform the duties of host."

"That's as may be, but is he safe?"

"Safe, sir?"

"I wouldn't care to stand with a man who isn't safe."

"I understand he's an expert marksman, sir." Knollys glanced at the list again. "Then there's His Grace the Duke of Bournemouth, who lives on the neighboring estate."

"Dear old Jerry. Good man. Hopeless shot."

"Not safe, sir?"

"Not in the least."

"Shall I strike him out?"

"Better not. The list is pretty undistinguished without him. I'll make sure he's well down the line from me."

"Claude Bullivant. He's a commoner."

"Ah, but he's a card. I like his sense of humor. This is getting damnably difficult."

'"There's Colonel C.D. Roberts, V.C."

"A V.C., do you say? That's our man. Blackball him. We can do without a hero turning the ladies' heads, eh, Francis?"

So the number was painlessly reduced to twelve. I had already run through the ladies' names. Two I hadn't previously met, which lent a certain relish to the week in prospect.

THE SUMMER RAN ITS ALL-TOO-FAMILIAR course: Ascot, Epsom, Goodwood, Cowes. I anticipated the shoot in Buckinghamshire as a change from my customary October *battue* at Sandringham or Balmoral. And a change is what I got. A never-to-be-forgotten week

CHAPTER 2

Those of my readers who haven't seen Desborough for themselves may care to be informed that it is approached by a mile-long avenue of beeches. It is an extremely large, moated, brick built Elizabethan mansion much extended by its eighteenth-century owners, who added a monstrous Palladian portico at the front and two extra wings. They also coated the Tudor brickwork in stucco, something I find as incomprehensible as putting a pretty face behind a *yashmak*.

We were graciously received. As custom decrees, our host and hostess, Lady Drummond and her brother Marcus, stood at the entrance flanked by their principal servants. Then in a charming, youthful manner Lady Amelia came running down the stone steps to greet us, bunching her skirt for ease of movement and affording glimpses of slender, white-stockinged ankles.

Beside me, Alix murmured, "No longer in mourning, it appears."

The young widow curtsied and gave us her well-rehearsed greeting. She had a most engaging voice, with what I can only describe as a gurgle when she spoke certain sounds.

"Welcome to Desborough, Your Royal Highnesses. I hope your journey was agreeable."

"It is becoming so by the minute," I said.

"Your suite is ready, sir, and your servants are installed."

"Capital, my dear. What are the rules of the house?"

She looked uncertain how to respond, so I jocularly explained, "For example, my mother, the Queen, has a horror of smoking, and prohibits it absolutely indoors. At Windsor one evening, the German Ambassador, Count Hatzfeldt-Wildenburg, who cannot live without a cigarette, poor fellow, was discovered in his bedroom lying on the hearth rug in his pajamas, blowing smoke up the chimney. I hope I may light up an occasional cigar in your house without performing gymnastics."

I had brought the dimples briefly to her cheeks and now she found that winsome voice again. "No, sir, there are no rules."

"No rules at all?" I arched an eyebrow. "Isn't that rather reckless?"

She colored charmingly.

Then Alix remarked, "Rules are unnecessary when people know how to behave. Shall we allow Lady Drummond to show us to our rooms?"

Our hostess had spared nothing in making us welcome. Each suite was newly decorated, Alix's in cornflower blue, mine in green and white stripes. Log fires were blazing merrily and producing pretty effects on the crystal decanters.

"When is dinner?" I asked Lady Amelia.

"At half past eight, sir. I would like to present my other guests at eight, if it pleases you."

"I am sure it will please us enormously."

When we were alone, Alix asked what time we were wanted.

"Seven," I said firmly. It's a constant battle with Alix. At Sandringham I have all the clocks permanently put forward half an hour.

She gave me a suspicious look. "That seems rather early."

"It's the country life. Everyone eats early and retires before midnight."

The result was that we got downstairs at twenty past eight.

I spotted a few familiar faces in the anteroom: Sir George Holdfast, of Holdfast Assurance, and Lady Moira, his wife (good people, supporters of many charitable causes, but *so* staid); Claude Bullivant, once the most eligible bachelor in London; and dear old Jerry Gribble, the Duke of Bournemouth, hand on the shoulder of a suit of armor, chatting noisily to a pretty young woman in black velvet. Trust Jerry to lose no time, I thought.

Our hostess made a deep curtsey that Alix later described as theatrical. It didn't offend me in the least. I seem to remember that Lady Amelia's dinner gown was apple green, or it might have been pink. I retain a very clear picture of the corsage, which I am certain was of cream satin, cut distractingly low and decorated with pearl beads. She had her hair bunched high and adorned with a posy of white blossoms. I do like to see a lady's neck and shoulders unadorned except for a few pearls.

Alix said pointedly that we ought to meet the Chaplain.

The Reverend Humphrey Paget demonstrably wasn't one of those clerics who practice fasting as religious observance. He was "Broad" Church, if ever a man was. And we had more in common than that, for he claimed to be a sportsman, in spite of his girth.

"An angler, if I am not mistaken," said I at once. "Did you land many trout today, Padre?"

His face was a study.

"Forgive me," I said. "I have recently interested myself in the science of deduction."

"Deduction, sir?"

"Yes. That distinct and even discoloration around the base of your heels suggests that you recently stood for some time in soft mud. Moreover, your toe caps, although splendidly polished, have several dull patches that could only have been made by splashes of water, say when a catch is landed. These indications, taken together with the knowledge that the River Ouse nearby is well stocked with trout, and the season ends on Saturday next, compel me irresistibly to the conclusion that you are a trout fisherman."

He glanced down at the telltale shoes. Then cleared his throat. "Your acuteness of observation is truly remarkable. Your Royal Highness."

"Anyone could do as well if he applied the method," I modestly remarked, passing on to another guest, a tall, pasty-faced young fellow with eyes like rock oysters. I should explain that the ordeal of meeting me has curious effects on some people. He was introduced as Mr. Wilfred Osgot-Edge, a poet.

"What's a poet doing at a shooting party—writing elegies on pheasants?" I jested.

He was tongue-tied, so Lady Amelia sprang to his assistance. "Wilfred also has the reputation of being the best shot in Buckinghamshire, sir."

"Good for you," I said generously. "A shooting poet."

"It is n-not so uncommon," he stuttered, then seemed unable to expand on the statement.

"Who else is there?" I asked. "I wouldn't care to hand dear old Tennyson a shotgun and stand nearby."

My wife, ever sympathetic towards the nervously inclined, said, "Lord Byron was a sportsman."

"And much else besides." I tried to animate Osgot-Edge with a nudge from my elbow. "Have you noticed how the ladies go pink at the mention of Byron? I really ought to read him."

The poet wound himself up. "I m-must say I like By-By-"

"Bicycling? You *are* an all-rounder."

The poet had no more to contribute. Casting about for deliverance, I caught the eye of Jerry Gribble, the Duke of Bournemouth, still in close proximity to his companion in velvet. "Jerry, you old bore," I shouted across the room. "The lady and I have been winking at each other for the past ten minutes and I still don't know her name."

She was brought to meet me, and I saw at once that this was no shrinking violet. The walk, the shining eyes, the knowing smile, the curtsey—all sang out "actress." Now I'm not one of those who regard treading the boards as the next thing to streetwalking. I pride myself on my encouragement of the dramatic arts.

"May I present Miss Queenie Chimes, sir?"

"Miss *what?*"

The lady giggled. "Queenie, sir. Queenie Chimes."

I said, "Queenie? Queenie? What sort of name is that? I didn't see it on the guest list."

Jerry coughed nervously. "My mistake, sir. I should have said Victoria."

I frowned.

Miss Chimes explained. "Girls who are called Victoria are nicknamed Queenie, sir, after her Majesty."

"Thank you," I told her formally. "The connection is clear to me."

She said, "Do you think it common?"

I stared at her. I am not used to people addressing me so directly. I said, "As a matter of fact, I have a daughter of my own called Victoria"—I paused—"but we don't call her Queenie." And then I smiled.

Everyone smiled.

I resumed, "You're quite right, my dear. Victoria is a common name. I also have a sister Vicky and a niece Vicky. Very common. Very confusing. I shall be happy to call you Queenie. Altogether more distinguished."

Quick to sense my approval of the lady, Jerry Gribble took

care to say, "Queenie and I are well acquainted. I would go so far as to describe myself as one of her patrons. She's with Irving at the Lyceum, you know. The great man personally thought of her stage name, didn't he, my dear? She was born Victoria Bell."

The lady gave me an endearing smile. "Bell . . . Chimes."

I chuckled. "I like it! Clever man, Irving. He obviously sees a fine future for you in his company."

"Oh, I don't know if I shall be good enough, Your Royal Highness," Queenie spoke up. She had an alluring, husky voice, as if she spent her mornings drilling the Irish Guards.

"I'm all for modesty," said I. "Are you currently in a production, Miss Chimes?"

"I am preparing a part, sir." Her eyelashes fluttered,

I glanced behind me to make sure Alix was still busy with the poet and said, "Would you care to read it to me?"

At which Jerry said, "It's a nonspeaking role, sir. Have you met Miss Dundas yet?"

"Miss Dundas?"

"The Amazon explorer, Isabella Dundas, a most remarkable person."

At that point the announcement was made that dinner was served. Hastily the remaining guests, including Miss Dundas, the Amazon explorer, were presented to me without time to discuss their remarkable attributes. We formed the procession, Alix, the lady of highest rank, on the right arm of young Pelham, leading us in, the rest following, and Lady Amelia and I last.

The banqueting hall is one of the notable features of Desborough, having somehow escaped three centuries of so-called improvements to the rest of the house. The only embellishments to the original oak and plaster are the escutcheons displayed high on the walls, the heraldic bearings of the Drummonds and their ancestors. Amelia (we agreed to be informal) pointed out her own. As a Pelham, she had a most exotic coat of arms with griffins and birds that I didn't recognize. Alix tried to convince me later that they were harpies.

The hall was such a barn of a place that Amelia had thoughtfully located the dinner table at the far end, where a grand fire was blazing and screens were strategically placed to keep out drafts. A small string orchestra played zestfully as we stepped between the ranks of liveried servants to take our places at the oval table.

The Chaplain said the grace and we were seated. Amelia was to my left, Alix to my right and Queenie the actress directly opposite me, too far off, I estimated, for our feet to make contact unless we sank down in our chairs with our chins resting on the table.

Queenie was flanked by Jerry Gribble and Claude Bullivant, and it was Bullivant, a delightful, black-haired rogue with a moustache as curly as a candelabra, who opened the conversation. "If I were a padre, I think I should object to saying grace on a Monday."

"Why is that?" someone asked.

"Monday, surely, is a padre's day off He's busy all weekend, marrying people on Saturday and taking services on the Sabbath. He's entitled to a rest."

The Reverend Paget gave a half smile and said nothing, so Jerry Gribble took up the running. "The Church is a calling, not a profession. A churchman can never have a day off like the rest of us."

"Oh, he *needs* a day to himself," piped up Lady Holdfast from one end of the table. She was desperately dull, poor old thing.

"I'm sure our friend the Chaplain isn't deprived of recreation," said I, mindful of the trout fishing.

"Perhaps he would care to enlighten us as to how he amuses himself when he is not at his devotions," suggested Bullivant, and all eyes turned on the Reverend Paget.

"I, em, fit in a few private pastimes when time permits," he said. He seemed not to want to own up to the angling.

"Yes, but do you ever get a day off?" persisted Bullivant, wicked fellow, unwilling to let the Chaplain off the hook, so to speak. "How did you pass your time today, for example?"

"Today?" The Chaplain wiped his mouth with the edge of his table napkin. "I was, em, outdoors this morning."

"Fishing for trout?" said Alexandra.

He went extremely pink and twisted the napkin as if he were wringing out washing.

"Out with it, Padre," said Bullivant. "A man of God has a perfect right to fish. St. Peter was a fisherman. Is that what you do?"

"I may have given that impression. Inadvertently." The Chaplain now had his fist wound up in the napkin. "To be truthful, I was officiating at a funeral."

"A *funeral?*" said I.

"And this afternoon?" Alix asked the Chaplain after a pause.

"A baptism."

Mud on his heels and drops of water on his toe caps. I was forced to conclude that I hadn't altogether mastered the science of deduction. To avoid one of Alix's looks, I turned to our hostess and congratulated her on the soup.

This markedly relaxed the atmosphere. The diners turned as one to their neighbors and struck up conversations. I learned from our dear little hostess that she expected a record bag from the week's shooting. The woods were said to be better stocked than the head gamekeeper could remember for years, and it appeared that most of Buckinghamshire would be beating for us.

"Curiously enough, I have never shot here in October," I told Amelia. "I once had a day's cock shooting after Christmas. That must have been when your father-in-law was alive. So you see, most of these guns around the table have the advantage of me. Your brother Marcus, Jerry Gribble, Claude Bullivant, they're all regulars. I don't know about the poet."

"Wilfred? He was at last year's shoot," she said. "He's quick and accurate. But you're wrong about my brother. Marcus was never welcomed here while Freddie was alive."

"They fell out?"

She hesitated. "There was some jealousy between them."

"Over you?"

"Marcus and I were very close as children, sir. Don't misunderstand me, but I think he felt that Freddie broke up the family when he married me."

I glanced at the others along the table. Couldn't see much family resemblance when I studied Marcus Pelham. He had straight, straw-colored hair and one of those pink faces that turn bright red in the sun, or under scrutiny from the Prince of Wales. "And now that you're alone in the world, he's supporting you on occasions such as this. Good man," I said, privately thinking he ought to be tarred and feathered.

I refused to let it spoil my appetite. After the *consommé* came Dover sole poached in Chablis, followed by the dish that never fails to please me: ptarmigan pie. Presently something was said across the table about sleeping in strange houses. It's curious, isn't it, how even when half a dozen conversations are in progress around the table one intriguing remark secures everybody's attention? We all stopped talking except Jerry Gribble.

"Personally," he said, "I never have any trouble. I'm used to sleeping in strange beds."

"Ladies, take note," murmured Bullivant.

"That isn't what I meant. I've slept under canvas, on a train, aboard a steamship, under the stars—"

"In a haunted house?" put in Queenie the actress.

"Not to my knowledge—until tonight," said Jerry.

"Good God—this house doesn't have a ghost, does it?"

said Sir George Holdfast in some alarm. His wife gave a horrified squeak.

"Oh, it must have," said Jerry, straight-faced. "In three hundred years it must have acquired one."

"A resident spook!" said Bullivant with relish.

Around me the unease was palpable. It was all very well joking about ghosties over dinner, but before long we'd be shown to our bedrooms by candlelight along dark corridors.

Osgot-Edge the poet spoke up. "I don't believe in gho-gho-"

"Going to bed in haunted houses?" said Bullivant. "Nor I, old man. I shall sleep in an armchair by the fire. You're welcome to join me."

Beside me, Lady Amelia drew herself up to speak. "I know you only say it to amuse, gentlemen, but there's something I would like to say in all seriousness. There is no ghost of Desborough Hall. If there was, I should have heard of it—and I wouldn't have remained here, least of all invited my dearest friends to stay."

"Well said, my dear," I told her and clapped my hands. Everyone did likewise—even Bullivant, looking sheepish—and the congenial atmosphere was quite restored.

Over the roast lamb I surveyed the party and amused myself pairing them off. Queenie of the Lyceum had, regrettably, to be linked with Jerry Gribble; it was perfectly obvious that she had been invited at his request. The Holdfasts looked likely to live up to their name, and they were such a dreary pair that none of us would object. Claude Bullivant was resolutely hacking a path to Miss Dundas, the Amazon explorer, though it was far from clear how she would receive him. The set of her mouth was daunting and her eyes glittered ominously. It crossed my mind that she might be stalking bigger game than Bullivant; once or twice she had looked my way and smiled.

As for the rest, I absolved the Chaplain and Osgot-Edge

the nervous poet from any amorous intent, and I could see that Marcus Pelham had eyes only for his sister.

What of the winsome Amelia herself, then? Up to now, she'd been scrupulously charming to everyone, as a hostess should. If you want to know whether I bedded her before the end of the week you had better read on. But one thing you must have gathered: noctambulations would be infernally difficult under Alix's nose and with a jealous brother roaming the house.

I was inquiring from Miss Chimes about Irving's latest production when there was an alarming cry from Lady Holdfast: "A bomb!"

Fortunately, Inspector Sweeney, my bodyguard, wasn't in the room looking for anarchists, or the cook's *pièce de résistance* might have been grabbed and flung out of the nearest window. It was a *bombe glacée Dame Blanche*, a veritable monument of ice cream and fruit carried high on a silver charger by the cook himself in his tall hat to the strains of "See the Conquering Hero Comes."

I am at pains to describe faithfully what happened. The mood around the table, as I recall it, was high-spirited. We shouted "Bravo!" and the cook warmed his knife over a flame before making the first cut. Then the portions were served. Jerry Gribble joked that this was obviously the ghost of Desborough Hall, the *Dame Blanche* herself. Alix asked for a portion with a cherry. Osgot-Edge knocked over his wine in the excitement.

Then Queenie Chimes pitched forward and collapsed—without a murmur—face down in the *bombe*.